DANCER
OF THE
APPALACHIANS

James Everidge De Forest

Old Seventy Creek Press 2018
Printed in the United States of America

PUBLISHED IN THE UNITED STATES
BY OLD SEVENTY CREEK PRESS
RUDY THOMAS, PUBLISHER
P. O. BOX 204
ALBANY, KENTUCKY 42602

ISBN-13: 9780615538495 (Old Seventy Creek Press)

ISBN-10: 0615538495

This Book is dedicated to the People of Appalachia and the Austin Peay State College 1963-64 Basketball Team

My mother Mary Stewart, was born in a log cabin in the Appalachian mountains. My middle name is Everidge I was named after Sol Everidge, one of the founders of the Hindman Settlement School. Mother told me stories of her people. I remember one well. Her mother, Cindy, was tired of a chicken hawk that that was raiding her chicken yard on a regular basis. So she got her house rifle and waited for him. Sure enough he came flying in and she took aim and fired. She missed the hawk but did blow the horn of their cow off. Neither the chicken hawk nor the cow was ever seen again.

The people of Appalachia live in a world different in the relationships they have with their families, neighbors and religion. They share a bond that has been developed for centuries from family to family. You will find folk songs in the book taken from the Appalachian history that are still being passed on from generation to generation today. The American flag is in several stores and places showing the respect these mountain people have.

One of first African-American basketball players L.M. Ellis started with Austin Peay State College. In this book and in the next, most of the basketball incidents were based what Coach Fisher, Ellis and the Austin Peay State College team went through.

Now, as time passes, we should not and cannot let the changing of history by Basketball Coach George Fisher (1962-1971) his 1964 team and Austin Peay State College President Joe Morgan (1963-1976) be forgotten

They were the one of the first, first coach, the first basketball team, the first college president and college to allow the first African-American L.M. Ellis the opportunity to play college basketball.

At a time when few had the courage to do what was right they stepped forward and made their mark in history. A mark that none shall ever surpass.

1963-64 Austin Peay State College Basketball Team

Coach George Fisher

Blakey Bradley	Doug Stamper
L.M. Ellis	Riley Holiday
Jim De Forest	Henry Murrey
Steve Miller	Sheldon Sledd
Richard Keller	Roger Putty
Jimmy Darke	Dwight Norris

Forest Adcock

Now Every Day I have a grateful attitude remembering every day is I live a gift from God

James De Forest
Austin Peay State College Class of 1965

Author's Afterword

The following article about Austin Peay State Basketball Coach George Fisher is from the Clarksville, Tennessee *The Leaf-Chronicle*, by sports Editor Jimmy Trodglen, January 25, 2009:

Fisher Made Statement When Needed

George Fisher was the first. He was the initiator, the trendsetter, the man with a conscience who believed he had the responsibility of helping correct a social wrong.

At a time in American's history when color defined what opportunities were possessed by a man, Fisher tore down a social boundary.

Three years before Perry Wallace signed with Vanderbilt becoming the first African-American to play basketball in the SEC; Austin Peay had already taken the initiative, thanks to Fisher giving L. M. Ellis an opportunity to play college basketball in his backyard

Ellis was a standout for Burt High School in 1961 when it won the National Negro Basketball Tournament. Ellis originally signed with Drake, but wanted to transfer after a year and half.

Fisher didn't hesitate to welcome Ellis when he wanted to transfer to Austin Peay.

For all of Fisher's coaching success during his nine-year run, all of the wins failed in comparison to giving Ellis an opportunity.

"That was the greatest thing I ever did," Fisher said, "Nobody else wanted to do that and

we had to do it. He loved it and we loved it and we loved him."

Ellis became the first African American scholarship athlete in the OVC and one of the first in the South.

Fisher along with Ellis was on hand Saturday to celebrate and recognize Austin Peay's 1963-64 team, the school's first OVC member team.

All members of the Gov's historic collective are still alive and all but one was on hand for the Team's 45th Anniversary.

Steve Miller, the team's captain of the 63-64 team organized the reunion to honor Fisher, who was one of the most beloved coaches and figures.

When Austin Peay was on the road, Fisher and later Miller, was Ellis' roommate.

If a restaurant wouldn't serve Austin Peay because it had a black athlete, the whole team would find someplace that would.

"I knew when he (Fisher) came out if he was all red faced and upset, they had told him that they would not serve me," Ellis said. "So we went on down the road."

Ellis, who describes Fisher as a father figure, said those social statements left an everlasting impression.

"I was never embarrassed by having to eat someplace separate from my teammates," Ellis said. "And even if we had to get burgers, we stayed together. That to me was important to have their respect."

When Fisher informed the Gov's in the spring of 1963 he was signing a black athlete color was the least of their concerns.

"Coach Fisher was talking about it, and one of the guys jumped in and said, Coach we don't care what color he is. All we want to know is can he play ball?" said Blakey Bradley, a center on the 63-64 team. "That was the attitude of the team."

And the attitude of a man who remains a beloved figure to his players 45 years after the conclusion of their historic run.

ABOUT THE AUTHOR

James Everidge De Forest had an Interesting
career.

1959 Lindle Castle- Coach Clinton Co. High School
Who played at Rupp at UK and Morehead

Jim Bechtold Freshman Coach Eastern Ky. State

Red Shirted under
Paul McBrayer Coach Eastern Ky. State College

Doug Hines Assistant Coach University of Kentucky
Former Lindsey Wilson Coach invited him to UK

Went to see Hines who was gone turned ran into
Adoph Rupp Coach University of Kentucky

Rupp called recommending De Forest
Dave Aaron Coach Austin Peay State College

The year he arrived he had a new coach
Austin Peay State College
1962 George Fisher Coach

Chapter 1

It was a beautiful fall day in the Appalachian Mountains. The trees were all shades of gold, brown and other colors of the rainbow. However, a figure ran down a leaf covered path paying no attention to the fall surroundings. He was dressed in old bib overalls, faded blue shirts and worn, dusty boots, carrying a shotgun in one hand and gripping his fist with the other. Reaching his destination, he leaped up the old wooden steps, across the creaking porch and though the half opened faded white wooden door.

"There is a haint on Bald Mountain," screamed Windy Marlow as he burst through the doors of Troublesome Creek General Store.

The usual group sat around the old pot-bellied stove gazing intently at the faded checkerboard on the old nail barrel. There was old Rust Stevens, dressed in usual gray flannel shirt, bib overhauls, smoking his old pipe. Across sat Parson Brown, in his church habit, complete with stiff collar and thick horn rimmed glasses. Leaning on an old cane back chair, stood Sheriff Cletus Evarts, dressed in his usual brown uniform, with a very shiny star pinned to his left shirt pocket. And finally watching Windy intently was the store's dog Cat, a large black wolf like dog with orange and white vertical lines between eyes that never left Ma's side except to go hunting with Dancer or Windy.

Watching intently from across the old oak counter between two large glass jugs of stick candy, was the owner of the store "Ma" Thomas, who was the first to speak. "Windy, you been hitting the shine again, haven't you?" she said in a calm voice.

"Cletus, you better check him out before he shoots someone," she stated matter of fact, "He never could hold his shine."

"I ain't tached a drop," Windy said defiantly, looking at the group until his wide. Bloodshot eyes fell on Parson Brown. "Parson, you know since I got saved, and coming to meeting, I been a changed man. I ain't even stole no seng or anything this year. "

"Tell em," he pleaded with a shaking voice, "tell em, please!"

Parson Brown looked up from the checker game through his thick glasses and shaking his head with agreement said in his best understanding voice, "I don't believe Windy has been drinking and I certainly don't believe there are ghosts on Bald Mountain. Put the shot gun in the comer, by the door and tell why you think you saw a ghost on Bald Mountain."

Windy turned to set the shot gun in the corner and slowly sat down in the chair that Parson Brown brought up the stove for him. "I didn't say I saw a haint on the mountain", he said more calmly while holding his outstretched hands close to the stove, "I said there was one. When I was little, my daddy used to tell me tales about such things happing at Old Christmas when ghosts and spirits tried to catch you and you could hear animals pray. But it ain't Old Christmas time."

This was a Jack Tale. Windy always loved Jack Tales, stories of the strange happenings in the hills and mountains passed from down generation to generation told by the men of the mountains whenever they came together. Now Windy had his own Jack Tale.

Continuing his story, with more confidence, since he held everyone's attention, "I went a squirrel hunting this morn before daylight. I was a leaning back against this big Oak tree, come daylight. I never heard so much cutting coming from them big oaks. They must have been a hundred of them hungry critters. Wall, I took Old Blue and started a blastin. I must have kilt at least ten or twenty in a minute or so."

Glancing appreciatively at Ma, "I knew that would be enough for Ma to make her Squirrel Stew." Taking a deep breath and spitting into the old coal bucket at his feet, he continued, "I got my grass sack out to fetch up the squirrels. Only there warn't none to fetch." Looking at the sheriff he said in a high voice, "Something had done stole them squirrels right out from under me. It had to be a haint, I didn't see or hear nothing."

"Well, maybe in the dim light you missed the squirrels," said the Sheriff looking at Windy, "It has happened before."

"Not to me it ain't", Windy declared, "And that ain't all, the haint knew where I lived."

"Are you saying a ghost stole your squirrels, and followed you home?" Ma said shaking her head, looking at the group and starting to smile.

"No, I ain't," he stared. "It beat me home. When I come to my cabin, on the front porch was twenty squirrels. Seven of the twenty had been shot. But the rest didn't have a mark on em", he raised his voice, "explain that if it weren't no haint."

Before anyone could speak, Ma replied, "James Dancer."

"What do you mean, James Dancer?" Windy quickly asked. "I never seen him."

"And you won't," Rust Stevens spoke for the first time, "that boys' a ghost in the woods. I went hunting with him last fall and it was a wonder the way he moved, just glided over the ground and he wasn't trying to do it, it just came naturally."

Windy looked up from his coffee, "Dancer, I shud a known," he said shaking his head.

Then he looked up at Ma, "Where is your room Ma?"

That question come out of nowhere and puzzled everyone in the store for the moment that is except Ma. Windy was getting ready to come up with one of his "colorful" remarks and she almost dreaded it.

One that came to her mind was when it was his turn to get a bucket of coal for the store's stove one very cold, snowy Saturday morning in December when everyone was at the store around the stove keeping warm.

Parson Brown, like everyone else, loved her coffee on a cold morning and this morning he was starting on his second cup that Ma had just taken off the stove.

"How cold is it outside, Windy," he ask as Windy was shaking the snow off of his knee high rubber boots as he set the bucket of coal down near the stove.

Windy was taking his gloves off and he turned to face Parson Brown and in a seemed like a stupid question deserved a stupid answer voice, "Why it's colder that a well diggers ass in January."

The Parson had just filled his mouth full of the coffee he loved. It was either spit it out or choke. You can't laugh with a mouth full coffee. Out it came hitting the floor near the stove. He was followed by Stevens and the rest that had a mouth full of coffee that morning.

But Ma also remembered one time his "colorful" answers came in handy. It was a beautiful spring day. Everyone had just come in from the fields for lunch. Most were in line getting bologna sandwiches, cheese and a cold drink of coke or RC Royal Crown. Others were reaching in a gallon jug filled with a long roll hot bologna.

A short young man outfitted in a black coat and pants with a white shirt and red bow tie was following Ma everywhere she went. He had his hands full of different pots and pans. He was a drummer or a salesman and had been following Ma for over three hours telling her how good his products were.

Like every daily lunch on the store's front porch they were sharing the latest news. Everyone looked forward to listening to a Windy story. Ma came out with some of her freshly made lemonade. She was being followed step by step by the young salesman.

The salesman, Nathan House, knew from experience that to get rid of him she would finally buy something. It had never failed him. But it was about to.

While Ma was pouring the lemonade, House looked at his watch. It had stopped. He reached over and grabbed Windy' shoulder interrupting Windy's daily story, a mistake that he was about to pay for.

"My watch is dead what time it is?" he asks in a demanding voice.

He got his answer. Windy turned his head and looked the salesman in the eye and in a loud voice, "Why hell, it's time for all pain in the ass salesman to die. You feelin sick yet?"

Everyone sitting on the steps and in the their rocking chairs laughed out loud as the red faced salesman turned and left in his car leaving a cloud of dust as he hurried up the gravel road.

Now it was Ma's time to answer a Windy question. Everyone stopped drinking coffee and waited for the answer and the Windy response.

"What kind of room do you want Windy," she ask in a slow voice knowing there was about to be a lemonade spitting response.

"Why an ass kicking room, Ma for people like me that should a knowed it could only be Dancer that could a done sometin like that."

Again everyone laughed out loud and Cletus laughed slapped his leg three times.

"Only Dancer could a done it. Why he barked them critters by shooting just close enough to hit the bark and knock em out of the tree."

Pausing, Windy continued now with a low voice, "I know how good he shoots. Dancer saved my life with his rifle gun."

All eyes were on him now, and Windy was not called windy for nothing. He loved to talk and he loved to be the center of attention, just like he was now. He continued, while looking at each one of the gatherings around the porch. In his best story telling style, he started his latest tale, "James Dancer saved my life the day. That is why I went to meetin and was saved."

Ma, who had seen this attention stalling before from Windy, said, "Get on with the story. Windy, everyone knows when you went to church and was saved. I was there," scratching eyebrow and shaking her head at the same time, she continued, "and I confess I never saw anyone, walk into church and to the altar with a shotgun in his hand."

"It was a first for me too," smiled Parson Brown.

Windy took a deep breath and lowered his voice to emphasize the importance of his story. "I was looking for seng up over at Hell-for-Certain and fell on some rocks under the leaves. I started to get up when I looked at death. I looked eye to eye with the biggest copperhead that that God ever made."

Windy now was using his hands to describe his actions. "It was about a foot from my nose and its head was bigger than my fist," he held up his large gnarled, brown fist," and it was ready to strike."

"I knew I was a goner. I had once seen a man who had been bitten on the jaw take a week to die. His face turned purple and swelled bigger than a pumpkin. He suffered awful."

Lowering his head in reverence, "I closed my eyes and told God, I knew that I was a sinner, but if he could save my life now, I would walk the line and be in meeting tonight and every time the church door opened."

"Then I felt something hit my face and I screamed. I just laid thar with my face in the leaves, a screaming and a crying, and a waitin for the hurt to start and a wondering if anyone would ever find me."

And pausing, glancing at Parson, he said, "A wondering if it was too late to set things right with the Almighty."

He continued with a smile and an embarrassed look all around, said, "I heard this laughin. There was James Dancer and Cat. Dancer was holding his rifle gun over his shoulder and a grinning at me. I looked up and that big copperhead didn't have no head. It was a writhing on the ground about a foot away from my face."

Pausing, "I reched got a hold of old Blue and looked up to thank Dancer, but he was gone. Just like he always does he disappeared. I counted fifty paces to where he was a standing, when he blew that Copperhead head off. I didn't believe no one alive could shoot like that. I didn't get to thank Dancer that day, but at meetin that night I thanked God for sending him to save me that day. I ain't missed a day at the meetin house since."

Parson was moved by the story and placing his arm on Wendy's shoulder, said, "God moves in mysterious ways."

"Amen to that," the group chimed in unison.

With that everyone stood and waved at Ma and each other as they went back to work some at the farm and others getting ready for their shift at the mine.

Windy leaned back in his chair with most of the store people gone and his mystery solved, he looked up from his coffee, "I always wondered where Dancer, Nada and Star came from Ma? I used to see them around the store, then one day they wuz all gone except for Dancer."

Ma sat down across from Windy and was sipping tea. "Well it started about sixteen years ago, in the middle of a December snow storm around midnight. I heard this knocking on my door. I put my heavy night coat on and opened it expecting to find Windy, drunk wanting a place to sleep and out of the cold," she paused looking at Windy," it had become a habit."

Shaking her head, Ma continued, "Instead, here was a half frozen young Indian girl with two little ones clinging to her she said she had gotten separated from her group and lost in snow storm."

"Well, to make a long story short, Nada, a Cherokee from the Carolinas, was a real lady and beautiful. She stayed here and worked at the store, while her children James and Star went to school. She said her entire village had moved to avoid the Green Death, whatever that is and it would be years before she could go back. Her family thought it would be safer for her and the children here."

Looking at Windy she continued, "Nada once told me she had to go back home every year or so because of ceremonies that she was required to do being the daughter of the tribes shaman and she had become the tribes Keeper of Secrets. Dancer is not her real son. She just raised him with her own daughter, Star. She never did say where he came from."

She stopped and looked at Windy, "Windy, you spend more time with the Indians that anyone, do you know anything about them leaving and Green Death," asked Cletus who had listened to all of the stories.

Windy, having regained his breath, answered, "Can't say that I do, but I will try to find out."

Cletus, who stopped sipping his tea shook his head and said, "Nada left about six years ago. Ma here raised Dancer and Star until Nada's people came after Star. Dancer stayed here and worked at the coal mines. He went to school in the day and work at the mines at night."

"A real shame too," I mean he did not get play basketball in high school," Ma said, "look at how tall he is now. He finally had to quit school because he had to support his sister and help out here at the store when I was sick with the flu."

Ma continued looking at the group," I watched him practice basketball with Coach Fisher for hours when he could between working here and his mine shift. He was really something to watch."

"Coach Fisher knows his stuff all right. After all he is a retired college coach from Northern Tennessee State. He came back here to stay with his daughter and her son after her husband, Donald was killed in the mine cave in five years ago.

"It was a sad time for everyone," Parson Brown said quietly

"It always is," said Ma as she rubbed her eyes to keep from crying, "Let's all pray that there will never be another one."

"Amen," everyone around the stove said in unison.

Standing, Parson Brown started scratching his right leg.

"I started this yesterday and paid no attention, now it starting to hurt and I am not feeling well either."

"Did you look at your leg where it itches," Ma asks?

"I did last night but I did not see anything."

"Let's look at it again," Ma got on a chair and leaned down to look at the Parson's leg as he pulled his pant leg up.

On the inside of his knee, almost invisible, was a small black spot and another above his knee.

"I'll be darn, it's just a little tick that has been causing me all of this trouble," as he spoke he started to pick the small tick off.

Ma caught his hand, "No, don't pick it off. It is a Deer Tick. If you just take it off it will leave its head and poison inside of your leg. Wait just a minute," she turned and went around behind the counter.

"They're fine as frog hair. I had two of those little critters, one on my neck and the other on my ankle. If Ma had not spotted em I would for sure been sick as a dog eatin cat food," Windy said as Ma came up holding tweezers in on hand a bottle alcohol in the other.

She dabbed both of the ticks with a cotton swab of alcohol. Then carefully she used tweezers to remove the two small ticks.

"Well, there you go Parson that should do it. Your new to Appalachia and it will take a little time go get use to ours ways and new dangers," she said as she went behind the counter put the alcohol and cotton back in its place to be ready for new Deer Tick treatment,

Meanwhile unknown to the group Fisher had come through the door that was partially opened and had heard most of the conversation without being seen because of the large stove and stacks of flour and wheat that he was behind. Only Cat had noticed him but paid no attention to him. He had been in the store many times before talking to Ma and the others around the stove. Cat considered him no threat. Cat yawned and went back to sleep.

Instead of going around and joining the group, he hesitated remembering that he had the same experience with the Deer Ticks. It was one of the reasons why at first he had wanted to leave with his daughter, Sara, after her husband Roger, had died in a mining accident.

One sunny spring afternoon Fisher and his daughter Sara, were sitting in rocking chairs on the porch. Fisher had just taken her daughter, six year old Sara to the school pick up place and came back to sit on the porch with her like he always had. As always he ask why she did not want to go back to their home. And as always she knew her father was puzzled why she had not wanted to come back to their home.

This time Sara had reached out and held her father's hand. In a moment she looked at him with a felling a daughter gives to a father she loves.

Sara then explained why she wanted to stay. She told him it would be some time in the future when her son, Donald, got older. Someday he would want to leave to explore the country around him and discover what his future held for him as most young men did.

It was something that Appalachian people had done in the past. But now, until then, she would watch him grow up here where his father had grown up and loved.

Fisher had tears in his eyes as the daughter he loved had reached into his heart for his understanding.

Now Fisher understood. It was the people with their ways, the forest with its ever changing colors and mountains of Appalachia that never changed had just seemed to say to him here is where you belong. Now he would stay until Sara decided it was time to go.

Now it was Dancer that brought him back from his past. The first time he had seen Dancer was still pictured it in his mind. It had been an early fall morning almost three years ago and the coal mine night shift had just gotten off work. Fisher was sitting in an old rocker on daughter's Sara's cabin porch enjoying the beautiful golden colors of the trees and watching a band small ground squirrels playing under the large Oak in front of the cottage.

Instead of going around and joining the group, he hesitated remembering that he had the same experience with the Deer Ticks before. It was one of the reasons why at first he had wanted to leave with his daughter after her husband had been killed in a mining accident. She had refused. She had tried to explain why to him with little results.

Now he knew why. It was the people with their ways, the Appalachian forest with its ever changing landscape.

Then on a well-worn path in front of the cabin came several slow moving men both young and old wearing hard hats, covered from head to foot with black coal dust carrying their black tin lunch boxes. There was little conversation. Fisher had thought how hard and long these men worked facing danger every day to support their families. After they had had passed he stood, stretched and started in to get a cup of morning coffee when he heard a familiar sound in the distance. He turned and saw two more miners coming up the path.

Unlike others, these two were talking and even laughing. What really stopped Fisher was that one of them was dribbling a basketball up the path. Since he was covered with coal dust and the hard hat covered his features Fisher could not really make out his face. He sat down again in his rocker and watched as they came closer. Using his coaching eye he judged the dribbler to well be over six feet in height and he walked with long stride not looking at the bouncing ball and changing hands from lunch box to ball while talking to the other miner. He never looked at the ball.

Fisher immediately became interested anyone that could dribble a basketball up the path covered with rocks and tree roots and never looked at the ball. It showed some promise.

They had just gotten past the porch when they stopped and the tall miner took his steel hard hat off revealing black cropped hair and a dark complexion under the fine coal dust. He just smiled revealing white even teeth and gave his hard hat to his friend. Fisher always remembered what was said next.

"If you can do it, I'll bring lunch for both of us tomorrow night, if you lose you will bring the lunch," the shorter coal covered miner stated with confidence, "Dancer you know how I like my ham sandwiches made with plenty of mustard."

He closed his eyes and could still see what Dancer did the next moment. A tall Oak had a large limb that stretched high across the path. The young man had taken one step and holding the basketball like a baseball in his right hand brought it over the limb and caught it with his left hand on the other side.

Holding the ball with one hand he turned to his friend, who was still shaking his head, "Mickey, remember, I don't like much mustard on mine." They both had laughed and continued up the path leaving an astounded retired basketball coach staring after them.

After they had disappeared into the woods, Fisher had gone out and looked at the Oak limb.

He had stood under enough basketball goals in his thirty years of coaching to know that the limb was over ten feet high and he had just seen a miner hold a basketball in one hand like you would hold a baseball, jump over ten feet while wearing his heavy mining gear. The old basketball coach's fever again began to grow in him. First he would go see Ma at the general store to find out everything he could about the young miner named Dancer

He had walked through the door at the general store and before he could speak Ma and Dancer came around the counter. She had introduced him to Dancer. Dancer had said he would give anything to be able to play basketball in college.

Fisher had believed what he had said and for several years he had worked with Dancer to do just that, prepares him to play basketball in college, but not just any college. He was preparing him for his former school, Northern Tennessee State College. Before long he knew that he had never seen any player with the natural ability that Dancer possessed. Simply put, Dancer was turning into the best basketball player he had ever seen. Suddenly he shook his head, cleared his thoughts and came on into the store.

"Hello coach," Parson Brown said, "come have a seat, we were just talking about Dancer and his mother."

Windy could not be left out, "And all of the powers she had," looking at the group, "I never seen anything like it."

As Fisher sat down on an old stool he nodded to everyone who responded the same way and ask, "I haven't seen Dancer for a few days. Does anyone know where he has gone?"

"We won't be seeing Dancer for a while," Ma said looking at the group, "you might as well know, he got his draft notice Wednesday. He leaves next Friday for Louisville," she said pausing, "He went into the mountains this morning; I look to Cat leave shortly and am with Dancer when he camps tonight. I think he will stay here to protect me as long as he can."

That evening, after Cat had found Dancer, they started hunting like they always did. It was getting dark when they stopped under a large Oak tree that provided shelter if it rained. Known only to a few, when Dancer found time like tonight, he almost always read books from Louis Lamour to Shakespeare.

His favorite poems were *Invictus,* by Henley; a poem from a dying man that after he read it, the polio crippled Roosevelt became president.

And the poem *If* by Kipling was a guide that helped him get the best out of his life. At times he even wrote poems and short stories, but sharing them with no one.

Over the years he had read almost all of the beloved Jesse Stewart's stories about Appalachia and he people that lived there.

Now as he sat under the Oak, while there was still light, he began reading another chapter of Lamoure's *Dark Canyon*.

It was almost dark when he started the small camp fire and after a while was about to pour some hot coffee into his battered tin cup. Then for some reason he stopped and looked up for Cat who had always found a place next to him and the fire. Cat had moved away from him and stood at the edge of the woods when he heard a wolf cry. Then another howl came that was much closer. It was Cat, who stood on the edge of the fire light and looked toward the woods.

A moment later several dark shadows with glowing eyes moved into the fire light. Dancer counted five of the gray, orange eyed wolves. As they approached, he raised his right hand. The wolves stopped and looked at palm of the hand with the glowing red circle and the image of Azar the White Wolf of Death, Stealer of Souls in the middle of it. Whenever Dancer wanted, the hand came alive with a red circular image with a wolf's head image.

The wolves then turned and formed a circle around Cat paying no attention to Dancer, who watched the ceremony without fear. Soon what he thought was a large bush in the darkness, came alive. One of the largest wolves he had ever seen came into the circle. It was almost black with a white stripe running between its eyes that glowed as he came forward.

He circled around Cat, who had orange and white stripes between his eyes, stood very still and looked straight ahead. In a moment the leader of the pack came in front of Cat and nudged his nose with his. At that time all of the surrounding wolves raised their heads and howled in unison and then the pack faded into the woods with the leader in the front.

Just before he disappeared into the darkness, Cat turned and looked at Dancer, as if to say these are my people and I must go. Dancer nodded as if he understood. Cat, satisfied that Dancer's approved, turned to catch up with the pack.

The next morning Dancer was moving at dawn through the green forest and hills that he loved until he came to the base of a mountain that rose beyond the low morning clouds. He then followed a narrow dangerous trail around the face of the mountain. It was almost hidden by the rocks. Finally he came to a crack in the solid rock wall that he could not see where it ended. The crack was among several along the mountain side. But unlike others this went through the mountain and was only wide enough to enter in some places if he turned sideways.

As he moved through the cave it opened wide and he could see daylight at the other end several hundred feet away. When he came through the other end he stopped and looked at the surrounding mountains whose tops formed a shear wall on each side as far as he could see. He looked with awe every time he came here.

Few had been from one end of this untouched land to the other or from side to side. It lay unknown by today's civilization and he hoped it always would be. Below were valleys, streams and green forest that formed a green blanket as far as he could see. Clouds drifted over the land each day and stayed low making it almost impossible to be seen from the air. He walked down a little used trail through the woods until it opened into green meadow with a wide stream of crystal clear water running through the middle of it. Several deer looked up at his coming and disappeared into the forest.

He stopped with Cat and drank the clear cold stream water to quench his thirst from the hike. As he stood up, he saw on two Indians dressed in buckskin, with different colored feathers in their long black hair, holding bows, and smiling at Dancer. Dancer smiled back held his right hand up and went across the wide stream on a log that had been put there for that purpose.

Dancer recognized them as chief Yellow Elk and Deer Runner, the best hunters the tribe had. In greeting each placed his right hand on the top of each other's shoulder, "It is good to see our warrior friend Dancer and the son of Keeper of Secrets and his warrior wolf Cat once again, it has been too long."

"You are right, it has been too long. It is good to see the great hunters and warriors chief Yellow Elk and Deer Runner again."

Dancer stood and looked at each of his friends, "I have to go and fight a battle in a faraway place and came here to see my brothers before I go,"

"Then come and stay as long as you can brother of the wolf. We will hunt and celebrate your visit and our shaman will ask our Great Father to watch over you." Yellow Elk replied and led the way toward their village.

As they entered the village, they were greeted by Yellow Elks wife, Blue Bird, who came forward to hug Dancer. "Dancer it is good to see you once more. We have prepared a feast in your honor, come."

Dancer, Yellow Elk and Deer Runner looked at each other with surprise. "How did you know that I would be here today," Dancer asked, shaking his head in disbelief, "I told no one that I was coming here."

Blue Bird looked at Dancer, "Yesterday a message was brought here for you by a warrior as tall as a tree," She pointed to a mark on an Oak tree, "I knew you would not believe so I marked a spot on the tree with a knife."

Yellow Elk walked over and held his hand up to the mark on the tree. Knowing that his wife would not make up such a story, he looked at Dancer, "We thought that you were the tallest warrior that I have ever seen. Now there is one that we saw at least three hands taller."

Dancer smiled, "No, it is more like five hands that was Kana, he guards my mother. But how in the world did he get through the crack in the rock and why did he come here?"

Yellow Elk said, "He had a very hard time but managed to crawl through the crack."

She then reached into the leather bag she was carrying and handed Dancer a letter. "Before he left, the giant one said we should give you this."

My Son,

I am sorry that I could not be there for you before you left, but as Keeper of Secrets I must keep my vows to complete my training Just after you were born I saw in the future that you were going to fight in this war, that is why you were trained by the best instructors in the world on every method of combat through the years you were growing up. It was told that the training was to protect me, but really it was done to protect you in the future. You will face many dangers and hardships. I look forward to your return. Take care and may the Great Spirit watch over you

You're Loving Mother
Nada

It was then that Running Bear said "Come Dancer, we honor you tonight with the gathering of our warriors and the Elders. You must hear Elder Brown Bear share secrets know only to the Elders."

Dancer quickly stood up went to the waiting fire with figures dancing around it to the beating of the ancient drums.

Dancer and Running Bear sat cross legged across from the five Elders of the tribe all thin and showed signs of age. The one in front stood up and the drums and dancing suddenly stopped. Everyone joined in the circle around the fire and watched as Brown Bear walked to the middle facing Dancer and the other warriors of the tribe.

He was tall, thin, and brown faced from many years in the sun, dressed in his best buckskin leather with colorful beads on his necklace. He looked through dark, shinning eyes at Dancer, "Tonight we honor two great warriors of our tribe. Dancer summons the other warrior to take his place with you."

Dancer nodded, held his hand right hand up and there was a red glow on his palm. Then a flash and standing in front of Dancer was a giant white wolf with red eyes. It looked at Dancer who pointed to place beside him. Azar the White Wolf of Death, Stealer of Souls, slowly walked leaving no tracks in the ground to his side moving his giant head from side to side at the crowd who sat frozen watching the legend join the group beside Dancer. For a short time all looked with astonishment at the legendary giant white wolf whose red eyes were glowing in the fire light.

"Tonight we honor Dancer and Azar who have proven them to be great warriors by having faced death many times in protecting members of our tribe. First we honor Dancer with a warrior's gift from the Ancient Ones."

Brown Bear nodded his head and a bundle wrapped in white beaded skin was handed to him by Running Bear. He turned to Dancer and held it out with both hands. Dancer accepted it with both hands and opened his gift. It was a knife with long wide, shiny blade that had inscriptions on both sides. The handle itself was of white ivory it too was engraved with inscriptions on it. Dancer had never seen anything like it.

He looked up at Dancer and with a smile said, "It was made by the Ancient Ones centuries ago from metal that came from the stars. There is only one and they gave it strange powers. It was sent to you by our Keeper of Secrets, I believe you know her well."

Dancer grinned and thought of his mother. She was always finding ways to protect him from what she had read in his future.

Brown Bear stepped forward taking the knife and holding Dancers right hand he cut into the palm and said, "Hold the knife until the burning stops."

Dancer did as he was told. At first the blood came through his fingers and covering the ivory handle. It was very hot. Then the handle became cool again. When Dancer looked down there was no blood on his hand or the ivory handle. The strangest thing was that he had no cut on his hand!

"Now it has tasted your blood, its power belongs only to you. Here take the knife and throw it at the feather in the tree over there,' Brown Bear pointed to a feather on a tree at least twenty feet away, "You must look at where you want the knife to go."

Dancer took the knife and looked at the small feather in the tree. At first he thought it would be impossible, but he knew the tales of the Ancient Ones. Whatever seemed impossible was found to be true. He took the knife by the handle and threw it as hard as he could toward feather.

The second it left his hand it had a red glow and was like rocket going toward the feather. It struck the feather with such power that it cut it into tree and vibrated it for a moment. The red glow went away. A loud gasp came from the all of the Indians of the camp.

Brown Bear looked at Dancer and pointed at the tree, "Now only you can handle the knife and it will always be like that until you choose to pass it to another warrior as I have done tonight. Only you can get it from your target. It will destroy not only any living thing but even evil spirits that it hits. Look at the tree."

The tree had turned from a green, healthy tree to a dead brown, shrunken tree with almost no leaves. The knife from the Ancient Ones was true to its legend.

"Now open your hand and point it at the knife. Suddenly the knife came from the wood and with another red flash it was back in Dancer's hand. It had flown from the dead tree. This time there was no sound from anyone in the surrounding tribe. Everyone just looked with amazement and could not find words to speak. For a moment Dancer had the same problem.

Dancer then turned and bowed down to Brown Bear," You have honored me with a true warriors knife I will use it well."

"Your mother Keeper of Secrets knows that you will use it well," Brown Bear answered with a smile and a quick hug.

Dancer left the next morning thanking all of his Indian friends for the celebration that they had last night. As he went through the forest with Cat, who had sat with the Elders during the ceremony, he thought of what was going to happen to him in Viet Nam and how he was going to use his special knife that his mother had sent him. He shook his head. There was no doubt because she saw in the future.

Chapter 2

Back at the store, Cletus took a drink from his coffee, "I hope Dancer gets back in time to catch the bus. He has to take his Viet Nam physical just like the entire draftees do. I am surely going to miss him," then looking at Ma, "I know some others that will too."

"Don't you worry none, Cletus," Ma said, while pouring him another cup of coffee. "He told me he would be here at the store to catch the Sheriff Everts ride to Prestonsburg. He has to catch several buses to get to Louisville. Dancer just wants to see his people and his mother before he leaves. But she is Nada the Keeper of Secrets for her tribe and she is away a lot."

Ma stirred her coffee, "We all miss her."

"I remember when her Indian kinfolk would visit and James would stay in the woods for days at a time with them and then go visit her people in the Carolina Mountains every year when he could get time off from the mines." Ma said pouring herself some hot coffee.

"I asked what he did when he went to visit his people and he said that since his mother was the Keeper of Secrets, he must be trained to protect her from harm if need be."

Turning to Windy, she continued, "That is how he learned to shoot so good and do other things to protect her. One time he came in from a visit and he had black burnt wood lines on his body. He said that was how he learned to fight with knives using wood from a camp fire as knives, other times he had bruises all over where he had been taught to fight hand-to-hand in different ways.

"The strangest time was when came in with needle like scratches all over his body. He would not say anything except the people who trained him was from all over the world and he would be called on some day," pausing Ma continued, "I think they were preparing him for something besides Viet Nam. I just don't know what."

Looking at Windy, Ma said "For some reason, Dancer brought me a mess of squirrels without a mark on em. What do you know about that?"

They all glanced at Windy who quickly looked up at everybody wanting their attention. That was a reason they called him windy.

"I told Dancer that they make a lot better stew because you don't crack your teeth on the shot. He barked em. That Dancer is the only one that could a done it."

When he saw a puzzled look come over Ma and the others it was time again to become the main speaker, "If you are one them people that can shoot squirrels on the run with a rifle gun and hit close, the bark can throw em such a way that the fall kills em."

And looking down and patting his old two barrel shot gun, "But I have Old Blue and she has always been good nuff for me."

"I figured you had something to do with it. Now the stews on the stove," Ma said turning to go into the kitchen at the back of the store.

"I'll be there shortly Ma," then turning to look at the group again, Windy added, "Almost reminds me of his mother Nada. She has powers that almost make me scared."

Rust Stevens spoke up, "You better believe she did. Last Spring, Windy and I were hunting some deer in a little meadow. There was this big buck"..... .that was as far as he got before Windy joined in.

As always Windy could not stand it any longer. He had to get his word in, "Before we could shoot, she came out of them woods carrying a basket of flowers and a walking calm as you could please right past them deer. She and the big buck looked at each other and she nodded. Why she even patted the big buck on the nose," he said with a shaking head.

It was Stevens turn, "She came on and looked at us or a moment."

Then she said, "The great one says it is not a good day to die. Come back another day," then she went on down the path."

"We looked at each other and then we turned to look at the deer. They were gone," shaking his head, "in all of my days I never seen nothing like it."

Stevens continued, "Another thing I will never forget is that when my wife, Cindy was sick with the fever and we couldn't fetch a doctor over the mountains because of the snow. She stayed with her and gave her some herbs or potions of some sort. In two days she was up and around. We tried to pay her but she wouldn't take a dime. She told us that she didn't do anything, it was the Great Spirit she called on that did the healing."

"Nada was good with her medicine all right," Cletus said shaking his head in agreement, and, "she was a fine person, it's just that she seemed to know what you were thinking and what you were going to say before you said it."

"Nada had the gift. She knew what would happen before it happened. Remember when she told the Martins not to go home after church," Ma said coming through the kitchen door and joining group around the stove again.

"I remember," Rust Stevens spoke slowly, like he was trying to recall all the details," Jacob Martin laughed and tried to get his wife and family to go on home, but Marie would have none of it. She said if he went home now he would go home alone and sleep alone." That brought a smile and laughter from the group

"Anyway, they didn't go home that afternoon they stayed here with Ma, and..." Before he could finish, Windy again lived up to his name and could not be quiet any longer.

"The mountain slide run over their house that day and now you can't even see the roof of the house where it is buried," Windy said loudly looking at the group.

Parson Brown had remained quiet and listened to the stories told about the Appalachian people as they were sitting around the stove. Then he thought of how he got here and why he loved these mountain people. He was the only one of the group that had not been born and raised in the mountains.

A new comer to the mountains, Brown was determined to understand the ways of these mountain people. They were much different from those in Louisville where he grew up. He was raised in a caring and loving family, his father worked in the post office and his mother in a clothing store. His problems started in school where it was a different matter.

Parson Brown tried to fit in, but was constantly harassed by others because he refused to join a gang or play any sports. His early childhood was miserable and he prayed nightly for a way out.

His prayers were answered when he was finally accepted by a private school where he worked after class to pay his tuition. Then after graduating from a Baptist Seminary, he was sent on his first mission into the Appalachian Mountains to not only serve in a church, but to study the everyday life and customs of these mountain people. He was tested quickly right after his arrival.

The first day he had visited this very store, Parson Brown had been offered to join the group in a cup of coffee. Wanting to be sociable, he agreed and when the steaming coffee was poured, and he started to drink. It was then that Ma had shaken her head ever so slightly. Then he had politely put his cup down and coughed lightly. The surrounding group had looked at each other and grinned.

The group proceeded to pour their steaming hot liquid in their saucers a little at a time, sipping and talking at the same time, until it was safe to drink it straight from the cup.

Parson Brown had later thanked Ma for saving him from embarrassment and a badly burned set of lips. She had laughed and said, "It weren't nothing. The boys just wanted to see if you would be pilgrim enough to put boiling coffee in your mouth. They were just deviling you a little."

Later something that he always wanted to know came to mind one day. "Ma, why do you call that big wolf dog that always watches you Cat?"

"Well first of all he was raised by a cat, Scratch," she answered turning toward the door.

There was a large orange and white mother cat lying on the porch washing a small protesting orange kitten's bottom while the rest of the kittens fought battles and rolled around on the stores porch.

"I found him on the porch one morning, a small puppy, nestled with Scratch and her kittens. The second reason is that he is now as quick as a cat and he watches over me."

Again they both looked at Cat in the corner that was now aware of the presence of a new comer around Ma. Alert now, he turned his head eyeing Parson Brown.

Turning to Brown she said, "He has proven it several times. One day last year a man came in with a pistol in his hand and grabbed me by my arm to move me to the register."

"That is as far as he got wasn't it, Cat," she said smiling at Cat who was satisfied that no harm was going to come to Ma and had relaxed, lying on the porch.

"He hit that man so fast and hard he knocked him through the door. If it had not been for me he would have killed him. He ran into the wood shooting his pistol at Cat. No one has seen him since."

Ma continued, "Then just last week, Scratch was playing with her kittens on the porch, when I heard her growl and looked out the door. Something had been killing dogs, cats, cows and other animals around here the last month, and I saw what it was. It was the biggest coyote I have ever seen moving toward, Scratch and her kittens.

I went to the door and yelled and picked up an ax, but he kept coming."

Ma watched Cat as he moved to the porch, "Cat came out of nowhere and squared off against that coyote. One look at Cat was all that was needed. It turned and ran into the woods with Cat after him. An hour later Cat came in covered with blood. It was only after I washed him off did I that discovered that most of the blood was not his. "

Smiling now, she asked, "Look, is that a killer dog or not?" She nodded toward the store's porch. On the porch Cat, the killer dog, was covered, by four small yellow kittens that were playing on his back and crawling up to his ears as their mother Scratch watched contentedly.

What Ma did not know was that Parson Brown had a good friend in the state police and Trooper Thompson had told him the story of what had really happened. Dancer, Sheriff Everts, Windy and two men with rifles from the other side of the mountain had come in an hour after the man had fled. Ma pointed out the way the man had run and then they all went into the woods following Dancer and Cat.

The robber turned out to be an escaped killer who had broken out of jail in Virginia, stole a car and had fled to the mountains. Three hours later, Dancer and Cat came back to the store just as Captain Allen had arrived with two other state policemen. Ma explained what had happened. The captain had looked at Dancer and Cat. Dancer nodded, and then the captain told the troopers to report back to headquarters.

One of the new troopers asked the captain why they did not start a search for the dangerous killer.

The captain had looked at the new trooper and said. "You are new to the mountains. These people take care of their own. The killer will not be bothering anyone else." He nodded to Ma and Dancer as he went out the door.

Since then, whenever Brown had a question about the local customs or what to do or what not to do in different situations, he tried to consult Ma. He was finally accepted because he had   been invited to join the group that sits around the stove and plays checkers on Mondays at the store.

One Saturday before the men began to gather Parson Brown walked in and watched Windy tapping on a coin with a spoon. His curiosity got the better of him.

"I've seen you do that before, Windy," he said, "but just what is it you're doing?"

"Well, it's a wedding ring for Bobby Stewart to give to Doris Macon," Windy said.

"May I see it," Parson Brown asked?"

"Ain't you never seed a fifty cent piece silver ring, Parson?"

"No, I've never seen or heard of such a thing, Windy."

"It just takes a lot of Spoonin."

"What?"

"I'm spoon hammerin the edge with a spoon all around."

"I can see it was a shiny new Kennedy half," the Parson said, turning it around and then flipping it over.

"How do you turn it into a ring?"

"Well," Windy said, "I take this here string's that the size of Doris' ring finger and I drill a hole through the center..."

"When it's the right size?" the Parson asked, grasping the concept.

"Yeah, but I have to file away everything that ain't the ring size. I keep spoonin until it reaches the right size. They's other ways to do it."

"Reminds me of Michelangelo and how he told someone he chipped everything away that wasn't David."

"Are you all right, Parson?" Windy ask with a concerned look.

"I'm proud to say that you are an artist, too, Windy."

"Thank you mightly, Parson," Windy said, but was too puzzled to ask anything else.

"Where have you been all week Windy," Ma ask coming around the counter and sat between Windy and Parson.

"Well, I been a helpin Joseph Turner divide his land into three parts for his daughters, Cindy, Mattie and Mary."

"I'm surprised he waited so long, everyone I know of has already divided their land into sections for their children so that they will have a place to build a house and live if they go away and want to come back," Ma smiled, "I bet it was hard with them three girls, they never could agree to anything in church."

"I done this a lot, but I never seen so much fightin and screamin. But old Joe finally just said, "I decide who gets this and who gets that. I don't want no more yelling, you ain't too big for me to take my belt to."

Windy grinned, "Why it became quiet as your nose bleed and it just took us four hours to put rocks and mark trees for the three sections. We drew it out and he had everyone sign our drawings. He gave each one of them a drawing and he kept one to store away."

Then Windy looking at Ma, took a deep breath and speaking with a serious voice said, "Ma I am in need of your help if you will."

Ma was startled. Windy ask for help only if it was very important. The last time was when the mine fell in and he asks if he could get food to take to the missing and badly hurt miners.

Parson Brown, recognizing the serious voice from Windy, turned to pay attention to the request.

"Well you know after meetin every Sunday we all go to eat dinner at a different people's homes. I counted and everyonc has done it but me. I was a wonderin if you could invite them here for me. I promise that I will work out for you until you say it is paid off."

Ma looked at the Windy who had his head down, being Appalachian born, he was ashamed that he had to ask for something he could not give or buy.

"Windy, I'll tell you what. Widow Craig and I have sows about to give birth. If you carry buckets of coal up the mountain to where we have them penned in starting in the morning and feed the sow every day until you think it's safe to leave her I'll fix your churches Sunday dinner"

He stood up and hugged the surprised Ma, "Gosh a mighty Ma I couldn't ask anything better. It is a good thing you are startin early, why old Joe said he lost ten out of fifteen new born pigs because he forgot to get the sow coal. Why he was lucky he had five left if you don't feed the coal she will eat everyone that she bored."

Soon Rust Stevens, Sheriff Evert and several of the other locals started drifting into the store to play checkers or just sit around the stove and share stories and jack tales of the mountains.

One of his favorite Local Tales was about a revenue officer, Lee Stewart who with his men known as Lee Stewart and his Seven Disciples searched the mountains high and low for illegal whiskey stills.

It seemed that one time the moonshiners were escaping and accidentally ran over Lee when their truck went out of control in the wet leaves on the narrow mountain road. They stopped the truck and knowing he would not survive without a doctor's care. They loaded him up and took him to the hospital at Prestonsburg where he recovers.

Later, one of Stewart's men had wounded a bootlegger in the leg while he was escaping a raid. When two other men came back for him, he was aiming to shoot them also. Stewart stepped forward and pushed the rifle down as he pulled the trigger. Stewart looked at the frustrated young man and said, "Those men have families and friends in these hills. I am different because I consider our job is to break up the still, nothing more. Do you understand?"

Looking up as the men disappeared over the hill, he saw one of the men raise his rifle, holding in the middle, above his head and nodded his head to them. It was then that another man with a rifle stepped out from behind a tree not fifty yards away, did the same and followed the others over the hill. It was then that the young man knew that had he shot at the running men up the hill, he would have been shot dead by the man hiding with the rifle.

He understood and looked at Lee who smiled, "I saw that man win a shooting contest for a pig at the fair. You are a bigger target than the walnuts he was hitting at fifty feet.

And so as Parson spent more time in the store he began to understand the spirit of the people of Appalachia

The group was sitting around the stove one fall afternoon discussing who the best hunter was. A few were named but everyone knew that none were better than Dancer. "You know besides being a good hunter, Dancer is a pretty good basketball shooter too," Cletus said.

"I saw him playing outside at the settlement school with the King and he was holding his own."

"I would have to see that," said Rust Stevens, "I saw the King get at least fifty almost every games last year."

"Dancer is the best overall player that I've ever seen, and that includes the King. At least at six-six or more, he is taller and quicker. But I will say, I don't think he is a better shooter than the King."

"There never will be a better shooter," said Ma.

It was time for a Windy remark. "Well, if they think they are better than them tell em to bring their lunch, because it is surely gonna be an all day job."

Everyone laughed and then there was a loud "pop" followed by a yell. Everyone turned, in time to see the two Everidge boys; both had shaggy brown hair and eyes. They were dressed the same with old shirts, jeans and dirt colored bare feet.

Bill, the older and taller of the two, was in the sixth grade, Bob was in the fourth. They were both aiming with what appeared to be wooden sticks at a helpless Mary Stewart and her sister Mattie, both were dressed in homemade dresses made out of flour sacks and their brown hair was in pig tails.

"Give me those pop guns," Ma said as she reached for the wooden sticks, "and empty all of the Dogwood berries in your pockets into the can by the stove."

"Do we have to, Ma, we picked the best Dogwood berries we could find and me and Bob promise not to shoot in the store anymore."

"Yeah," said Bob, "this Elder is just the right size for the berries this year."

Looking at Windy," We paid him a dime apiece for them."

Windy, shook his head and said, "Boys, I made you the best shooters I could this year. Ma, she might give'm back if you promise not to shoot Mary and Mattie no more."

Mary, who had been taking all of the conversation in finally spoke, "Give'm back, Ma, they done worked with us in tobaker all day for the quarter."

Then looking at Bill and Bob, "If they shoot me again, I'll tell you and you won't sell them any more rock candy until Christmas."

Then looking at Windy, Mary continued, "I told em they was worth only a nickel. But they wouldn't listen."

Windy, who was taken aback by this remark, said, "I got that there Elder from top of the mountain, hollowed it out, and carved the shooter out yesterday?"

Then he took a shooter from Ma and looking around, he said in proud voice, "This is the best work I ever done. I could hit anything ten paces away," he said holding the hollowed out Elder and its Dogwood plunger.

Windy took a two Dogwood berries from Bill. He put one berry in and pushed the plunger moving the berry to the front stopping where you could see the berry stuck in end. Then he put another berry into the other end of the hollowed out Elder. He turned aimed the shooter and pushed the plunger into the Elder. There was a pop and the berry shot across the room and hit the door knob leaving a berry stain.

Windy bowed to the applauding group and handed the shooter back to Ma. "When they get through tellin how good of a shooter you are, get a kitchen rag and clean up the mess by the door. Don't forget to clean the knob too, great shooter!"

This brought another round of laughter as they all watched a sad Windy go through the door into the kitchen.

Since it wasn't the boys' fault she turned and gave the shooters back to the boys who were standing with the saddest look on their faces they could muster.

"Now you know what will happen if you shoot them in the store or at dog or cat, now scoot," she said with her hands on her hips.

Bob and Bill nodded their heads yes. They turned quickly and ran to the door before she changed her mind. Their faces turning into laughter as they escaped out the door, loading their Elder shooters and looking for a legal target for their red Dogwood berry as they ran.

Pointing to the large gray cat by her rocker "No wonder President Truman and Scratch won't go outside, you were using them for target practice." Windy standing in the kitchen door with a rag in hand, blushed and everyone around the stove laughed.

Suddenly Bill stuck his head back through the door, "When are you going to get our red rubber sling shots done. We want to go squirrel hunting with em."

"Yeah, we can shoot at rabbits too," Bob joined in putting his head across Bill's shoulder, "they will be worth at least fifteen cents, red rubber is hard to find."

"Boys, I just got an old red rubber inner tube from Sheriff Evarts, when I helped him change tires last Monday. It was in his trunk. He found it in an old wreck and forgot to give it to me. You will have to bring me the forks to put the rubber on and don't forget an old shoe tongue for the pocket," he replied as the boys went out the door.

He turned to Ma, "Don't worry none Ma. I'll charge them only fifteen cents for both of them and if they shoot anyone I promise to tell you and you can take them away."

"It better be that way," Ma replied as she watched the boys and Windy hurry out the door and disappear into the woods. Suddenly she thought, he had done it again. Anytime there was a chore to do Windy tried to find a way to escape and not do it. Oh well she thought I should have known better as she picked up the dropped kitchen rag and started cleaning the door.

It was getting late and she stepped aside as everyone nodded to her as they went through the door home. They all had smiled a little to themselves. Windy had done it again.

Ma stood in the door watching them disappear into down the path. As she turned to step back inside the store she looked out into the woods. Her thoughts went to Dancer and wondering how he would do if he got in the army and went to basic training. Ma knew unlike most other raw recruits, Dancer had been trained by experts in everything it would take to survive from hand-to-hand fighting to how to survive in all kinds of situations. The army had a surprise coming.

As Parson Brown started home he stopped to watch a marble game between Bob, Bill and their friend Tommy. He had never seen a marble game before.

Bill drew a line on the ground, stepped back, "Alright time to leg to see who gets the first shot and is ruler."

The boys stood beside him and carefully rolled their marble toward the line. Bill's rolled and stopped directly on the line."

He took his marble up and looked at Bob and Tommy, "First rule no steelies, Tommy."

Tommy shrugged and put his steel ball bearing back into his pocket.

He turned to Bob, "And there will no bombing. You are too good a dropping on the marbles and you want to hold it lower that your belt."

"Three's," Bill announced and everyone put three marbles in the middle of the circle where he put them in a group.

Bill said "Leg for first shot," and they did. This time Bob won.

Smiling, he reached in his pocket and held up a red crystal like marble. "Best shooting tawl you can find. I gave Wendy a nickel for it. He found it after a car hit a tree. It came out of the round cap over the headlights."

He took aim and the red marble hit the group of nine, scattering them around inside the circle. One went out of the circle.

He jumped over and put it in his pocket. He got four more before he hit another marble and it stopped inches away from the circle and did not go out.

"Thanks Bob," Bill said as his point blank shot knocked the marble out of the ring. He got two more before his last shot was almost across the ring.

"Time to clean house," Tommy said as he knocked the last marble out of the circle and put it in his pocket.

They were beginning a new game as Parson Brown started for his house. His thoughts were that Appalachian people young and old like to compete no matter what the game was or the stakes were.

Chapter 3

At the Troublesome Creek General Store, it was a sunny afternoon. Sitting and relaxing around the old cold stove were Parson Brown in his church habit that he never changed, Rust Stevens dressed as always in his gray flannel shirt and bib overhauls, and Sheriff Cletus Evarts in his brown uniform with a badge above his left shirt pocket.

Sheriff Evarts looked at the group around him, "I passed Windy this morning going up the old gravel road to Big Rock carrying a shovel. I stopped and ask he wanted a ride. He said no, he was on his way to finish digging the outhouse or Window Marcum and her two daughters. He had finished digging the new hole for it Thursday. Her older son Jason would be coming over the mountain to help him finish it this morning."

"Windy knew It would take two to tip the outhouse over and with a rope drag it over put it up right over the new hole he had measured."

"He brought the extra shovel today because he and Jason would take an hour or two to fill in the old toilet hole with dirt from the new outhouse and get the two wasp nest out. Finally, just as he left, he asks me if I had any old newspaper in case they had no toilet paper."

Just then there were a few drops of rain falling on the stores side windows. There was a large American Flag on a round Oak pole sticking out from the large Oak post across from the door supporting the stores porch.

Parson Brown had been inside the store

before and every time there was as sign of rain Rust Stevens had stopped what he was doing and went outside to remove the flag. As he did he was always careful not to let the flag touch the ground as took it off of the pole. He took it either on the porch or inside depending on the power of the rain where he and another person, most of the time Wendy or Evarts could fold the flag.

Parson Brown had always wondered how a flag was folded now he watched as Stevens and Clark again carefully spread the flag out each holding their end with both hands. They folded the lower striped section of the flag over the blue field. Then they folded edge again to meet the edge. Stevens then started a triangular fold by bringing the striped corner of the folded edge to the open edge. He turned the flag inward parallel with the open edge to form a second triangle When he was through the he took it in and placed it in an glass box on the counter next to the cash register where everyone could see it.

Stevens saw it was starting to rain harder and turned hurried out the door. It was Stevens turn to roll up the cars and pickups windows at the sign of rain. Next time it would be Parson Browns. It saved everyone running out and coming back wet. Now only one gets wet in a rain storm.

While Stevens was gone, Clark turned to Parson Brown, who he knew was wondering why Stevens was so careful with the flag. "That flag was given to him at his oldest son, Lewis's military funeral. He was killed in Viet Nam. Ma let him take the old flag down and put his son's up. One of us takes it down at sundown and put back up in the morning. As you can see the American flag means a lot to people in Appalachia. We have always and always will defend American whenever we are needed."

"I know you do, I have never seen so many American flags on houses, cars and flag poles. Parson asks, "What happens to the old flags?"

"They are burned when they are tarnished or damaged. That is why we are very careful when we either take it down or put it up.

Just then Stevens came through the door. He was wet but not completely, the rain had stopped and the sun started coming from behind clouds.

He sat down at the table wiping his face with a towel Ma had just given him, "We did not get much rain but just over the ridge it was raining something fierce."

A few moments later they heard a stomping on the porch. When Windy opened the door and stood there for a moment. He was soaked to the skin from head to toe and covered with mud.

Ma looked up and down at the soaked Windy. Then she asks a question she should not have asked. When you do that to Windy you are about to get something right back at you.

She shook her head looking at Windy standing there dripping water on the floor, "Is it raining that hard out there Windy," Ma ask

For a moment Windy just stared at her and nodded his head," Yep sure is," then he said in an eye to eye answer "Yes Ma, it was just like standing under a cow pissing on a flat rock."

Parson almost fell out of his chair laughing and was joined by Stevens and Clark.

Finally after everyone had stopped and wiped their faces to keep people from thinking that they had been crying, they sat back down in their chairs, and the conversation continued.

"How did you get the mud on you," Ma asked as Windy turned to face the group. Then he sat down in an old chair and looked at the group surrounding him wanting he hear the latest Windy story. It had to be a great story for him to sit here in his wet and muddy cloths.

"Well you know me and Jason went to move the outdoor toilet today after digging the new hole yesterday. We was just getting started on the outside. I was pushing it over and Jason was holding it on the other side until I went around helping him let it fall so we could drag it over to the new hole we had dug. Then we would fill the old toilet hole with the dirt we had piled from the new toilet hole."

Windy took a deep breath and everyone knew that here comes something to laugh about. "Well everything was a gonna good when here come Widow Marcum's daughter Aza out of the house, skirt raised and leaving dog piles behind her Then seconds later here come Nadaene right behind her doing the same thing. There was a line of piles goin to the outhouse one big one small.

But the difference was that Aza could get in shade under a clothes line and it would take a coal truck at noon to get Nadaene out of the shade.

At that everyone knew he was telling the truth and started laughing. They could see the race with skinny Aza and big Nada both with their naked bottoms dropping a trail that their dogs would have to cover up. Everyone laughed but they knew it was going to get better because Windy wasn't excited yet, but it would come on big tales when he got the end.

Aza , holding her drew up over her head, went into the toiled and Nads stopped and squatted leaving the biggest pile I have ever seen. Why it was bigger that a bull stuck in the mud.

Then the door flew open and here come Aza out with her dress in the air and a band of wasp after her."

Windy stopped for a moment as everyone was starting laugh, "Well sir, Aza ran square over the squatting Nada and they both fell on the big pile that Nada was sittin over."

Now the store shook with laughter from everyone even Ma.

Windy shook his head, "After they had all gone inside, Widow Marcum came over to us. She said that she wanted a two seater out house and to be sure to tell Ma she would have to get another box of EX-LAX because Aza and Nadaene had eaten it all up a few minutes ago but she didn't think it would happen again. If it did the two seater would take care of it wasp or no wasp."

Me and Jason just shook our heads and figured we are going to have to get some mighty big four by fours at least to get started."

The whole group could not hold their

laughter anymore. Everyone knew that only one chocolate tasting EX-LAX would make your bowels move in a short time. Aza and Nadaene must have thought they were eating chocolate candy.

Windy took a deep breath and went inside the next room where Ma had filled a big wooden tub that was half of barrel that had been used to ripe whiskey.

Ma yelled, "Windy that is lye soap use the other bar. And don't make a mistake like you did last time.

'Don't you worry, Ma, I can still feel my mouth that was almost burned out."

Then Ma produced a bar of lye soap that had a set of teeth marks on it where he had bitten it last year. Again everyone laughed shaking their heads thinking how Windy must have felt with a mouth full of fire.

This reminded them that it was almost soap-making days and everyone knew what that meant. Lye soap is made every year at the store. Ma has a large caldron that is heated over a wood fire and every one brings their own wood ashes to make lye and then mostly from left over cooking fats, lard. The lye soap is carefully poured into a loaf pan lined with parchment paper most of the time. Then it takes a day or two for the soap to become solid enough to be cut into bars.

During that time the women sat and talked away as a group of women do. Most had not seen each other for a while and brought their own lunch for the two days. Ma always supplied those that did not bring their lunch with sandwiches and other food. Everyone had free tea, water and in the morning coffee. It was one of the few times that none of the men that were always at the Troublesome Creek General Store. showed up. It was for women only and they knew it.

Now everyone had laughed about as hard as they could about Windy again. It was almost an hour, when Parson Brown ask "Where is Windy, he should be through by now?"

Before anyone could answer Windy, dried up and dressed in old bib overhauls with a faded green shirt came out the door of the store.

"I think it's time we had a Saturday Night Dance Party." he held a banjo across his chest and began picking it before long everyone was tapping the floor keeping time with the banjo beat.

"By golly your right, it's time we did just that," Sheriff Everts turned and in a few minutes returned from his car with fiddle and joined in.

In a moment, Ma shook her head with agreement and in a minute came through her bed room door carrying her dulcimer.

Parson Brown went behind the counter in the store and came out with a banjo that Ma had let him borrow to take lessons from Windy. He joined in.

Then, like the Pied Piper of the mountains, Windy led them out the door where they stood on the store's porch spreading their music through the hills, forest and mountains. It was a call that generations of Appalachia people answered to come and join them. And they did just that.

They came down the still muddy road with guitars, banjos, juice harps, to name a few instruments. There were even jug blowers who settled around the group on the porch.

In a short time they were all joined with pick-up trucks, cars and even a two horse drawn wagons all packed with families. They parked off the road, where they let the truck's wagons tail gates down to sit on. Others brought chairs sitting them around to watch and listen to the their music It was their Appalachian music, some of which had gone through centuries was passed down and was now still being played.

Even though the grounds were a little damp, but it could no longer hold back the music's call that came from their souls for generations whenever their music was played. The people were clapping, yelling, dancing and singing as their forefather and those before him had done.

From the past their music came

Barbra Allen was going to be sung by Cindy, Mattie and Mary Turner. Everyone knew that their voices rang loud together. It brought silence to the crowd as they began the sad story of Barbra Allen.

Twas in the merry monthly of May
When green buds all were swelling

Sweet William on his death bed lay
For the love of Barbra Allen

By the time they had finished with:

*Out of sweet William's heart, there grew a
rose
Out of Barbara Allen's a briar*

*They grew and grew in the old churchyard
Till they could grow no higher*

*At the end they formed a true lover's knot
And the rose grew round the briar.*

The music brought about tears in some
eyes as there always had been and always would
be for decades past and future.

While Ma played the dulcimer, and sang
Wild Rose of the Mountains Everts joined in with
his fiddle.

There was a story behind every song.
Legend had it that a certain fiddler fell in love
with a certain young lady who he saw repeatedly
at local dances. Because he proudly repeated the
music the fiddler could never stick up an
acquaintance with her because she strayed from
one fellow to another and she became known as
the *Wild Rose of the Mountains.*

Windy played his banjo and sang *Ruby
With Eyes That Spark.* The whole crowd stopped
to listen to the words of the songs that had been
handed down from generation to generation.

Then it was time for Old Bob dressed in
his worn red shirt and old blue overhauls as he
always was limped on the store porch with his
old fiddle in his hand He looked at everyone
nodding his long white hair hanging down his
back and his brown face that was tanned by age

and the sun. Some thought he was over a hundred years old. He had been in the mountains long enough that everyone remembered him as they grew up.

He had said nothing; he just put his fiddle under his chin. Now everyone knew what was coming and young couples stepped onto the foot pounded made clay dance floor. They formed a circle with young Gary Tucker in the middle.

Old Bob's fiddle came alive and he was joined by several others. Everyone else clapped hands and kept rhythm by pounding the clay. Then couples started going in a circle holding hands as they went around singing:

Skip, skip to my Lou
Skip, skip to my Lou
Skip to my Lou, my darling

Lost my partner what will I do?

Gary sang as he looked at the all the girls passing around him. Then he kept his eyes on the beautiful, red haired, Mary Cole, who was dancing with her boyfriend Bob Morris. Then he sang;

I'll get another one prettier than you

Gary grasped Mary's hand and took Bob's place. Bob now had his place in the middle and sang:

Fly's in the buttermilk, Shoo Fly Shoo

He sang it three times then he
picked Mattie Stewart out, whose date was his friend, Roger Gillis?

Lost my partner what will I do?

The same as Gary did and got another girl and her dancing partner went to the middle and so it went on for over an hour before Old Bob took his fiddle from around his neck and bowed to the applause Everyone that came from everywhere would go just about anywhere to dance to Old Bob's fiddle.

Finally it was getting late and several had to drive roads that at night were very dangerous while others had arrived on horseback it would even be longer more dangerous.

The churches usually joined together and sang *Amazing Grace* and the first stanza of America.

Parson Brown stepped forward, "With your permission I would like to sing the last verse of the *Star Spangled Banner* that I feel is something we should all know besides the first verse. My English teacher in high school, Mr. De Forest had us either memorize and say it to him or write it twenty five times."

"Go ahead preacher, it will warm us up for tomorrow," a yell came from the crown that was followed by laughter and a serious "Go ahead, my son is in Viet Nam and this is what he is fighting for."

Parson stepped to the center of the crowded porch. None had ever heard him sing and did not know what to expect. They found out on his first lines that came from a deep baritone voice no one had ever heard before. They looked with awe at the sound that came from this man of God they all knew.

They were also stunned by both the words that came from the last verse of the Star Spangled Banner that few had ever heard.

Oh! Thus be in ever when freemen shall stand
Between their loved homes and the war's
desolation!
Blest with victory and peace, may the
heaven-rescued land.
Praise the Power that hath made and
preserved us a nation.
Then conquer we must, when our cause it
is just
And this is our motto:
"In God is Our Trust"
And the Star - Spangled Banner in triumph
shall wave
Over the land of the free and the home of
the brave

There was silence for a moment. Then the crowd broke out in cheering and clapping hands. People moved to shake his hand and several with sons still in the service hugged him and thanked him with tears in their eyes. Now almost everyone wanted the Star Spangled Banner last verse to sing in their church tomorrow.

It was getting late and almost everyone was gone. They had left as fast as they had arrived disappearing into the Appalachian night.

Some stayed to watch the flag as it was taken down. Then they waved good-by and they too disappeared into the night as their neighbors had done.

Old Bob watched from the edge of the forest as everyone left. As he watched them go into the night as he had done for years now he closed his eyes and his memory of the past came into mind just like it was tonight. Over sixty years ago when he was young, he was in the same dance.

He picked out Maggie Wilson from the circling crowd. Maggie had looked at him and smiled. That was all it took and he married her a month later.

They had moved back to her family's land here in Appalachia and built a log cabin. At the time she was the only child of the Wilson family. She had lost a brother at birth.

Being the only child, everything was left to her by her parents after they had died in car accident during the early spring. Some of the roads in Appalachia are hidden by mountain shadows. Most of the ice on the road is melted when the sun is directly overhead around noon. As soon as the sun passes over the narrow roads between two mountains the melted ice on the roads become clear solid ice.

That day a coal truck going around a curve spun on ice and the driver did his best to get in under control, but it hit Maggie's parent's car head on.

Soon Bob began raising cattle in their bottom land and became very successful. Later they had three boys Adam, Peter and Joseph.

Their life together was a happy one until she died of a sudden heart attack.

Of his sons, Adam the youngest was the joker. He laughed at everything and people liked to be around him. And with his brown eyes, tall broad shoulders, and brown hair attracting girls was not a problem. He was a natural in classes and had to study little to keep his grades high.

Peter was built the same as Adam except he stood six foot one, with gray eyes and brown hair. He laughed daily at Adam and studied with his friends. He had to study hard to keep up with his brothers.

Joseph the oldest was also built like his brothers. But he was six-four with black hair, gray eyes and was serious about everything. He was the one that loved to hunt and live in the Appalachian Mountains most. He never said much, but what he said was what he did. He had graduated from high school but had decided he did not want to go to college until later.

Bob taught all of the boys how to fight with everything from hand, knives to different types of guns. But it was Joseph who had wanted to know more about hunting, fighting and everything he could from his dad Bob. He was definitely his father's son.

Trouble came when the beautiful, dark haired, blue eyed, tall Johnson twins May and Marcy had turned away from the Baker boys, Eli and Iza to Adam and Peter.

The feud between the Bakers and the Johnson's had been going on years. It what had caused the argument had changed several times, but had come to a stop when there was few left on each side to fight. Nothing had been going on for years but now it was about to start again.

The Baker boys, Eli and Iza, had waited with wooden clubs to beat Adam and Peter when they were walking home from the Johnson's house one Sunday afternoon. Unfortunately for them Joseph saw them waiting and in a short battle he left the two Baker boys beaten and staggering home. After that both dropped out of high school and were rarely seen.

Adam and Pete did well in high school and accepted academic scholarships to Eastern Kentucky State College in Richmond. The Johnson twins, May and Marcy were accepted at Eastern also. Bob had watched the feeling that had grown between his son Adam and May. It was the same that way with and

Summer had passed and it would be soon be time for college to start. As always it was Sunday all of the boys gathered around Bob on the porch one evening. Before they Bob said anything, Adam stood to speak. He grinned at everyone, 'Dad, Peter and I have something important to say to everyone."

At first this startled everyone. Neither Adam nor Peter ever said anything at the family meeting. Everyone except Bob, who just sat and listened while rocking slowly in his old chair and smoking his old pipe. He knew what they were going to ask.

"Dad, Adam and I want to ask for Mr. Johnson permission to marry his daughters. Adam wants to marry May and I want to marry Marcy. I know we are young but we are going to college and to become teachers. Adam and I want to teach math and May and Marcy wants to teach in the elementary school. We are going to find a school where we teach together if we can or at least not far apart. What do you think?" Peter asked hoping for an accepting answer from his father.

What puzzled him was that Joseph just sat there with his sneaky grin. He was always up to something when he did that.

"Well to tell you the truth, Johnson and I have talked about it already. He and his wife Joan think it would be good because they know you boys and they respect our family," Bob finished looking at the surprised and happy boys.

"Now both of you get together and go over tomorrow and ask May and Marcy about it. If they agree then go ahead and ask Johnson permission to marry his daughters."

Bob hesitated and then with a grin said, "Johnson and I agreed for you to meet at five when everyone is finished with their work."

Adam and Peter looked with amazement at their father. What he said had really startled them. How did their father knew what they wanted to do and when? It did not matter. They both grabbed their dad and hugged him.

"Well you might as well her the rest of it. Dad sent me to Eastern weeks ago to make sure you had two of the married houses on the campus. I got there just in time. Your two have the last ones. They are not new, but they are side by side," then Joseph said with a grin, "it will be a good place for me to stay every once in a while."

Everyone laughed at that remark. There would be no room for him at their small homes.

The next day, promptly at five, Peter and Adam, dressed in white shirts and black pants with shiny black shoes, knocked on the Johnson's door. It was opened by two smiling dark, haired beautiful twins, Marcy and May For a moment the boys were frozen from the beauty they were looking at. It was always going to be like that.

The girls each held their hands for a moment looking at their young man they loved and were ready to spend their lives with. Then they stepped aside and pointed to the kitchen. May and Marcy came over to the nervous Adam and Peter.

They each hugged their future husband .Then May whispered to Adam, "You and Peter can do this. We will be waiting for you here. Mom and dad know how much we love you and Peter. As she pointed to the kitchen door and said with a whisper, "Now go."

Robert Johnson and his wife Joan were sitting at the table in the kitchen drinking cups of coffee thinking about what Bob had said. Bob had come over a week ago and told them about how his sons felt about their daughters. It was sudden and unexpected to say the least.

Then Robert and Joan started paying more attention to their twin daughters and Adam and Peter. The two couples as they   sat on the porch in their swing or rocking chairs in the evening. They would always talk a while, laugh a little, but never take their eyes off of each other. It did take long to see the feeling each couple had for each other. They never walked anywhere without holding hands and looking at each other with that I-love-you look in their eyes that could be seen by anyone.

Finally after days of discussions they agreed that it would be difficult for their two girls to find young men like these. They knew all about them since they were born and what they knew was the kind of young man they wanted their daughters to marry. It was a little soon, but after talking with their daughters May and Marcy they convened their mother and father that these were the ones for them. Something else that Johnson and Joan thought was very important to them. They were all from the Appalachians and their children and grandchildren would always be close to come home to see them. They hoped they would not be separated and their new families gone to other places or states.

Just before the boys were to arrive that day they called the girls into the kitchen and ask them how they felt about what was about to happen.

They heard the boys coming through the door right on time. Joan looked at Robert and grinned a little. She remembered when her husband had come to ask the same thing.

Then Peter and Adam came through the door. Each one was a little pale. That was expected. The Johnson's looked up at the two young men that would be part of their family.

Peter looked at the future parents of their wives, took a deep breath, "Mr. and Mrs.

Johnson, my brother and I are asking permission to marry your daughters. I will marry Marcy and my brother Adam wants permission to marry May. We promise that we will love them, take care of them and always be with them."

Johnson stood up. And to their surprise he extended his hand, "I know you will boys. Her mother and I could not ask for anyone better. We will be proud to have you in our family."

Mrs. Johnson stood and hugged both of them while Mr. Johnson shook their hands.

The twins had been listening outside the door and ran into the room to hug their future husbands. It was a great day.

The couples were married by Parson Brown on Sunday afternoon after church. Then there was opening the presents, cake cutting, changing of cloths and they left for Eastern in a used Ford purchased by both of the parents. They would have a honeymoon in their old apartments. They would probably be there for the next four years.

Bob and his Joseph were walking home from the wedding. Bob knew there was something bothering his son. It came out soon.

"Dad, when I went to Eastern for their college apartments, I stopped at a marine recruiter. I decided to join. I will leave next Thursday."

"I did not tell them because I thought it might spoil the wedding and upset you," he took a deep breath, "Dad, I just want to see the world. I just hope you understand."

Bob turned to his older son, "I do understand. I did the same thing when I was your age. Now before you go I want to tell you some stories about me that you need to know about. It is about what I did and where. You can tell it to Adam and Peter someday."

Joseph listened with care and was amazed at what his dad had done in his life. There was his raising in Texas and how he learned to use his Colt. He talked about the Rough Riders and their battle a San Juan Hill. Then he grinned as did the pistol and the clapping of hand trick with his Colt forty-five.

Joseph could not believe the quickness of his dad's draw and the hitting of cans with every shot. He blinked at the speed the old Colt got back into his holster.

Bob still remembered the next morning when Joseph was leaving. They looked at each other and hugged each other like it was the last time they would ever see each other. As he went down the path, Joseph turned again to wave at his dad for the last time. They both knew it would be the last time they would see each other.

Bob still lived in the same log house he had built decades ago. Now he sat in his old rocker on the porch and watched the sun set over the Appalachian Mountains that he loved again and again. It was one of the reasons he could never leave. But he knew things were changing.

Yesterday he had gone to Maggie's grave as he had at every evening, but this was different. He went that morning and finished digging his grave beside hers. It had taken several days because he was forced to stop anytime his heart reminded him that it was just about done with this life.

As he sat there his rocker on his porch, Old Bob or his real name Robert Smith, again thought for the last time the memories he had told his son Joseph from past life.

He had started with the beginning. Bob was born and raised in Texas near El Paso. His mother and dad had been killed by an Indian raid. He was six and his mother had put him under a dug out hiding place under the rug under their table when she heard shots outside.

The battle did not last long and he heard moccasins above his head. Someone pulled the rug away and before his hiding place was opened he heard shots and the Indian fell on the floor above his head.

Later it was opened and there was a rough looking man in a black hat, an old heavy gray shirt with blood on it. He reached down with one hand and pulled Bob out. He just looked and they went out the door passing his dead mother, dad and the Indian that had tried to get him.

Outside were four similar looking cowboys and four dead Indians. He put Bob in the saddle with him. "Bob I'm your grandfather Clay. I had come to see my daughter's family and you. You will have to stay with me at the ranch until I think it is time me leave."

Bob always remembered what he had said and thought it was strange. He grew up and worked as a cowhand on the ranch until he was eighteen. Then a call came for a need of cowboys to fight the Spanish in Cuba after the sinking of the Maine. He along with several of his friends joined the Rough Riders. Over half of his friends missed the boat to the war.

On July 1, 1898 he was one of the Rough Riders to follow Teddy Roosevelt up San Juan Hill. It was a fierce fight that day. To his left moving up the hill with them was the 10th all African-American Cavalry let by Captain "Black Jack" Pershing advancing, ignoring the deadly fire. All around them men were dying.

Finally they all rushed the Spanish block house and trenches together. The Spanish fled. Smith joined a group of men that after reaching the top they drove the yellow silk flag of the cavalry and the Stars and Stripes their country into the soft earth of the Spanish trenches.

Old Bob memories came back to him about that day he had to use the pistol and holster he was holding. He reached and put his holster on for one last time. It was an old leather holster that held a worn, ivory handled Colt forty-five six shooter He tied the holster to his leg, checked the cartages in the cylinder. Then in one blur of a motion, he drew and fired sending the can that was fifteen feet away high into the air. He looked with satisfaction as he put his pistol back in his holster before they can hit the ground.

Then he put two cans up and did the same except this time he fanned the Colt with his left hand and two shots rang out almost as one and the two cans flew high into the air.

Old Bob sat back down in his rocking chair and the memories came back to him. He had been taught to use the Colt when his grandfather spent time with them in the Texas winter on the ranch. His grandfather Clay had been a Texas Ranger and had faced many outlaw duels and had never lost one.

Clay and Bob practiced shooting in summer and fall. In the winter he showed Bob how to draw the pistol. After several years when he left for the last time he had given a used Colt forty-five and holster to Bob.

"It's a good outfit Bob, the Mexican fast gun I got it from will never need it again," Clay remarked as he handed the outfit to Bob.

"Well Bob you are fastest I have ever seen with a six-gun. Too bad you were born at the wrong time. You would be a legend by now with me in the Texas Rangers. Remember someday you will need it. So keep practicing," he then tipped his hat to his ranch friends and rode into the hills where he had come from. They never saw him again.

The skills taught to him by the Texan would soon prove what he had learned. After he battle for San Juan Hill was over, the Americans were all getting together to have their picture made. Roosevelt and other were walking in front of Bob when a wounded Spanish soldier in front of Bob rose up on his knees to shoot Roosevelt in the back. Bob still didn't remember what had happened that day but he had drawn and shot the soldier in the back and put his pistol back in his holster before anyone had turned around.

Roosevelt and his group had spun around and saw Bob standing there and the dead Spanish soldier with a pistol in his hand lying dead across the path they had just walked over.

Soon they were surrounded by men who had heard the shot and were afraid that Roosevelt had been wounded. But everyone was puzzled because only Bob was standing there and he did not even have gun in his hand, only a rifle.

Then a tall, heavy red headed Irish soldier stepped out of the crowd. "I seen it all sir, it was the lad there that saved the day."

One of the men with Roosevelt stepped forward, "I could not have been him, and he was holding no pistol."

"Aye that's the lad. He wasn't because he put pistol back in his holster."

"Are you telling me that he drew his pistol, shot the soldier and put his pistol back in its holster before we could turn around?"

"Aye that is what I saw," nodding his head with appreciation."

"That is impossible, no one could do that, let alone this young soldier," with that the surrounding veteran soldiers who had just won a battle agreed. It would be impossible.

Roosevelt stepped forward, "First I want to thank you for saving my life. As far as being doubtful I have been out West and have seen many of what I thought was impossible handling of the Colt by men who looked no different. I think this young man just might be another one."

He smiled and nodded his head, "Will you show the Rough Riders something to remember?"

Bob handed his rifle to the Irish soldier

and waved the doubtful soldier to him.

"Spread your arms and clap your hand three times,"

To this the soldier humped his shoulders with doubt and began. He clapped his hands the first time making a loud noise.

"Faster," Bob told him twice and the soldier was beginning to think Bob was trying to make a fool of him. On the third time, he brought his hands together as fast as he could.

But there was no clap because Bob had his pistol between his hands for a second and back in holster it two.

Everyone looked with disbelief except Roosevelt, who stepped forward shaking Bob's hand. "Bully for you, and I thought I had seen it all with Buffalo Bill, Earp and others in the West but now I see that we have a Rough Rider better than any I have ever seen or heard of."

With that there was cheering and shaking hands with Bob as the gathered to make the picture.

Now it was getting dark. Bob was sitting on the cabin's porch as he and Maggie had done countless times. He was about to go in when his old hound, Roosevelt, stopped and stared at the dark woods. The hair on his black and brown back came straight up and he made a low growl. Bob did not look around, but he patted the upset Roosevelt on the head and led him inside. He knew what Roosevelt's growl and raised hair had meant. They had arrived and he was glad of it. Tomorrow he would settle something that had worried him for a long time.

But now his heart was struggling for the

last time and he knew his last day was tomorrow one way or the other. But he did not fear it because he would be meeting Maggie soon and they be together forever.

The next morning his heart told Bob it was almost his time to join Maggie. Out of an old trunk he took his cowboy outfit that he had worn that day on San Juan Hill. He wrapped his Rough Rider blue polka-dot handkerchief around his neck. Roosevelt had worn one that flowed like a guerdon for men to follow that day. After the battle they had all had decided it to be the sign of the Rough Riders

He looked in the mirror. His clothes fit well and he thought he looked pretty good for his age He belted his pistol on and again watched it jump from his holster in a blur. He smiled to himself. If he was right today he would face someone again in battle for the last time one way or the other.

It was Saturday and Bob almost all ways went into town to visit his friend Jacob, the president at the bank. Most of the time business was slow. They sat around his president's desk where they had always liked to discuss war battles. Jacob had been in WWII and fought with the 101st at the Battle of the Bulge and was wounded seriously.

They had even discussed the Battle at San Juan and the Rough Riders. Bob had never said anything about himself. Still it puzzled Jacob because he knew so much about battle especially the Rough Riders in Cuba.

Bob walked through the bank door that morning and faced the two men he had hoped to meet for the last time somewhere or somehow today. The older tall man facing him had a black beard and dark eyes that showed both hate and satisfaction was pointing a double barreled shot gun at him. Both had old black hats, rough looking tan shirts, muddy boots and black suspenders holding up used jeans.

On the other side, with the same shot gun, stood a shorter, stocker man with a black beard and dark hate filled eyes. He showed the same family hate and satisfaction.

"Well, look at this, the last of the Baker boys, Eli and Iza, my old hound, Roosevelt, smelled you boys out last night," Bob said as he stopped and faced the hatred stares from the two men.

"We waited a long time to get you Old Bob. We still hate the Roberts for what they did to my great grandfather Azra."

"Azra tried to steal my grandfather's daughter and he killed him for it. Since that time three of my relatives have been killed and all of yours except for you two," Bob smiled, "It time for me to go up and you two to go down with the rest of your back shooting family."

"Before we kill you, we want you to know what is going to happen to all the rest of your family, tell him Eli," Iza said with a grin and look of satisfaction.

Eli, who looked with satisfaction, grinned, " Well when they bury you and all of your children and Roberts kinfolk come to see you off, we are going to be there to send them off. We were sparkin May and Marcy before they came along. They will pay too. What do you think of that?"

"Well, Again I was thinking that you two are about to go down and I hope I am going up," he answered.

Jacob looked at them as they spoke to each other. He knew his friend Bob would probably try to stop them, but there was no way to for him to beat the two killers with cocked shotguns pointing at Bob.

Jacob decided it was time he did something to give Bob a small chance. He had been in situations like this during the war. If you did nothing you were sure to die and on the other hand if you tried to do something you had a chance to live. It all depended if Bob was good as everyone thought.

He quickly raised his right hand, pointed at the door and yelled, "Come on in sheriff."

The Baker boys turned their head for an instant. That was all it took. Jacob watched as Bob drew his pistol and fanned the hammer. It was a blur. Two pistol shots sounding as one. No one else could have drawn a pistol and shot two men who had shotguns pointed at him. The bullets fired from Old Bob's Colt forty-five blew Paul and Bob across the room.

There they lay with bullet holes in their foreheads. Each bullet had hit them in the middle just above their open eyes.

In a blur Bob put his gun back into its holster, smiled and nodded with thanks to his friend Jacob, who had not moved because he was still in shock. He could not believe the impossible shooting that had just saved his life and the others in the bank.

Jacob came out of it and raced across to his friend, Old Bob who had fallen to the floor.

On his knees, Jacob quickly looked for a wound of some kind on Bob, but he could find none. He looked down at his face expecting fear or pain. But Bob looked like he was asleep with his eyes closed and a smile on his face. Bob had gone out the way that he had wanted. He had saved a friend with his last fast draw.

Old Bob's funeral was held at Parson Brown's church. It was held outside because Parson Brown estimated over a hundred of his admirer's young and old had come to pay their last respects to the old man that would never again play the dancing fiddle that generations had learned to love. His children, their wives were all there shaking hands and listening to stories about their dad, but keep some stories they only knew to themselves. Joseph was not there and they did not know how to contact him in time for the his dad's funeral

After the service, he was buried on the mountain in the grave he had dug beside his beloved wife Maggie that he had shared a life with for over sixty years.

After the funeral and everyone left, Ma opened brown sealed envelope he gave her a year ago in the store. His instructions were that it was only to be opened on his death.

Ma looked at the picture of Roosevelt and the Rough Riders that was made on top of San Juan Hill. There was a young and fearless young man standing with the Rough Riders. Old Bob had circled his picture. You never could tell about the people moving here to the mountains.

She would put his picture on the wall with the rest from police, gun fighters, solder's from wars, and more. Now a man who played a fiddle for decades turned out to be a Rough Rider.

Dear Ma

I know that the only reason you are reading this letter is that I have passed away.

My tomb stone is made with this year's date on the ground by my grave next to Maggie's. Windy knows where it is.

The map of my land divided up into three even parts should be sent to the enclosed addresses of my three children.

Also please send a copy of the picture of me on top of San Juan Hill with the Rough Riders to my children with it I never told anyone about it.

Keep the gun and holster. Learn to use it and it will serve you well someday.

Finally enclosed are two ten dollar bills for Windy for taking care of our graves and to care for my old hound Roosevelt

My life with Maggie and the people of the Appalachia could never have been better. I will miss the dancing and the fiddle I played. It goes to Parson Brown. Now he has one of his own and I hope he learns to replace me.

Now I am with Maggie forever.

I will see you all some day
Old Bob

Chapter 4

After Old Bob's funeral Dancer had taken a bus to Louisville for his physical. During the ride up there on the crowded bus, there were several other men trying to figure out a way to be ruled 4-F and avoid going the army. They were doing anything to avoid being shipped to Viet Nam. One put soap under his arm to try to raise his blood pressure another as putting something in his eyes to produce temporary blindness and there were many other strange methods being tried to go home.

However, the next day at their physical exam they found out that the veteran army doctors were experienced with most of these methods and paid no attention to them. They went in groups where they stood naked and turned their head and coughed as the doctors inspected them.

The immunization shots were different. The recruits put their arms into a large yellow smiley face. Someone grabbed it and held it steady. When your arm was finally released it was full of shots and holes where your blood was drawn. Dancer passed his physical and was then cycled into a basic training company ending up at Fort Knox.

Dancer's training day sometimes started at five in the morning in rain or snow six days a week. The day consisted of digging foxholes, bivouacking in the woods, and hand to hand combat training. On Sunday, his only day off, he looked forward to reading any mail he had gotten the past week. It was mostly from Ma, his mother and at times Fisher. Others received mail that was either good or not good news. It was mostly about breakups with girl friends or illness in their family. When received no mail he just caught up on his sleep.

One of the most intense training was on the M-1 Garand rifle that he had to disassemble, clean and reassemble with his eyes closed. Dancer learned to shoot it under any conditions. The M-1 also proved to be dangerous to the recruits as drill time. Some found out the hard way that the M-1 required other skills. One was that during inspection, you had to open the action of the rifle and close it by pushing down with your thumb. If you pushed down and did not get your thumb up quickly enough, you had a mashed thumb. Every day you would see recruits with swollen thumbs on their right hands.

Also it was dangerous when recruits were cleaning the M-1 because the long spring that had to be carefully put coiled back into the rifle had a tendency to break loose. It shot across the room hurting anyone anywhere it hit and it often hit them is some bad places.

Later Dancer was in one of the first groups to be trained on the new AR-15. The AR-15 was lighter, shot the .223 and was easier to handle. But his M-1 was more dependable and shot a larger the 30-06 round. His old rifle back home was a bolt-action 30-06 WW I Springfield a black bear with cubs came out of a berry patch going toward him. He shot into the air and it stopped the bear, but if it had kept coming, he doubted he would have had the time for one or two more shots using the bold action.

In basic training he caught the attention of the several of his trainers. One was Drill Sgt. Pierce a veteran of WWII with the 101st Airborne. He was a tall man with blue eyes that went right through you when he wanted them to. It was enough to make every recruit do anything to avoid the look and what was following. He knocked on Lt. Lee's door, "Come," replied Lee.

Pierce was a young man with little experience and he trusted anything his sergeant had to say. Pierce stood at attention before the desk, "At ease, what can I do for you sergeant?"

"Sir, I spoke to you about the new recruits and the one that could hit dead center the first shot, but could not hit the target on any of the others"

"Yes, I remember, Dancer, I believe, you didn't think he was trying and he was just lucky on the first shot."

"Yes, sir, but I was wrong," stepping forward he laid the target on the desk, "sir, at first I didn't notice that the hole near the middle is actually too large for one bullet hole."

"Sergeant, are you are saying that he put three bullets that close to the same hole?"

The sergeant took a deep breath, "He is from the Appalachian Mountains in Kentucky, sir."

Lee stood up and held the target out and looked at it again, "That explains part of it. He has probably been shooting and hunting since he was born. I wish we had a division of those men. They're the kind that will stand up for their country and you will never have to worry about your back in combat."

"There is more sir, Sergeant Thomas, who teaches hand to hand combat not only to our recruits but to the green berets was using him as an example because he was tall and looked like he needed to learn about protecting himself in combat."

"Yes, I know Sergeant Thomas, he has third degree black belt and was the champion in the recent company combat test. Did he accidentally hurt Dancer?"

Pierce stood with his hands behind his back, answered slowly, "Not exactly sir. It seems that Dancer was better than Thomas. In fact this morning Thomas told me he had never seen the type of hand to hand Dancer uses.

Lieutenant Lee started rubbing his head with his hand, "You are telling me that a young, raw recruit can out shoot and out fight the best that we have in this company."

"Yes, sir I would like to train him to be a scout. He said he had been trained on hunting and survival in the woods and jungle before."

"A jungle in Kentucky!" Lee shouted, astounded.

"No, sir in the Everglades, he was trained by the Seminoles," Pierce replied.

Lee went behind his desk and said, "All right we need men like that, I'll send this through," as he filled out forms on his desk," he added, "recommending him to jump school at Ft. Campbell and scout training for the 101st. If half of what you say is true, the VC's in for a shock."

Chapter 5

Dancer came home after his basic training. He spent most of his time around the store just resting and talking to the checker board crowd about basic training. One thing everyone wanted to know was how it felt to jump out of an airplane. Dancer described it and answered their questions and started to relax, he looked forward to hunting with Windy and Cat.

Today this hunt he wanted to try out his special jungle boots. His Indian friends made a set of waterproof moccasins for him that was suited for the Vietnam rainfall and jungle. They were as high as his boots, but they allowed him to travel silently through the jungle. With the leather soles on the bottom of his boots, his feet could feel the ground before he put a step down allowing him to avoid any sticks or other things that would make noise. Dancer could now walk through the forest or jungle almost without any sound. But Cat had been gone for several days and it worried everyone.

It was late at night when a strange sound came from the store's front porch. As Ma started to get out of bed, Dancer, had already dressed in his army scout clothes, rushed past and opened the store's front door. In the moon light he saw Cat washing the faces of two wolf dog cubs that were close to his legs. Dancer looked at Cat, who stared at him for a moment, then raced back into the woods with Dancer right behind him. He knew Ma could take care of the cubs. She had a way with the creatures of the forest.

Ma looked at the small wolf cubs looking up at her. Both had white and orange stripes between their eyes, but one was built like a husky, with a bigger chest and shorter ears. She smiled, "Well it seems to me we are going to be together for a while."

They sat and watched as she crossed the stores porch and emptied what was left of potatoes out of large cardboard box. Reached and got a large towel that had dried in the sun and placed it in the bottom of the box. She picked up the cubs, gripping each of them on the back of their necks and as they curled their tails between their legs she placed them in the box. She then carried them inside.

Ma and Windy had milked their cow that day and were going to make buttermilk. She now had better uses for the milk. She took a large metal dish out of her cabinet and filled it with milk.

Ma looked at the deep gray, larger cub who was protesting the most, "Now ain't you the bad one," she smiled and stuck his protesting nose and mouth into the dish.

He wiped his mouth with his tongue and began to lick the warm milk out of the dish. On the other side of the dish the other cub did the same. Soon they were rolling around and attacking each other. They were acting just like little boys always do Ma thought.

A short time later, she took them both outside, where each dug a small hole and used it and covered it. Ma picked them up and went back into the house and placed them in their box. In a short time after trying to find a suitable place in the box they were asleep back to back.

She looked at the two little cubs sleeping soundly, "Something bad must have happened to you and your family, but don't you worry none, we will take care of you like we did your dad," she slowly said while watching the empty trail.

They came up the trail at daylight. Dancer carrying a large gray wolf that she thought must be Cat's mate. Dancer laid her quietly on the front porch of the store and went inside and returned with a small medicine bag. He quickly found the wound, two large puncture wounds at the base of her hip. Using a large hypodermic, he began to suck the poison out of the wound. It was a strange green fluid.

"Keep away, it is deadly to just to touch," he said glancing at Ma. After adding some of his personal herbs, the spot began to bubble. He then covered the wound with layers of bandages. Cat lay down by his mate and kept his eyes open watching her slow breathing.

Dancer looked up with frustration on his face and said, "I can't save her, the poison has no cure."

Then looking down with admiration he added, "She had four cubs, and even knowing she could not win, she fought to give these two time to escape and Cat found them hiding on the trail here."

He bent over and softly rubbed Cat, who never took his eyes off his mate who was resting comfortably.

"Unlike humans and other animals, the wolf can mate for life. I think Cat will have a hard time without her," Dancer said as he went to his room.

A short time later, he came out. At first Ma did not recognize him. He was no longer the Dancer she had always known, he stood as an Indian warrior from his leather moccasins to his buckskin pants. Then there was his painted body and face. She thought he knew who did this and he wanted them to pay.

Dancer walked to her holding out both hands and hugging her, "If I do not come back, thank you for everything you have done for me. And please take care of Cat and find a good home for his little ones. I will always love you," he kissed her cheek and went out.

She watched him going into the woods down the same forest path that he and Cat had taken before. At the edge of the woods he held his hand up in the air and said something. There was a flash of light and a large white wolf suddenly appeared, looked at him and they began running down the trail together.

Ma had heard legends about Azar the White Wolf of Death Stealer of Souls. Now she had seen him. She would not like to be the one Dancer and Azar were hunting, she thought as she closed the door, for death was on their way.

It took the racing Dancer and Azar about an hour to enter the crack in the mountain and finally reaching a hill overlooking the Indian village. In the middle village were the chiefs and elders from thorough out the valley.

On the other side were a group of men painted green. In front of them was a large man painted green with a green and red snake headdress. Before him, coiled up was the largest green snake Dancer had ever seen.

He looked down at Azar, "It is time for us to destroy once and for all this evil,' and starting down to the village, he again looked at Azar, and half smiled, "at least you will be still standing win or lose," then as if he understood, the giant white wolf looked up with his red eyes and shook his large head several times.

Actually it was Azar's way to show smile and laughter. He understood what Dancer had said. Being over four centuries old, he had mastered the language of several civilizations and tribes. He often observed though the necklace when the wearer became frightened to see who or what was trying to harm them.

Of all of those he had served, Dancer was his favorite, because he was a warrior born without question. He reminded him of a tall, face painted warrior with a spear centuries ago. Azar saw him through the necklace. Although covered with blood, he was still fighting armored bearded men that had long knives.

The warrior had killed three, but Azar saw that he getting weaker by the minute and that he was needed, but could do nothing until he was summoned by the wearer of the black jeweled necklace. As the bloody warrior faced the remaining two, Azar saw that he was determined that they must not live to kill his wife and son.

The two started their final attack. It was then that the wounded warrior's wife, daughter of the tribe's shaman, had called on him. Azar destroyed the attacking men in seconds. He turned to face the warrior who was being held up by his wife and being hugged around his leg by his small son. The warrior was trying to lift this spear for one final attack to save his family. It was then that his wife put her hand on the spear and explained about Azar.

In the excitement, she had forgotten about him. As Azar approached the bloody, weak warrior he dropped to one knee. He smiled and rubbed Azar's ears and his small son hugged him around the large white neck. His wife had also rubbed his ears and nodded as she summoned him back into his home in the black jewel necklace she wore.

The other thing is he loved to run into battle next to another warrior on a mission to destroy evil. And finally he hated snakes and looked forward to destroying the one that had killed Cat's mate. However, he knew the Green Death Snake could possibly destroy him because he was a spirit snake. For some reason, he looked forward to a kill or be killed battle. After all, he was Azar, killer of evil whether it be man, snake or anything else.

When they arrived at the village, no one saw them as they stopped at the edge of the crowd listening to the Green Gods demands. The man was green with a snake head dress was speaking. "I am the Green God one touch from me or a bit from Satan," pointing to the giant snake curled in from of him," will bring instant suffering and death."

" I will explain this one more time," standing up, he turned facing chiefs and Elders, "it is simple, you leave here before sun up taking nothing except what you can carry, come back in ten days we will not be here."

One of the old chiefs, Bear Killer, stood up, "As you did before, you will take our entire crop we have harvested for winter, and anything in our homes we can't carry. How can we care for the old ones and the sick? You will kill all of our game; there will be nothing for us to live on this winter."

The Green God stood, "Well, unlike you, they will still be alive," and pointed his stick toward the chief and the green snake began moving toward him.

Dancer stepped out of the crowd, "I challenge you and the snake to combat to the death."

He raised the green stick and the giant snake stopped and came back.

"Oh, my! Another hero with a wolf no doubt... We had one challenge Satan yesterday. She escaped, but will die because she was bitten. She died fighting over her two little wolves, which by the way fed my snake yesterday. There is no wolf that can beat the mighty Satan!" he said yelling and raising both of his hands in the air.

The surrounding families knew he was speaking the truth as he had done in the past. They would be forced to do as he said again and lose many of their men, women and children. There had been no one to stop him. But now he was being challenged by the legendary Azar and Dancer. Now everyone had glimmer of hope at last.

The Green God stepped forward, "As far as killing me, it can't be done except by the poison generated by me and I am not going to kill myself. Well I don't mind a little sport,' and pointing at the chief that had spoken up, "you will be desert."

"Now let's get this over with, bring out your champion," as he pointed his green stick toward Dancer. The green group of men began cheering and shouting, "Green Death! Green Death!

Dancer stepped aside and Azar walked toward the snake. Now from the Indians who recognized Azar came a chant of Azar! Azar! The two stopped about eight feet from each other. This was exactly the distance Satan could strike and kill in less than a second. Azar did not crouch, but stood looking at the giant snake. Everyone stood silent knowing that death would soon come to one or both of these combatants. Suddenly the snake struck at Azar and the two were lost in whirl wind of dust, white fur and green scales.

The green men and their chief were confident about who would win. It had always been this way, a challenge, a fight to the death and all in village leaving. Then they would take everything left, kill everything they could. After that they would leave.

Suddenly, there was a loud crunching noise from the cloud of dust. The green group looked at each other. There had never been a sound like that. Oh well, Satan had probably coiled around the wolf and broken its back they all thought.

Then it was suddenly very still as the dust cleared and the two were visible not moving on the ground, neither Satan nor Azar moved where they both lay. Then Azar stood up and carried something to Dancer and dropped it at his feet. It was the large head of Satan with its eyes and mouth showing its fangs open still dripping green poison.

The Indians suddenly broke into a cheer, Azar! Azar! While the green men and the Green God looked on with disbelief.

The Green God looked at his headless green snake that had killed and terrorized with him for years. How could this be? Nothing had ever even touched Satan, the giant snake. The more he thought of it the madder he got. How could he replace the giant snake? Then he looked across at Dancer. He would die for this. He would die now!

As the Green God moved across toward Dancer, Azar started forward to meet him. Dancer stepped forward and stopped him.

"No old friend, you have done your part, now it is my turn." Azar stepped back and sat down to watch Dancer. This is why he loved Dancer, a warrior born who faced death and was not afraid.

They stopped at about six feet away from each other. The Green God said, "Now you will die, nothing you can do will kill me. Sooner or later," he showed his hands with needles sticking out from the end of each finger 'one of these will touch you and then you are dead."

Dancer had seen the needles before. He had been trained to fight and destroy this killer of innocents. His trainer had taped needles to his fingers. At first he was marked and bleeding all over. Gradually he got better and better until he could dodge the needles. Now it was time to see if his training had paid off.

Suddenly the chief swung at Dancer with both hands, Dancer stepped back and slapped him hard across his face with his right hand causing bleeding from his nose.

Dancer stepped back and smiled as cheering came from the Indians. "Never been slapped before have you. Your snake is dead. Your men are losing faith in you."

Dancer was right, if he kept getting hit his men would lose confidence in him. He must kill him now!

The Green God ran forward. Again he swung with his right hand then spun around bringing his left hand around to where Dancer was standing. Only Dancer was not standing. He had dropped down and brought this foot heel into the side of the left knee of the Green God, who let out a howl of pain and dropped to one leg. He tried to stand up, but staggered. His knee was shattered.

The Green God staggered up and raising both poisoned hands he lunged at Dancer. He was slow because his right knee could not hold his weight. As he started to fall forward, Dancer stepped aside and caught his left arm and forced it down. He came up with side of his right hand striking the exposed throat.

The Green God gagged and held his throat with both hands at he fell on the dirt. Too late he realized what he had done. His throat was pierced by the poison needles on both of his hands. He struggled to get up, but the poison was now going through his body. And what he had witnessed so many times in the past, the choking, coughing and the final uncountable jerking of the body before death was happening to him. In a moment it was over.

The tribe cheered and chanted Dancer! Azar! Dancer! Azar! The green men began to back slowly away from the approaching Indian warriors. Suddenly they started to flee leaving their green cover, spears and cloaks behind.

As everyone celebrated the death of The Green God and the snake Satan they cheered Dancer and Azar. But no one got close to the giant white wolf with glowing red eyes.

Then old Bear Killer and the Elders gathered around Dancer and Azar. The rest of the tribe formed a circle them. The chief stepped forward and put both of his hands on Dancer's shoulders "Once again you have proven to be a true son of Keeper of Secrets and with the help of Azar you have defeated those who would have destroyed our way of life. We will tell of the battle to all of our brothers in all of the tribes everywhere. They will speak of it over their campfires for a hundred lifetimes."

Then looking down at Azar, he dropped to one knee and held the large white head with the red eyes, "You too have proven once again, to be Azar the White Wolf of Death, Stealer of Souls to any and all evil as you have done for hundreds of years. Your story will be told with Dancers."

Dancer received a thankful nod from all of the Elders and cheering as he and Azar ran past rest of the tribe. They had to hurry back to where Cat was and his dying mate.

As they ran, Dancer looked down at Azar, "I know you understand me, would you like to go on a hunt someday, just you and me?"

Azar looked up at Dancer, the only person that ever believed he could understand what they were saying. He let out a quick howl.

"I look forward to it, now you must go and I must get back to Cat and his poisoned mate."

He nodded his head to Azar who understood what was about to happen

"Home, Azar." He said as they reached the top of the hill overlooking the store.

Then Azar disappeared in a flash and cloud of smoke.

In the mountains far away, Nada stood, looked out the window into the stars and said, "My son I could not be prouder of you for what you and Azar have done this day. Another evil destroyed. Now I must work on protecting you from something you think does not exist."

Chapter 6

Back at the store, Cat's mate had died. At dawn, Dancer covered her in a black wool blanket and buried her under a large Oak tree in a meadow in back of the store. Cat stayed at the grave day and night. He ate very little.

On the morning Dancer was being driven to Prestonsburg by Sheriff Evarts to catch a bus to Knoxville, where he would board a bus to Ft. Campbell he had said good bye to Ma and the others at the store and was leaving when he heard Cat's wolf cry.

Dancer told Sheriff Evarts to stop the car. The sheriff looked with concern at Dancer, "Is something wrong?"

"No, I just forgot to say good-by to a friend that I will never see again," he said as he got out of the car and hurried up to the meadow where Cat was.

As Dancer neared, Cat ran to him just like old times and wagged his tail and licked his hands as Dancer rubbed his ears.

They sat down by the grave. Dancer had made a small wooden marker with a carved wolf's head. As he sat down, Cat moved over and placed his head in his lap.

From a distance Ma and Sheriff Evarts watched the two as Dancer talked and moved his hands and Cat sat up and watched him. Finally, he got up; Cat put both paws on his chest and licked him as he hugged the one thing that he would miss forever.

"What is he doing, Ma?" Sheriff Everts asked watching Dancer and Cat.

"He is saying good-by to his best friend. They both know they will never see each other again," said Ma as Dancer came toward them.

Dancer hugged Ma again and got in the car. Everts said nothing about the tears he saw in Dancer's eyes.

A week later, a pack of wolves showed up at night in front of the store, Cat ran out and left with them while Ma watched. She stepped out on the porch and watched as they faded into the forest. Suddenly Cat came racing back and stepped up on the porch and stood before Ma, looking up at her.

She dropped to one knee; she knew he was saying good-by. "I will miss you too Cat, we share a lot of memories."

Then holding him close, "Don't you worry none about your sons, I will take good care of them, " and in a final rub of his ears, "and remind them of what a father they had."

He stepped back looked at her for the last time and ran into darkened woods to the waiting gray wolf pack. Cat disappeared into night never to be seen by them again.

Ma or Dancer did not know it but Cat would become a legend known throughout and written about for decades. A month or so later Windy came in with what had happened to Cat.

Dear James,

The back of a deer skin... This year they came again with another story on a deer skin that will be legendary.

It was the story how Cat died. The first

100

drawing showed a mountain lion with a bad right foot. Under the lion were seven Indians, three men and four women on their backs. They were killed by this lion. Next there was a drawing showing several warriors hunting for the lion. The next was a girl getting water from a stream with the lion above her in a tree. Then it leaped for the girl but was met in midair by a black wolf with orange and white stripes between its eyes, it was Cat. They fought until a hunting party came.

Although he was part wolf, Cat was no match for the lion and lay dying there as the lion tried to get away. The little girl ran to Cat, who though he knew he was dying, wagged his tail. The hunting party were going to kill Cat but were stopped by the girl who held Cat's head in her lap. The hunting party then ran past them and killed the lion, it had a twisted front paw which made it impossible to hunt, and it is why he hunted the Indians. His other front leg was also broken by Cat.

The Indian chief knowing that Cat had given his life to save his daughters had Cat carried back to the camp where later he died with his head on the little girls lap. On the final drawing it showed Cat being honored by the tribe's best warriors.

In fact each had a black wolf face with orange and white stripe between the eyes on their chest. Windy told me it was the sign of a warrior who would give his life to save a member of his tribe.

I know it hurt you as it did all of us that Cat died, but he died bravely and is now a legend in the making. His two sons look the same black, gray with orange and white stripes between their eyes getting bigger every day.

When your mother came by for a visit, one of the cubs came over to Kana and sat on his foot. Kana picked him up and asked permission to play with him. You should have seen a giant like Kana playing with a puppy he could hold in his hand. Your mother Nada, saw what was happening and asked me if he could keep it or should she wait until you got back.

I thought about it and I knew you would like it if I gave him a good home, so I gave him to Kana, who was so careful taking it out the door and thanking me every step of the way. Your mother thanked me also and just shook her head when she saw him acting like a little boy with his first puppy in the car.

James, the other cub looks different. He is growing fast and is already almost as big as Cat was. I think he has a little husky in him. We call him Ready because he is always ready to do something good and bad just like his dad, he never leaves my side.

Windy has dug a grave for Cat beside his mate's grave. Of course he is not in it, but it serves the purpose. Ready hunts with Windy now and then, but most of the time he stays in the store just like his father.

It took me three days to finish this letter and let everyone here read it. I read all of yours. I take pen in hand to tell you the news of Cat's death and better yet of how he died. Last year we were visited by Indians who had you and Azar's fight with the Green God written on skin. I'll mail pictures of them when you have time to *send us a letter in reply. Windy is trying to find out the whole story about Cat and will tell it to you when you come home again. Now take care of yourself and we look forward to your safe return.*

God Bless

Ma and Everyone at the store

Dancer read the letter again and again when he could find shelter and it brought some relief from the constant rain in the jungle. Every time he read it. Tears came when he remembered the adventures that he and Cat had shared.

Later, Windy, after visiting the village and talking to the chief Yellow Elk, found out the complete story. It seems that the chief's daughter, Yellow Flower and her best friend, Morning Mist, had taken jugs to the creek to get fresh water. They had filled their jugs and were turning to go back to camp when they heard a growl and not ten feet away was a big tan mountain lion. It had to be the lion the hunting party was trying to find.

It had killed five members of the tribe within the last three weeks. Yellow Flower was chief's daughter and the oldest quickly dropped the jug and grabbed a large broken limb. She told Morning Mist to run for help.

The lion paid no attention to Morning Mist. It took two steps and jumped toward Yellow Flower. Although she knew she did not have a chance against the lion, she was buying time for Morning Mist. She bravely met the charge with the stick. But before the lion reached her it was struck by gray shadow that surprised it and knocked it over. It was a start to a battle to the death. Yellow Flower was surprised to see a large wolf but it also looked like a dog too. After it had knocked the lion down it had gotten itself between the lion and Yellow Flower.

Yellow Flower knew that it had no chance against the lion and she did not understand why it was willing to give up its life to save hers. The lion growled and leaped, this time there was no surprise, and the wolf stood its ground and met the lion in a death battle that took it around and around.

Just then the hunting party had come over the ridge and stopped in its tracks. Below them was the mountain lion they hunted, between it and Yellow Flower was a large grey wolf protecting her and fighting the lion. With a loud yell they started running over the hill with Yellow Flower's father Yellow Elk in the lead. The lion saw the men coming. Turned and struggled to get into the woods.

Cat fell to the grass, blood covering him. Yellow Flower looked at the strange wolf that knowingly had given its life to save hers. Her father Yellow Elk, yelled not to go near it, but she knew that there was something different about the wolf. As she approached, it tried to wag its tail. She sat down, held its head it her lap and slowly stroked its head as her father came, sat beside her and examined Cat's wounds. One look and he knew the brave grey

104

wolf was dying. It slowly tried wag its tail and licked his hand as the other members of the hunting party came up.

They had killed the mountain lion a short distance away; its right front leg was broken. With its disfigured left front leg, it could barely move. The disfigured front leg made it impossible for it to catch game and that is why it hunted the Indians.

Still Yellow Elk was not going to let the wolf that had given its life to save his daughters and seemed to have been raised by man, die here in the woods. Cat was slowly loaded on to a blanket with a hunter at each corner and Yellow Flower still rubbing it head, as he was moved to the village where news of the wolf's sacrifice had spread over the camp.

Cat died that night, with Yellow Flower at his side. The chief and the Elders met the next day and declared a new clan to be formed. It would be made up of those would be willing to give their lives to save others. Its sign was a black wolf with a white and orange line between its eyes. What had happened would be known by the passing of the story on the deer hide from tribe to tribe.

After Windy had told the complete story to Ma, she looked at Ready, sitting near the fire place. She sat down by him and rubbed his head, "Your father left a high road for you to follow."

Ma corresponded with Dancer as much as she could. She knew that the time to receive and answer her letters would never be consistent. Sometimes his letter would be back the in a week or so and other times it would be months before she heard from him.

Every time Ma got his letters, she would let Parson Brown read it to all the sitting around the stove group. Once in a while one would tell what was happening around the store and she would put it in the letter. Windy was the one who loved to add to Ma's letter with one of his happenings that everyone had laughed at. Ma had to always add it to her letter because Windy could not write.

Chapter 7

It was starting to snow hard when Michael Carty saw the light in the distance. He was tired and needed to stop to find directions to his motel room in Prestonsburg. He stopped and lowering his head against the whirling snow and cold wind stumbled through the old doors of the Troublesome Creek General Store. Inside he found an old potbellied stove with boiling coffee pot surrounded by empty chairs and an old checkerboard on a keg. Taking off his gloves and warming his hands by the fire, he wondered if anyone was here on a night like this.

"Coffee's hot," said a voice behind him, "help your1self. But, it's best to let it cool before you drink it. It might scald you, right off the stove."

He turned to see an older woman in a red flannel shirt, worn bib overhauls, boots that still were covered with snow and a hat held tightly on her head by a scarf. She set the coal bucket she was holding down near the stove and after removing a glove with her teeth extended a handed and said, "My name is Ma Smith, I own this store and am surprised to see anyone out on a night like this."

"Coach Michael Carty, assistant basketball coach at Northern Tennessee State, Ms. Smith," he replied shaking hands, "I got lost trying to get back to Prestonsburg. I came up here to see the King play."

"What do you think of the King?" She asked with a smile, pouring herself a cup of coffee.

"I didn't get to see him play," bringing his cup up, "I got lost trying to find the gym. Coach Fisher is going to have my hide for this", he said with a smile, "I'll just tell him he is one of the best shooters that I have seen."

"He is that. The boys that hang around the store figured his average to be around forty five points a game now," she said, leaning forward, holding her hands above the stove. "He gets letters from a bunch of colleges every day."

"I thought so, anyone that good is not going to a small college like Northern Tennessee," Coach Carty replied, shaking his head, "I just can't imagine anyone getting that many points game."

They were both sitting by the stove now, warm, relaxed and talking about ball players, teams and even the weather.

Finally Ma said, "I'm going to bed up stairs now, you can sleep in the rocker by the stove. The storm should blow itself out by morning. There is enough coal to last the night," pausing at the top of the steps, "have you ever heard of James Dancer?"

"Is he a ball player?" Carty asked looking up, "I haven't ever heard of him."

Ma stopped at the head of the stairs, "You probably won't, and he never finished high school although he was plenty smart. He had to work at the mines on different shifts to help his mother and his little sister."

Pausing, she added, "He has natural ability that cannot be taught. God willing and with your permission, when he gets back from Viet Nam, I would like him to go to Northern and try out for your basketball team. It might just be enough to keep him in school."

Carty was just finishing covering himself with the quilt, "Sure thing. Just send him to Northern and ask for me. I'll leave my card on the counter." Little did he know that the card would change his future and that of his team.

Four years later, at Northern Tennessee State College, basketball players and staff are preparing for the new season. Now head Coach Michael Carty, with his grey flat top and blue sweat suit, watched as his Northern Tennessee basketball team, outfitted in their gray sweat suits ran through their loosening up drills. Assistant coach Bob Roberts, tall with thick glasses and matching sweat suit, was at his side. "They look a little rusty," he said through a whistle in his mouth, "especially Keith."

The object of their attention was Keith "Hound Dog" Stamper; a slender six foot guard that was their second leading scorer and third leading rebounder from last year's conference team. Stamper was slowly doing his push-ups with a pained but determined look on his face.

Carty knew that look. He had seen it countless times before when the team was down and needed a basket. Stamper would almost always score or find some way to get the ball to their All-American center, Butch Reynolds, who would score. At six foot nine, he was almost impossible to stop. He and his twenty three point average would be sorely missed this year.

"That is because it is the first day of conditioning," Carty said smiling, "Hound was probably out all night, playing cards and came here without any sleep. He will be fine after you run him a week or so up and down the stadium steps and around the track. I just wish he had some to help our scoring. If we don't find someone to step up, it will be a long season," he said grimly, turning to go, "a long season." *Until the start of the second quarter*, he thought to himself and smiled.

Without telling anyone he had a surprise coming in when the classes started in September. Actually there were two surprises. One was Bill Forest, a transfer from Southern Kentucky State. A quick six foot five inch forward who the Southern coaches thought needed another year of practice without playing in any games, he was red shirted last year. He spent three to six practicing with the varsity and six to nine with the freshman team four days a week. All of that time he just played defense and guarded everyone from All Americans to seven foot centers. He got better and better until finally the players he guarded ask the coach for other people to guard them if they scrimmaged.

Although Forest had just played defense his red shirt year, he had averaged over twenty points a game in high school. A bad lower back injury he suffered in a summer pickup game forced him to drop out of college. At home his old family doctor, Dr. Bradley, told him to sleep on a board and his back would heal. After sleeping on a board for months his back healed and after examination, Dr. Bradley said he could play basketball again.

He got together with his friend, Lewis Brett, who played at Albany Jr. College and had accepted a basketball scholarship to Middle Kentucky University. The local gym was open all summer and they played every night during the week and Sunday afternoons all of the churches had teams and there was always spirited games a number of times with college players and those just back from Nam.

Brett saw daily improvement in his friend. Finally, he asked Bill if he wanted Middle Kentucky Coach Allen to contact other college coaches that might be interested in him. He could not go to Middle Kentucky State because of conference rules.

They had met Coach Allen in his office. "Coach, this is Bill Forest, he played at Southern Kentucky State last year before an injury forced him to drop out of school."

Coach Allen stood up and extended his hand to Forest, "I don't need an introduction to this young man. I saw enough of him when we scrimmaged Southern. I am sure Greg Smith remembers you too, as I remember he scored only 7 points while you guarded him. He was used to getting at least over 20," he said with a smile.

"Now what can I do for you," he said as he sat down and waved Brett and Forest to sit down.

"Coach I would really appreciate it if you could find me a place to play basketball. My back is all right now and I know that I can play if I could get a try out," he said slowly.

Then, looking the coach in the eye, he said, "I have to get a scholarship in order to finish college."

Coach Allen studied Forest for a minute. He knew the problem Forest had because after last year's scrimmage, the coaches had talked and he had found out about Forest's money problems and how he had cut tobacco all summer to pay for his mothers' electricity bill the coming winter.

"Wait here," he said and went out.

Bill and Brett looked at each other and Brett shook his shoulders.

In what seemed like an hour to Forest, Coach Allen came back into his office.

"Forest, I just called Coach Carty at Northern Tennessee and told him how good of a ball player you are. He said he would call you next Sunday at two at Brett's house since you don't have a phone."

Grinning he shook Forest's hand, "Don't make me regret I said that,"

"I promise I won't, Coach," Forest said with a happy grin.

Coach Allen nodded his head in agreement," I know you won't Forest. Give my best wishes to Coach Carty and his family."

Carty remembered the call. Coach Allen had described Bill Forest as a fine   player. On the freshman team he had been the leading rebounder and second in scoring. But Coach Allen said his strength was his hard-nose defense. In a scrimmage game he had frustrated his All-American Greg Smith and held him to seven points.

Forest could also score as well at six five, strong and could hold his own with anyone in rebounding. Because he had worked and supported his mother and two younger sisters, he had no way to go to college. But now his grandfather and mother were going to take his mother and sisters in with them later this year. It would free him to start to college again if he could go on scholarship.

Coach Carty had called him Sunday at Brett's house. He told Forest that he had been highly recommended by Coach Allen and asked if he was interested in playing for Northern Tennessee on a full scholarship.

Forest said an excited yes, but explained he had to work this summer to pay for his mother's medical bills. Carty said he understood, but he needed to go to summer school and attend two quarters to be eligible to play the last quarter.

Carty asked if he would like to work a summer job on campus where he could earn money for the medical bills and go to summer school? Another excited yes and Forest had reported the following week. After meeting him, he knew that he was everything Coach Allen had said he was.

The other surprise would either make him be remembered as one for the pioneer coaches or remembered as a coach that went too far, at the wrong time and was fired for his decision.

Carty had met with Northern President Bradley the week before and they discussed the possibility of being the first college to have an American Negro on their basketball team. He had told Carty that he would get back to him next week to give him his response.

He called Carty the following Thursday

and told him he had made his decision. Now Carty was sitting in a leather arm chair across from President Bradley, a tall man with brown graying hair, wearing his usual black suit with a red tie.

"Well coach, I decided to discuss the possibility of being the first college to have a Negro basketball player with several of the college staff and instructors. Here are some of their replies.

He put his glasses on and looked down at a yellow tablet.

"There are several remarks. I'll have to think about it, why we need to do that, it is up to you." Then looking up at Carty, "The one I really like are you crazy?"

From these remarks Carty knew what President Bradley would answer now and he started to get up, "Wait just a minute coach I haven't finished yet, when I told my wife about what I was going to do, she just looked at me and walked away. When she reached the door she turned, "If you do this, I will start packing and you should start looking for a new job."

President Bradley took his glasses off and looked across at Carty.

"Despite all of this, I like you, feel it is time to recognize the American Negro in both athletics and academic skills. However, you and I both know that this has never been done. It is a historic decision by the college, the college president and the basketball program here at Northern to allow Ellis to be the first to play basketball here at Northern."

Finally Bradley, hesitated of a moment

then looking at Carty, "The consequences could possibly be grave for the college, the president, for you and your team, especially at some colleges that are on your schedule."

Bradley came from behind his desk, and looked directly at Carty, "Coach I have thought about this, even in my sleep. If fact at times I got out of bed, sat down and considered all possible reactions to this decision to you, your team and Northern."

"Finally it comes down to this. Do you think that you and your team can survive the crowd slurs, the throwing of trash, finding a place to stay on away trips, a place that will serve you meals and you know that there will be more problems, some even here at home?"

Bradley bit down on his lower lip as if he was trying to determine what to say, "Now we both have been in restaurants where the Negro is asked to leave or eat somewhere else. Finally there are places that unless it has Negro on the door will not even allow your team to use the restroom."

Carty stood up and faced President Bradley with a look of determination, "Those are all good questions. I know that you are putting your career on the line. It will take a team whose players are molded into one to face the challenges that you have mentioned and more."

Carty looked at President Bradley and thought here is a man that could lose his job as college president and would probably never even be considered for another one because of the chance he is taking. How could he do less?

Carty stepped forward, "I checked on Ellis

before he graduated from high school and from what I know he is the answer for the first Negro basketball player here at Northern. We both know that Ellis will face just what you have said and more. You can be sure with our team that he will never have to face it alone."

"I know that if it can be done you are the man to do it. If there is anything I can do don't hesitate to call me," President Bradley shook hands with Carty and for a moment they looked each other in the eye knowing that each one would fight to the finish for what they believed.

Then just before Carty opened the door to leave, Bradley smiled and said "Another thing to remember is be on the lookout for another job, I will be doing the same."
A few minutes after Carty had left; Bradley looked out the window and watched him going back to the gym. He had his shoulders up and was walking in a military fashion. He was a combat veteran. He had fought for something he believed in before and this would be no different.

He had not told Carty about his meeting with Dr. William Perdue, head of the English department to get his opinion on Ellis. Perdue had taken his time then he looked at Carty, "The decision is up to you President Bradley, however a fitting thought from Shakespeare comes to my mind, "Uneasy lies the head that wears the crown."

Later he thought Shakespeare could not have said it better. It was good to know that even in centuries past others had similar problems making difficult `decisions.

There was a reason that Bradley has supported the first Negro basketball player here at Northern, even if it meant his job. It was a debt he felt he owed.

Known to few, he was in XII Corps' 26th Infantry Division that was assigned to General George S. Patton's Third Army as it raced across France. They were slowly and carefully approaching a field near the Siegfried Line when German machine gun fire cut the man in front of him it two. Then came the mortar fire. The radio man was calling in for help when a mortar round landed about two feet away. They were pinned down.

If they tried to fall back the machine guns would cut mow then down. If they stayed put, the mortars would eventually get everyone. As he lay down behind a small rise he said a prayer as just like everyone else.   But they all knew it was just a matter of time.

Suddenly from behind came a blast and one of the machine gun position disappeared in a cloud of smoke and debris. Everyone looked around and on hill behind them were American tanks. They were firing at all of the German positions. Soon what was left of the Germans were running away from the deadly tank blasts.

They all had stood up and cheered the tanks as they came in line slowly rumbling toward them. As the tanks got closer the men inside opened their turrets. What they saw was a shock for everyone including him. All of the tanks that had just answered their prayers were driven by Negros!

As the tanks went by, a man next to him yelled, "Who are you guys, you saved our ass today."

"Hey man, we are the 761st Tank Battalion, but you can call us the Black Panthers. Glad to be of service. Look forward to fighting with you guys and helping you kick Hitler's ass."

After they had passed, the man next to him had said, "If I get out of this war alive, anyone that says anything bad about a Negro to me he is going to get a knuckle sandwich."

As they watched the tanks go by, "That is a swell idea, what if you wife doesn't feel that way," to that there was silence and everyone around had a good laugh.

Bradley thought his payment was not a knuckle sandwich but something better. It was the opening of a new way of life for them.
Now he turned and sat down thinking of how his wife was going to take this. It was time he told her why he did what he did. It was the least he could do.
As he walked back to his office, Carty was thinking of what President Bradley had just said. It would take team courage of fight all of the problems President Bradley had mentioned and there would be more a lot more that neither one had even considered. But he was going to do his part. Few men in his position would have even considered what he had just given permission to Carty to attempt.
stand.

Now the question was how would the college, the fans and most importantly how would his team react to T.C. Ellis, who now will be the first African American ever play basketball in this conference and any other as far as he knew.

This was going to be the whole change in American history, one way or another. It had started with a phone call conversation he had with Ellis's mother two weeks ago.

"Coach I am Alice Ellis, is there any way my son T.C. Ellis can play basketball for Northern Tennessee? I know it will be a problem, but I don't know what else to do.

I have arthritis in my right hand and knee. It now is getting almost impossible for me to take care of the house, do my laundry and other things. It is getting worse. He is a very good basketball player. You can ask Coach Pickens at Western Iowa. Please can you help us?"

Carty had not responded immediately.

She had taken that as a polite no. "Well Coach Carty, I understand what I am asking has never been done and you could lose your job over it. Well, thank you for listening to me anyway. Have a good day and God Bless."

"No! No! Wait Mrs. Ellis send T.C. over tomorrow at ten. But remember I can't promise anything until I meet with him. Is there a problem with that?"

"Oh, thank you Coach Carty! I mean there is no problem with that. He will be there in the morning at ten."

Ellis had come over the next day and they had spent the morning together discussing the possibility of him playing for Northern. Each of them was aware of what could possibly happen.

Finally, standing up, his six foot six frame towering above Carty's six foot two height, he looked at Carty with concern in his eyes, "Coach, I want to stay here with my mother. She is the only family I have. I am asking you to let me play on a scholarship. I am aware that what I am asking could cause you to lose your coaching position. We both know that the whole team will have problems because of me. But I promise you if you will just give me this chance you will never regret it."

This time it was Carty who stood up to shake his hand, "I know my team, they will do what is right, and you playing here is the right decision. Be here in the morning at nine to sign your scholarship contract and meet Bill Forest your roommate in Stateland Hall for the summer. You will work and go to class this summer to get your required school eligibility. Be sure to have your transcript sent to the admissions office. Coach Roberts will be who you report to this summer. I am asking that you and Forest do not reveal anything about basketball until I tell you to do so. Now any questions?"

"Does that mean I have a scholarship, coach," Ellis said with an amazed look on his face.

"Yes that is what it means and tell your mother I hope she gets better," Carty replied, "See you at nine."

Ellis had gone out the door looking like he had just won million dollars.

In the morning, after Ellis had signed the scholarship contract, shaken hands with Carty and left, Carty had watched him as he walked to an old red two door Ford truck parked in front of the gym. As he had gotten closer he held his arms in the air and shook his head yes. His mother, with white hair, glasses and a long blue dress had gotten slowly out of the truck with a big smile on her face limped to greet him. They had locked in an embrace that only mothers and their children share.

Carty felt good, no matter what happened he felt he had done the right thing. Turning around to leave to tell Coach Roberts the news, he had walked past the office front desk, where Shirley looked up as he went by with a smile and tears in her eyes. Somehow she knew what he had done

Oh, it was just as well, he never could keep secrets from her. But in his heart he knew he was in the right no matter what the consequences.

For the whole summer, both Ellis and Forest worked hard in the classroom and the gym. After class, they both reported to the gym where they were assigned daily duties ranging from mowing the campus, lawn to cleaning the bathrooms at the swimming pool. Each also worked on supervised tutoring program to make sure that were applying themselves in the classroom. Grades were routinely checked. Both had proven to be very good students.

As Carty had said, neither Forest nor Ellis had been introduced to the team. Neither of them had told anyone about them joining the team. The students and people who saw them work daily paid little attention to them.

Everyone thought they were just campus workers doing their job. Some remarked how tall and athletic looking these new janitors were.

Coach Roberts worked with Ellis and Forest daily in the practice gym when the teams were through. They were in the weight room three days a week and after going through fundamental drills, they played one-on-one with no fouls called. Roberts said the pounding that they gave each other would force most players to stay away from either one.

After discussing the situation with Coach Roberts, they had decided to wait until the first day of official practice on October the fifteenth to introduce them to the team. Now his thoughts came back to the present, "Their all yours coach, get them in shape, October the fifteenth is right around the corner" He said over his shoulder as he walked toward his office.

Hesitating at his office door, he watched as Coach Roberts led them through the gym door toward the football field to run the dreaded stadium steps.

Carty went to his office, nodding to his secretary, Shirley, in her usual seat behind her desk in the little reception room. In her white blouse, buttoned to the neck, thick glasses and brown hair with a little gray, she was as much a part of the program as she was twenty years ago. She gave her usual good morning smile and handed him the morning mail.

He shut the door and sat down in the old wooden office chair. He paid no attention to the mail but instead put his feet on the old oak desk and looked at the team pictures of years past on the opposite wall.

Carty looked at the nineteen-forty-six team. There he was his first year of college after the war. He still had the Marine look about him, tall, straight and thin with a deadly stare. A real fighting machine he chuckled to himself. He still had the look, the stare. It was Jill that had changed him and for the best

Chapter 8

Sgt. James Dancer watched as his bus pulled away from the college bus stop, leaving him standing with his olive drab worn duffel bag with DANCER painted in white on the side. He was dressed in the usual green regulation army uniform complete with issued hat that he unfolded and placed over his closely cut black hair.

That morning he had just been discharged from the army because of a back injury and his time spend in combat. He had caught a bus that went by the college entrance.

As people walked by, most looked up at the tall young man, with broad shoulders, dark complexion, gray eyes. Some on the bus had watched and wondered why he had stopped looked all around just as soon as he stepped off of the bus. It was a jungle habit that had saved his life many times.

The bus driver, a Viet Nam jungle veteran just smiled to himself. He had done the same thing many times before he stopped. This young man would have the same problem judging from the decorations on his chest.

Ahead of him was a sidewalk going through a brick fence on both sides. On the right side a bronze sign embedded in the brick fence said *Northern Tennessee State College.*

Dancer watched the campus sidewalks that were milling with students going to and coming from summer classes.

Dancer stood there for several minutes running thoughts through his mind. Did he really belong here? He decided to think it over and sat down on a white steel bench under a big Oak tree beside the side walk leading to the college buildings. What he decided to do now would determine what his life would be in the future.

Still Dancer had his doubts. Just before getting off the bus he had ask the bus driver when the bus stopped here again. It was that day and it went by the bus station where he could catch a bus if he wanted to go home. He would just have to wait here for three hours. Then he would be back at the store with Ma and his friends by late tomorrow.

Again Dancer wondered if he could pass the college classes. He thought about the fact that all he had never been to a real high school. He had just studied with Ma and Parson Brown at the store to get his GED. It was then that Brown had gotten him interested in reading books and writing. Ma had helped with the math. He finally took the GED test and passed it with no problem. He had completed some college classes from the college. Now he was here sitting on a bench at the place he had dreamed of, yet he was still not sure of what to do. He was beginning to have his doubts again.

Then he remembered the main reason he was here. When he was growing up for some reason it was his dream to play basketball at a college. Since he did not get to play in high school and he did not know where he could learn about the game to prepare him for college, he told Ma about his dream.

Ma suggested that he contact the retired Northern Tennessee Basketball Coach Fisher. Fisher lived with his daughter and her son. Her husband, Ben, had been killed in a mining accident. Dancer had seen him on his porch every morning drinking a cup of coffee and watching Dancer and the rest of the night mining shift go slowly walking by leaving a black coal dust trail.

He wanted to get Fisher's attention. Dancer had spent hours of dribbling and handling the old basketball that Windy had to blow it up with an old tire pump every day or it was flat by noon. Finally it was when he dribbled the basketball past him and dunked the ball over a tree limb that he finally got Fisher's attention.

Dancer went to the store to tell Ma about what he had done. Dancer had just as he finished the story when Fisher came through the door and they had talked for hours. Fisher was making sure that Dancer would stand up to what he was about to go through to play basketball, most would not. Finally it came down to whether he wanted to test the skills Fisher had given him to play basketball, get a college education or go back home to his mountains.

Dancer remembered his training. At first they had only use their old rubber ball that now went flat every twenty minutes every day. Windy was there most of the time to pump it up with Parson Brown's car air pump.

Fisher had watched Dancer when he first started to shoot basketball in the barn. Anyone who could do what Dancer could do with nothing would be something to watch if he had the right equipment and training. Fisher decided it was time for Dancer to get serious with his basketball training.

Then as if by magic new basketball shoes and two new college basketballs appeared at the store. A week later a set of weights arrived. A week after that a new basketball goal, complete with backboard, arrived at the store.
The local mail man Big Bobby Brown delivered all sorts' mail to the Troublesome Creek General Store besides the Dancer's basketball and gym equipment for different people. There was just no way to find some people in the mountains. Sometimes envelopes had a name and that was addressed to the store that no one had ever heard of before. But they would almost always show up in time.

On the shelf on the other side of the counter were twelve small card board boxes six on top of each other. Each had a two letters A-B, C-D written in black ink except X-Y-Z.

If you were unknown, you had to have an ID of some sort like a driver's license or someone that could vouch for you.

Under the counter were page size manila envelopes that would be opened only in emergencies or the death of the owner with who to contact if something had happened.

After the basketball goal and backboard delivery Brown had asked Ma if there was anything else like the heavy backboard and goal he could expect for delivery to the store. If so he was going on a vacation.

It took Windy and Parson Brown a day to put the goal on an old telephone post they found. From then on he and Fisher practiced for hours after work and on Saturdays, outside in the summer. If you missed the goal or dribbled off of your feet you had to run very fast to keep the basketball from going over the hill to the creek down below.

Windy tried to be there and stayed behind the goal to stop the ball when he could, if it got by him, Dancer was on his way over the hill.

In the winter the practice moved to an old abandoned barn with a flat floor that was kept dry. Windy and Parson Brown had nailed old lumber to cover the cracks in the walls. It helped keep out of the cold wind

Dancer mastered how to dribble with one hand while tossing a piece of coal in the air with the other. Fisher drilled him every day until he could dribble behind his back, between his legs and shooting from every position was another.

Despite of what he had said Big Bobby Brown delivered sets of weights after which he took two days off. Dancer worked out and grew muscular and improved on his already quickness what seemed to get better every day.

It was from the heavy weight lifting, exercise and jumping rope for three days a week. Fisher was molding him into a competitive player.

In over thirty years of playing and coaching basketball, Fisher had never seen anyone with the natural born athletic ability that

Dancer possessed. He taught him moves that he had, up to now, only imagined basketball players could do. He was amazing.

Later in the army Dancer had wanted to play but he rarely did and when he did play he held back what he could do with a basketball because he had seen people show out. He did not like what other players thought of them.

Now he was here. He made his decision. Standing up, he saw the gym across the campus and with his duffel bag over his shoulder and his Army cap on straight, he headed that way. As he walked across the campus he thought, James Dancer from Appalachia is going to try to play basketball in college and graduate from college. This time trying out for college, if he just got a chance, he would hold nothing back.

As Dancer walked to the gym he noticed two young men, one was an African American working in a flower bed next to the gym front as he passed What caught his attention was that they were both tall and looked very athletic to be janitors. They both stopped what they were doing and watched him go through the gym doors. For some reason they both looked at each other, there was something about the tall, dark soldier that made him stand out,

As Dancer went down the gym hall he again thought to himself who would ever have believed an Appalachian mountain boy with a GED who had never played any kind of school basketball would be trying out for a college team? Then he took a deep breath and thought he had to do it. If he didn't try out, he would always wonder if he could have made it.

It was when he was passing the open gym doors hearing yelling and basketball dribbling, he stepped inside and watched group of boys playing basketball on one end. That did it. Now he was getting excited and thought that could be me. No, on second thought it will be me.

Dancer looked down the hall and on the right was a white painted sign on a gray steel door, *Michael Carty, Basketball Coach.* Again he hesitated, took a deep breath and stepped inside.

Behind the desk facing the door was an older, neatly dressed woman blue dress with gray hair. She looked up from her desk, "What can I do for you young man?"

"My name is James Dancer, if Coach Carty has time, I would like to talk to him about trying out for the basketball team," he said in a nervous voice.

She looked up at him, said nothing and went to office door.

As Carty sat in his office, his thoughts were interrupted by Shirley's knock on the door. He knew it was her by the light peck, three times in three seconds. She came in quickly and stood in front of his desk with an excitement in her eyes.

"There is someone to see you Coach. A *young man* that wants to try out for the basketball team," she stated in her precise English.

Coach Carty thought to himself, another walk on. A player from a small town that had averaged in double figures and had listened to his loyal fans on how great he was and he had believed it. He had seen so many though the years. Most never could stand up to the demands and ability the college level play demanded.

But on the other hand, few times Shirley had come into his office and said that there was a young man wanting to see him. Over the years he had come to respect her judgment in both people and athletes in general. Whoever this *young man* was, she had given him her stamp of approval already and that he had not seen that in a long time. In fact the last time was when a player named Brian Farley asked to see him, she had done the exactly same thing and he turned out to be an All American. So instead of sending him to Coach Roberts he said, "Well, send him in Shirley."

Holding the door in one hand she leaned out and said, "Come in James, Coach Carty will see you now."

Carty was at his desk leaning forward, rubbing his eyes, when he glanced up. There blocking his door way was a tall, broad shouldered dark youth, dark black eyes, close cut army style black hair, dressed in an army uniform and holding his army regulation cap in front of him with both hands.

Dancer stood straight and said slowly, "Coach Carty, my name is James Dancer. I would like the chance to try out for the Northern Tennessee basketball team. I know that I am late but I have just been discharged."

Being a coach he looked carefully at James Dancer. He must be at least six foot five or more, with broad shoulders, dark complexion and a quick smile with bright even teeth. As Coach Carty stood up and he stepped forward to shake his extended hand. And a grip like a vice, Carty thought to himself and his hand was so large it almost hid Carty's hand. Carty thought he had a large hand but it was nothing compared to the one he was shaking hands with.

Carty pointed to a chair, "James Dancer, where have I heard the name?" he said to Dancer as he waved hand for him to sit down in front of him.

Dancer handed him an old business card. It was crumpled and barely readable. Looking closely he saw it was his but it was when he was assistant coach years ago. Carty looked carefully at the card and then at Dancer.

"You came to see the King play and got caught in a snow storm and had to spend the night at the Troublesome Creek General Store. Ma told me that you said I should drop around whenever I could and that you might give me a chance to try out for the team,"

Dancer replied, with worry in his eyes, "I just hope the offer still stands after all these years. Coach Fisher, who used to coach here before you, worked with me a lot. I got my GED and I have been going to Northern Tennessee classes at Ft. Campbell since last year. I passed all of my freshman college classes."

Finally, taking a deep breath and holding his hands together, he looked Coach Carty in the eye and said slowly "I have looked forward to this all of my life, all I ask for is for is a chance."

While Dancer was talking, Carty was

looking him over. There was something familiar about him he could not place. At the same time, his uniform decorations spoke for themselves, combat infantryman's badge, tour medals, Purple Heart and the insignia of the 101st Airborne.

What really caught his eye was the Silver Star medal on his chest. Dancer had been through it and survived if the story told by his decorations spoke the truth of his past and most of the time they did. He had probably lost friends, seen things that will forever be burned into his soul. He had the look of someone much older. This young man had been through a lot in Viet Nam.

Carty asked Dancer about his education and where he was from. As he was answering the question, Carty thoughts drifted to his past and how it was similar to the young man standing before him. He knew exactly what all this was about. There always exists a bond between veterans that a generation gap could not separate now and then. Their memories had been etched with terrible scenes they would never be able to forget no matter how they tried. You just had to live with it the best you could. You took it day by day.

As Dancer talked he noticed Carty was studying him as if comparing him with someone else. He was comparing him with his memories that suddenly had come back. Memories of Guadalcanal a past that Carty had tried to hide in his mind came back. A combat veteran of the WW II, Carty had been on Guadalcanal. This is the memory he tried to hide and forget. It was one rainy, dark night. The fighting had been face to face hand to hand most of the day. It was getting l

It was getting dark when the lieutenant told them to take off their helmets and shoot anybody that wore one because of the infiltrators were everywhere and that is what he did.

Out of his platoon he and two others got off the hill. When Carty got home he would wake up screaming. When someone shut the door with a bang he would hit the floor and once when a truck backfired he jumped into muddy ditch. He did not know if living was worth the trouble. He knew that he was slowly worrying his mother to death because when he cried out she would be at his side. He had to get away and spare her and the rest of the family the hell he was going thought.

Carty knew what he had to do, but not how to do it. He had to get away. Then as if an answer to his prayers, he ran into his old high school basketball coach. And after the usual recounting old times, then Coach Daley had mentioned if he had ever thought of playing college basketball.

Finally Coach Daley had called his friend. Coach Fisher at Northern Tennessee and asked if he would give Carty a chance to play. Carty still remembered the first meeting. He had stood in the same door and looked over the same desk at Coach Fisher. And Fisher probably thought the same thing about him. He had given him his chance.

There for a while, Carty didn't think he would make it. The nightmares continued and he found it hard to make himself study and meet the physical demands of the basketball team. Gradually, he begin immerse himself into the basketball and his classes. He worked in the cafeteria in the summer and took classes that he had a difficult time with in the regular school year. He began to heal.

It was after the worst snow fall of the year in November of nineteen forty six that changed his life. He was on his way to the gym to practice, being careful because the sidewalk was slick where it had been recently shoveled. Ahead of him walked Jill Stevens, a cheerleader he had seen many times at the ballgames but had never had a chance to meet.

Jill too, was taking her time with the icy sidewalk. He had always wanted to meet her but she had always been surrounded by a group. She was a tall brunette with a quick smile and seemed always radiant He noticed that those around her always seem laughing and enjoying each other. He thought he had felt her looking at him, but when he looked up she was always concentrating on something else.

For some reason Carty made his mind up that his was the time to actually meet her. How could he do it? It was then that he heard a cry and laughter coming from a hillside they were passing. Several bundled figures both male and female were throwing snowballs at each other. He scooped up a snowball and threw it at the figure ahead of him. He missed.

Since Carty was behind her Jill didn't seem to notice the snow ball as it went by her. He tried again, another miss. The third time he was less than ten feet away when let it fly. Smack! It hit her right on the bottom. She tried to turn then her feet shot out from under her and down she went.

Carty panicked and quickly moved to help her up. He misjudged the distance and tried to stop. Too late, and down he went, right next to her right on his bottom. He looked at her and she was smiling and what else could he do but start laughing. She began laughing too.

"Are you all right," he asked as he got to his feet, "someone must have thrown a snow ball from the hill and accidentally hit you."

"I think I twisted my ankle," Jill said with a grimace, "if you could help me to the gym, I can get it wrapped before cheerleading practice."

Carty reached down and picked her up. "I'll just carry you and take no chances if it is all right with you?

Jill just nodded her head, buried it in his shoulder and he carried her to the gym. After his practice he stopped by the cheerleading practice to check on her'

Jill was sitting on the side line watching the last of the cheerleader practice. It was late and the cafeteria would be a long way to walk in the snow, ice and darkness with a bad ankle he thought and it was a good excuse to hold her again.

Carty waited until the other cheerleaders had gone to get dressed and Jill was struggling a little while getting up. He went over and asked if she would like for him to walk her to the cafeteria. The sidewalks had been cleared and even with her bad ankle, Jill could only walk slowly without the danger of falling. As they walked slowly, they talked and shared stories.

Carty helped her to a table and carried their trays to a table where they spent hours talking and laughing even after the cafeteria closed. As he walked her to her dorm she wrapped both of her arms around his again saying she did not want to take a chance and have another fall. He told her that he was walking slowly because of her injury, but the real reason was he just wanted to be near her for as long as he could.

Outside of the dorm it was just about curfew. Jill had to get to her room before they locked the outside doors and she missed her room check by the dorm mother.

As she had turned to face him, her face was outlined by the reflection of the lights from the dorm rooms and snow. She was the most beautiful girl he had ever seen. She gently placed both hands around his face and kissed him lightly on the lips and looked him in the eyes.

Everything stopped. This is who Carty wanted to spend the rest of his life with. His feelings of the past disappeared and were replaced by thoughts of the future. A future shared with the beautiful blue eyed girl that had captured his heart and soul. He had never forgotten that night and he never would.

That was how he had met Jill and with her help had put the nightmares and deaths of friends behind him. He still gives thanks to the good Lord every day of his life for her. With help from the Man up above, she had saved him.

They married, had a family any man could be proud of.

Now this young man was standing before him and asking for the same chance that had been given him by Coach Fisher. A chance to put a terrible past behind him and try to forget the violence that he knew was in his heart and soul. How could he do less than had been done for him?

Dancer had stopped talking and was puzzled by Carty's faraway look. "Is anything wrong coach?" he said as he stepped closer to the desk.

Carty blinked his eyes and quickly looked up at Dancer, "No, I was just lost in thought for a moment. You will get your chance James, and I want you to report to Coach Roberts in the gym in morning. He will direct you on what to do. Now do you have a place to stay?'

"No, sir I don't, but I will get a room somewhere," he said excitedly.

"There is a room available in the old dorm that you can stay in until we get you situated. I have two players staying there now, Bill Forest and T.C. Ellis. It is a short distance away from the gym and most of the other players are in the new dorm that is full at this time. Will that be all right with you," Carty asked?

"It will be great," Dancer said stepping forward to shake Carty's hand again.

"Coach Fisher said you should call him after I met you," Dancer said as he picked up his bag and started for the office door.

Standing up to follow Dancer to the door, Carty saw Stamper in the office waiting to see him. "Stamper, you wanted to see me," he said as Dancer started to the door?

Stamper and Dancer had exchanged a nodding of the head to each other as Dancer passed him going out the door.

"Coach, I just wanted to know if I could move over to Stateland Hall. The new dorm is too crowded and I miss being over there," he said while watching Dancer start to the outside door.

"Just a minute Dancer, Carty stepped into the hall, "you need to meet someone," motioning Keith to come forward.

Dancer turned and stopped in front of Keith and Carty.

"Keith Stamper this is James Dancer, he will be playing basketball with us later this year, Dancer this is Keith Stamper our captain, he is also known as Hound," he said as the two shook hands.

Smiling Carty added, "I have never discovered why he is called that name."

"Keith, I want you to room with Dancer the rest of the summer and show him around the campus. Make sure he meets Ellis and Forest."

Then he turned to Dancer, "I'll get a transcript of your classes from Ft. Campbell and send them to admissions. You may have to take some classes during the intersession period in order for you to be eligible to play the second quarter of this year."

Then as Dancer was going out the door, Carty stopped him for a moment, "The cafeteria will have your name down for meals starting at supper tonight."

As Dancer and Hound were going through the outside door, Dancer asked, "Why do they call you Hound?

Hound looked at this new roommate, "I knew you would ask that. Well, the first year I got here I went to big cook out down by the lake with some of the football players. They were drinking stuff that looked like water and handed me a glass. Hell, I thought it was water until I drank the whole glass full at one time. It burned my throat and that is the last thing I remembered until the next morning. I woke up in my dorm bed with a mother of headaches."

Then turning to Dancer, head lowered, he explained, "I barely made it to the cafeteria. When I walked through the doors everyone let out a big howl and laughed at me. I found out the stuff I drank was moonshine. It seems that night when I started looking at the full moon. I howled like an old hound dog. The name has stuck with me ever since."

Dancer could not help himself and his smile broke into a laugh as he shook his head.

Carty watched the two go out the gym door talking, laughing and looking around. Things were looking up. Then he thought of the remark Coach Carter had said at the end of last year's conference tournament after Southern Tennessee had beaten Northern by one point in overtime on a last second shot from the half line.

Smiling with an I won you lost look, extended his hand, "Get used to it Carty, you lose your best player and I keep all of mine plus I have a surprise for the whole conference next year."

Carty had smiled back and had wished him luck in the NCAA tournament left. Later in the deserted locker room, no one had seen him hit a steel locker with his fist so hard it had turned purple and had bled on his shirt.

Later at home, Jill had noticed the swelling and blood on his hand. Shaking her head and saying nothing she had put ice in a wash cloth and wrapped it around his hand with tape. Nothing had to be said. She knew her husband.

Now he looked at his secretary, "Shirley, I think you have done it again, this one looks like a real winner," he said as he returned to his office, "keep up the good work and get Coach Fisher on the line"

Shirley smiled and thought that makes three she had steered into this office. She had always listened to her first boss, Coach Fisher. Whenever he called about a player, she made sure the player got to see Carty. He had not been wrong yet. He called her last week and said James Dancer would be getting out of the army soon and make sure that Coach Carty was the one to see him.

She dialed Coach Fisher's number and told him that Dancer was enrolling. Fisher laughed and said, "Wait until they see him play, they will be in for a shock."

Coach Carty picked up his office phone and thanked Fisher for working with Dancer. He had told Fisher to remember that there would always be tickets for him and anyone else he brings to the ball games.

Carty was puzzled by Fisher's last remark of, "Coach, be prepared for someone who will make a difference."

It took two days to get Dancer's grades from courses he had taken while in the army transferred. Carty looked with satisfaction; Dancer had passed a quarter of freshman English I, European History I and math all with a B. Well, he thought to himself that took a major worry off of his mind. Now if he could only play basketball. He knew that even if he proved to not be a starter, he would still be on the team. Carty would see to that.

Dancer deserved a chance as Fisher had given him. Meanwhile he was assigned daily campus work with Forest and Ellis. He moved in with his roomy Hound. Finally that night he would be able to practice with Ellis and Forest.

Hound had gone home earlier for his father's birthday and would not be back until the next morning. He had decided that he would return early. There was a problem that he had to discuss with Coach Carty.

That night at the gym, while Dancer was getting ready to play for the first time, Coach Roberts met with Ellis and Forest.

"Now take it easy on Dancer tonight. He has just gotten out of the army and even if he is talented, it will be a while before he is ready to play. I mean after all he has never even played high school basketball. So take it easy on him and don't embarrass him, understand.'

Forest and Ellis both replied as Dancer came through the dressing room door, "We understand coach, we won't do anything to hurt or embarrass him."

The next morning, Hound was waiting to see Coach Carty as he arrived in his office the way he always did promptly at eight.

"Coach if you have time, I would like to talk to you about a problem," Hound said as Carty as he opened the door to his office.

Carty was concerned. Hound never asked to meet with him unless there was something was important.

"Come in, Stamper," and as he shut the door to his office, he nodded to Shirley. She knew that that was a sign he did not want to be disturbed, no phone calls, no anything.

After sitting down, "Coach actually there are two problems, you can help me with that concern the team," he began, " the first is that I would like to join the closed night practice with Ellis, Forest and Dancer."

"The second is that Dancer has a problem that I don't know what to do about," he said as Coach Carty listened intently.

Hound continued before Carty could reply, "For the last two days he wakes up in the middle of the night moaning, yelling names and breaking into a cold sweat. I wake him up and he sits up in bed, shakes his head and says how sorry he is about causing problems."

Hound looked at Carty, "We really like Dancer coach, and I would not be telling you this except it is something you should know."

Carty looked at Hound and said, "I am glad you asked to join in the night practice. Ellis, Forest or Dancer will not be eligible to play until the start of the second quarter. In the meantime, they can only practice with the team. You can show them some plays."

He paused, "On the other problem, I am asking you to be patient with Dancer; he will get better once he learns to cope with college life. It is hard for him to put his past memories behind him. I think basketball and belonging to a team will make a big difference."

Hound looked at his coach, "My dad was in the army. I know what all of those medals mean. He has been through hell hasn't he coach."

Carty looked at his team's leader, "I'm afraid he has and I am asking you to keep this between us, unless it gets worse."

Standing up, Hound looked at his coach, "You can count on me and the rest of the team to do whatever it takes to help him coach."

Before he could reach the door, Coach Roberts came through with the door with Shirley right behind him.

She gave a frustrated look and said "I tried to stop him coach but..."

Carty held his hand up stopping both Shirley and Coach Roberts, "It's all right Shirley", as he shut the door.

"Sorry about busting in coach but this could not wait, I did not want to talk about it over the phone and I told Ellis and Forest not to say anything about it until talked to you," Roberts said while getting his breath.

"Coach Roberts, is there anything that our team captain should not hear?" Carty said looking from first one and then the other.

"No, you both will find out soon enough,

but I just had to tell you first," Roberts said shaking his head and again catching his breath, "I would not have believed it unless I had seen it."

"Seen what? Was someone hurt," Carty asked concerned with what had happened to make Roberts so excited.

Roberts had calmed down and looking at each one ask, "Have either one of you ever seen James Dancer on a basketball court or do you know of anyone who has?"

Carty and Hound looked at each other and nodded their heads no.

"That explains it then and I did not know about it either until last night," Roberts said shaking his head as he understood.

Carty could stand it no longer, "Know about what?"

Roberts continued, "You know, you told me to let Dancer start working out with Ellis and Forest in the old gym. Well, last night was his first night, I did what you said about asking Ellis and Forest to take it easy on him until he got in playing shape again because we did not want Dancer to get hurt."

Roberts hesitated and shook his head, "Coach it should have been the other way," he finally gasped out. "James Dancers the best athlete and basketball player I have ever seen. He can do it all, he is as tall as Ellis, but handles the ball like a guard. He can go inside and score over Ellis or he can stop on a dime and drill a twenty foot jump shot. He has a sixth sense that allows him to pass the ball without looking. He shoots with either hand and can hang in the air and change hands before he shoots. He is one of the quickest big men I have ever seen that has the softest touch near the basket. And yes, he rebounds, handles the ball like it is a baseball and dunks with either hand, he is built like a block and he gave everyone fits. To be honest I have never seen an athlete like him,"

Pausing and catching his breath, "Coach, Dancer could play for anyone, anywhere. That is why I asked you if you or any other coach had ever seen him play. If they had, they would be beating on his door."

Catching his breath and looking at the surprised Carty he continued, 'He is a little rusty, but if he works hard he will be ready to go with Forest and Ellis in time for the second quarter and the Appalachian Conference Tournament. I told Ellis and Forest to say nothing about him until I talked to you."

Carty and Keith were stunned. They sat down and looked at Roberts. Carty knew Coach Roberts well enough to know he rarely exaggerated. If he said Dancer was that good, he was just that good. He sat back in his chair and put his hands together on the back of his head and started thinking on what to do. He had never had a problem like this before. A player that no one knows about that is better than anyone he has ever coached.

Finally Carty made up his mind, stood up facing Roberts and Hound with little smile on his face, "Coach you did the right thing. I don't want this mentioned to anyone."

Coach "Tell Ellis and Forest, we don't

want Dancer's ability   know by anyone else. Like them he will just be another janitor."

"I told them all that last night coach, I wanted to see what you wanted to do,"

As each shook their head in agreement, he said with a smile, "The team will find out the first day of practice about our "janitors". The rest of the conference will find out soon enough and we will be ready for this year's Appalachian Conference Tournament."

Fisher, that old rascal, that is what he meant by Dancer making a difference. Carty thought after all of those years as his assistant coach he should have expected it.

Chapter 9

Hound was hurrying to English class. You never wanted to be late to Miss Staton's English class. You would lose points on your next test. As he was walking across campus he noticed a group of students around several men. It was probably another Vietnam War protest. Different students and other people were taking turns speaking about the horrors of the war and why we should leave. Then one of the speakers caught his ear with his last statement.

"Every man in the army is a baby killer," said the tall red haired man, with tattoos over his large arms who was stepping down from the platform in a loud challenging voice.

"That right and they always have been," joined another big man with hair over his shoulders, in front with black Harley leather jacket.

"That is not true," came a voice from the other side of the group, "my dad was in the army and never harmed a baby." Hound looked at the speaker, a stocky, brown haired student in a blue Northern sweater on the back row, he recognized as Roger Thorn, the football team's quarterback.

Hound, could not stop from joining in, "That right, my dad and brother were both in the army and neither one ever hurt anyone except in combat where it was kill or be killed. How do you know they kill babies, were you ever over there or is it just hear say?"

"Calling me a liar," turning to the man in the Harley jacket, "I think they are both calling us liars, Chuck."

"I guess we will have to show them what real men think about baby killers JD," replied Chuck, as they ran through the startled crowd toward Hound and Thorn, who had moved to make a stand with Hound. They were about to join together in a fight they would surly lose. But they had to stand up for their family."

What happened next neither one ever knew. Suddenly Chuck seemed to fall flat on his face, and then JD was in the air falling on top of Chuck just as he was getting up. Both were dazed and did not move. Hound and Thorn looked at the two big men lying on each other.

It was the first time either had noticed Dancer in the crowd. "Are you two all right?" he said as he approached them. Each were surprised and stunned just nodded head yes.

Dancer had his books under one arm and was munching on a large red apple with the other, started walking toward the English Building

"We better hurry, roomy. We don't want to be late for Miss Station's English class."

Thorn and Hound looked at each other, shook their head in amazement, and started walking fast to catch up with Dancer. Just before Hound went thought the tall oak door to the English department, Thorn turned to him, "What just happened back there and who is the tall guy that just flattened those big men who would have surely have flattened us?"

"I don't know what happened, I thought we were going to get the hell beat out of us," then seriously looking at Thorn," his name is

James Dancer, my new roomy and one thing I do know is that I always want him on my side in a fight."

"I have to go to calculus now, be sure to thank Dancer for me," and smiling at Hound, "I wish he played football, I could sure use that kind of protection."

After that remark, Hound laughed all the way up the stairs to his English class. He was not late as he sat beside his roomy and savior Dancer who was busy going over notes as if nothing happened. Hound thought for a moment, to him he had acted as if the recent fight against two big thugs was nothing.

But if that had been nothing to him, Hound wondered what it would take to be something. Then looking at his friend Dancer, deep in thought over the English papers, Hound remembered the Purple Heart, the Silver Star, and the bad dreams he had. That answered his own question, compared to what he had been through, what had just happened really meant nothing to Dancer, nothing at all.

Then looking at Dancer as he sorted through the papers he noticed his big hands again. He remembered the first time he had seen Dancer pick up a basketball. It was in the gym as he and Dancer were leaving after lifting weights, when a basketball from a P.E. class bounced toward them.

Dancer was talking to Hound when he caught the ball in midair with one hand and threw it back to the startled player who was chasing the ball. He was so startled that the ball bounced off his forehead. Dancer quickly apologized to the player and after making sure he not injured, and then he and Hound went on to lunch leaving a startled P.E. class behind and a startled roomy.

It was then that Miss Staton, dressed in her long blue dress, came through the door and set her weekend assignments down on her desk. After calling the role, she handed out the writing assignments to the class. Each student stood, and told the class what they had written about. That is everyone except for Dancer who thought she had lost his paper and would mention it to her after class. He was surprised about what happened next.

Miss Staton stood up and said," I read all of your poetry assignments, most were very good, but I have selected one that I considered the best to be read by the author in class today. James Dancer please read your poem to the class."

Dancer, who was caught by complete surprise, "Are you sure it was mine, Miss Staton?'

"Yes, I am quite sure James, please share it with the members of the class," smiling she continued, "do not be afraid, Stamper will not bite you."

Hound turned red and the rest of the class broke out in laughter.

Dancer stood up, looked at the class with uncertainty and started reading his poem.

Never Forget the Alamo

*When I was growing up and sat on my
grandma's knee*

*She told me stories of battles and the way
America use to be.*

*The stories were of men who fought to the
death to make America free for you and me.*

I always liked the Alamo story best.
*It is about the men who faced death's final
test*

Over the Alamo walls that first day
*Looking at Santa Anna's thousands they
knew the price they would pay.*

But where did these men come from,
*these men who knew their last battles final
outcome.*

*It was from the valleys, hill, mountains and
plains*
As one these men came

*They were white, brown, black, red, brave,
strong and tough*
God made them out of that special stuff

*That flows through the hearts and souls of
free men now as it did then*
*At Lexington, Concord, Shiloh, the Alamo
and other battles without end*

Travis knew he had to give Houston time
With his saber into the sand he drew a line

All 180 men, Crockett, Bowie, Texans, Tennesseans and the rest
Knew to cross the line would mean certain death.

Looking death in the face was not new to these freedom fighting men
As one they all crossed the line and even smiled at Crockett's little grin.

Crockett and his buckskin Tennesseans with their long rifles
Slaying at half a mile wasn't even a trifle

Jim Bowie famous knife in hand in his death bed lay
Before he died under his knife many would pay

Travis with saber in hand stood on the ramparts tall
He would fight to the death until the Alamo's fall

Finally, late their last night they rested under the Texas stars
Free men who dreamed of green forest, family and friends so far

Never would these buckskin men walk the green sunlight paths or hear eagles cry

Never again would they hold a new born baby and see the first glint in its eyes

All knew that tomorrow into the face of God they would look
To a man they gathered strength from the holy book

The final day the battle raged, Crockett's long rifle, Bowie's knife and Travis's saber reaped a grim toll until none were left to stand.
None of the 180 was alive who crossed the line in the sand

Over a century has passed since the Alamo's fall
But some say on a cloudy starless night you can still hear the final bugle call

And a line suddenly appears in the blood soaked sand
And you can see ghostly figures of Crockett,
Bowie and the rest cross the bloody line again to a man

Always remember no matter who or where you are today
Take time out to bow your head and pray

Thank our almighty God for the men who crossed the line in the sand even if they knew the price they would pay
That gave their lives so we could have freedom in our land today

Dancer, with his head down, tried to get to his seat without looking up, but was caught by the hands of his classmates. With replies like, "I did not know you could write like that or do you have any more poems like that one and it was great."

Miss Staton stood up, "Thank you James, I think you surprised everyone, including me with that poem, because of that I am dismissing class early today and assigning no home work. Class dismissed."

At first the class just looked at each other, and then everyone made a dash to the door, except for Hound, thinking about his roommate Dancer who was putting his papers together.

Now he realized that he knew little about him except that he was the best basketball player he had ever played with. Now he was something else, he had to be one of the most educated people that had never even gone to high school.

Not only that, but today Hound had seen Dancer to be very dangerous. From what happened he was sure it would depend only on the situation on which Dancer you would see.

Hound shook his head and thought Dancer really doesn't know the limit to his ability in anything, then again and he probably never would.

Dancer stepped back into the door, "Hound if we hurry we can beat the crowd to the cafeteria for lunch."

"I'm with you Big D I don't want to miss

those bullet proof burgers,' Hound replied heading out the door with Dancer.

As they approached the cafeteria, Dancer turned to Hound with a smile, "Another important thing is if we get there early enough, you can stare at Kit."

"Hold it," Hound stopped just outside the cafeteria door and looking at Dancer asked, "What do you mean by that?"

"I mean she is a very attractive cheerleader that someone, like you, should ask out instead of staring at her every chance you get."

"Well, I'm going to when I think the time is right," Hound replied as they went through the doors.

Dancer looked at his best friend, "There is always Valentine's Day months from now."

Hound glared at Dancer and said nothing. He looked around the cafeteria and Kit was nowhere in sight.

Meanwhile, back at the scene, the crowd had gone and Officer Bixby was interviewing Chuck and JD, who had just gotten their breath.

"We want to press charges," red headed JD said to Bixby.

"Yeah, we was attacked," tattooed Chuck joined in.

"I see," Bixby replied, "do you know who it was?"

"We didn't see him; he hit us from the back." Chuck said.

A group of Northern cheerleaders had gathered around Bixby, "We saw the whole thing, Officer Bixby," Kit Simpson, a tall, very attractive brown haired and brown eyed cheerleader stepped forward, "and it was them attacking Keith and Thorn because they said their dad and brother were not baby killers in the army."

She continued, "We were going to practice when we saw those two running toward Keith and Roger. We started to find you when this tall guy stepped out of the crowd and tripped him," pointing to Chuck and "did something to him," pointing to JD in the Harley jacket, "causing him to fall on top of him," pointing to Chuck again.

"It was kind of funny," she hesitated looking at Bixby, "he stepped forward, keeping his books under one arm, held an apple with the other and talked a minute to Keith and Roger. Then he went on to class, like nothing happened."

The two beaten men glared at her. "We're going back to Nashville. We ain't gonna get no justice around here," Chuck said over his shoulder. "Come on JD. We are going to find out who did this to us and we will be back, no one gets away treating the Jackals like that."

After they had left, Bixby stood and began to think of just what had happened. Two big men, obviously experienced bar fighters, were both flattened by a student, who never even removed his books from under his right arm. Had he wanted to, Bixby was sure he could just have hurt them seriously or even killed them both just as easily.

Bixby stopped writing and stared at the notes he had taken His thoughts went back in time. He had known such a man in Korea,

Dawson, a short lanky man from Iowa, who laughed and talked just like everyone else but when it came time to live or die he had proven himself to be different and had saved Bixby's life.

It happened on a barren ridge in Korea on a bitter winter day. He was dug in trying to keep from freezing. Several of the men in his detachment of the 27th Regiment had frost bitten feet but could not go for treatment not then. No one complained, they just looked down the white ridge below and waited. They knew what was coming.

The Chinese infantry would be coming up the ridge in a wave of tan quilted, screaming men waving swords, rifles over the mounds of frozen tan bodies partially covered by the white snow and frozen ground that had come before. Some of the men around him were also frozen in their army uniforms covered in snow; they, too, would never move again.

Then the bugles blew and up the ridge they came. The M1's and the BAR's began firing, followed by the chatter of the Browning machine guns. The wave melted into mounds of bodies. But more came over the fallen front soldiers. Soon he was fighting hand to hand with his bayonet and rifle butt swing and slashing. He was knocked down and lost his rifle.

Bixby heard the roar of a machinegun close by but did not have time to look. Then one came at him raising a bayonet. Suddenly, he stopped in his tracks when a machine gun burst almost cut him in half. He fell at Bixby's feet. Then just as suddenly as the attack started, it ended.

The Chinese had retreated and it was then that he saw Dawson surrounded by dead Chinese. Dawson was standing holding his machine gun. When he saw Bixby looking at him, he just nodded and sat down. Soon replacements came and Bixby never saw him again. Before he had gone, they counted seventeen Chinese that were cut down by a hand held machine gun. Later they identified the machine gunner as Sergeant Dawson.

He shook his head and thought about the present. But this young man was not a soldier. He must be a basketball or football player, being that tall he was probably basketball player. He would see Coach Carty in the morning.

As he started to leave a voice came from behind him. "Mr. Bixby, there is something else you should know," cheerleader Melanie Ryan, who had waited until the others had gone, "he gave me his apple to hold."

'How's that again Melanie?" the surprised Bixby replied.

Melanie hesitated for a moment, getting her story straight, "After the first man had fallen and the other one was rushing in to fight, Dancer gave me his apple and said, "Hold this please." I looked down at the apple and the next thing I knew he took his apple, thanked me for holding it and went to class."

The amazed Bixby replied, "Thank you Melanie."

"I thought you should know about it, after all I have never held an apple for anyone, see you later," she turned and went skipping on her way to practice.

Bixby shook his head and went to his office.

In the morning after Coach Carty had been informed of what happened by Hound who was leaving his office when Bixby arrived.

"Stamper, I need to talk to you about the incidence yesterday. Is two o'clock at the gym all right for you and how is your ankle? You were moving a lot better when I saw you yesterday."

"Fine with me, Mr. Bixby, I'll meet you as soon as I get my ankles taped. The hot-cold really helped it. My toes are turning purple and that is a good sign," Hound replied going out the door.

Bixby described the student in the fight yesterday and Carty identified him as James Dancer, a new player for the basketball team. He had just told Bixby what Hound had told him, and then there was a commotion outside.

"Sweet Thing, Carty's door is always open to me, but actually I just come to look at you," said Northern Football Coach Mike Conner as he came through the door followed by a protesting Shirley.

"I am sorry coach he just barged in like he always does," she replied loudly "and I am not your sweet thing."

"It's all right Shirley," Carty said as he closed the door.

The Northern Football coach was a slightly overweight, stocky man who always wore a school football cap and a whistle. He had played at Northern was all conference and conference player of the year his senior year when they played Southern for the championship.

Conner had tackled the Southern quarterback so hard he had to be taken out of the game. He also broke his arm the fourth quarter and told no one until the game was over. If he lost a close game the next day he would show up with both hands taped. No one asked how he got them, they knew. He demanded and got the most effort possibly from each of his players.

Carty glanced at Bixby who nodded in agreement, both knew that they were about to witness obscenities few had ever heard out of the mouth of a human.

Conner looked at Carty and Bixby, then to Bixby "Sorry sir I did not know that you were here."

Then to Carty, "Carty I appreciate what your player Dancer did for my quarterback Thorn yesterday. "

Then he asked, "Do you know those two I-think-I'm bad- suckers from Nashville could have hurt my quarterback's hands or arm?"

He spoke louder when he started walking around the office, "Do you know that Thorn was all conference last year and will be up for player of the year this year? And if he had to fight, he could have broken his hand on some fat, beans-for-brains, funny home rejects and it could have ended his career?"

Finally he settled down, "Anyway, instead of the whole team coming over, I just wanted to personally tell you that the team and I will always remember what Dancer did."

Then turning to Bixby, he asked, "Sir is it true that he kicked the hell out of those two with his books under one arm and while eating an apple with the other?"

Bixby replied, "Yes, except a cheerleader held his apple for him."

Then turning to Carty, he exclaimed, "Held his apple for him! What kind of basketball players do you have, Carty?"

Carty looked up at Conner, and then said, "The kind that had three tours of Viet Nam and has a purple heart and a Silver Star."

Coach Conner backed up with surprise on his face, "Damn, after what he has been through, it's no wonder he didn't pay any attention to those two. Hell, why didn't kill the slobs?"

"I think he has seen enough death in his time in Viet Nam," he said. "Coach I would appreciate it if you did not tell anyone what I have just told you about James Dancer."

"Well, you can trust me, Carty, I won't say anything about Dancer's past, but with your permission I would like to show my appreciation personally," he said as he turned toward the door, "and you can depend on the football team to back you and your team up any time."

"I appreciate your understanding the situation coach, speak to Dancer anytime you wish and the basketball team will always be there to back your team," Carty replied.

Turning back, "Carty I just wanted to say I admire you for putting your job and career on the line for Ellis. He is the only player that wears a tie to class. And from what I have seen, he is a class act. Hell, I'm glad you did it, I have my eyes on a black half back and a linebacker that are both faster than the wind."

As he went out the door, he looked at Shirley and taunted, "I'll come back soon, sweet thing. In the meantime, you can always dream about me."

Carty listened to what was coming: a loud bang came through the door. Shirley had thrown her stapler again at Conner who could be heard laughing all the way down the hall.

Some days earlier, Carty had followed Conner out the door to talk to him about upsetting Shirley, but he saw Shirley smiling as he left, a smile that quickly vanished when she saw Carty looking at her with a small smile of his own.

As Carty sat down, he looked at Bixby and asked, "Why does Coach Conner always call you sir with such respect?"

Bixby smiled, "It seems that his father was a Marine in Korea in the same company as I was. He told him to respect any and all veterans from the Korean War."

As he left the office he turned to Carty and said, "I am sure that Dancer was capable of a lot more than just stacking them on top of each other. Between us, men like that never show what they can do unless they are pushed to their limit. I'm glad his limit did not come yesterday."

After he left, Carty sat and thought as Bixby had, the training to do what Dancer did is not from the regular army. No, someone else had taught him the skills he used today, but who and why?

Later that afternoon in Dr. Abston's American History Class, Dancer and Hound were listening to Forest read his paper on their assignment: *The Most Important Event in American History.* He was finishing up with ......"and that is why I think the winning of World War II was the most important event in American History."

Dr. Abston stood, a short stocky man with brown glasses. Who always dressed in a brown coat ,black tie and tan pants, looked at the class, "That was a good report Forest, you made some very good points on what could have happened if we had not won World War II." Then looking down at this roll book, "I believe I will call on you, Dancer, please read us your selection of the *Most Important Event in American History.*"

"Yes, sir," Dancer answered as he went up front to the podium, faced the class, took a deep breath and began reading.

The Battle of Brooklyn Heights

The American Army, under the command of General Charles Lee was defeated by the British Army under the command of General Howe at the Battle of Long Island in August1776. The Americans were forced to retreat and dig in on Brooklyn Heights. They were out-numbered three-to-one when General George Washington arrived. He quickly recognized the situation his army was in and it was not a good one. He knew that without aid or way to retreat, his army would be destroyed by the superior British forces.

Below General Howe started forming his British forces into attack positions. He knew that his troops out numbered the American forces and that the American force's back was to the East River where the British were moving their warships preventing their escape across the river. Howe was confidant this would end the war

A sudden storm came and made it impossible to bring the British canons up through the mud and swollen creeks. His troops also were at a disadvantage because battle formations were very difficult in these conditions. Howe called off the attack to wait until the ground was dry enough to commence his attack with his canons and troops in their battle formations.

Howe was in no hurry. He knew that Washington and his army had nowhere to go. In the front they were facing his veteran British troops and superior canon range. Behind him was the East River with the British warships preventing his army from crossing it to safety in Manhattan?

However, unknown to Howe and the British, the rain also prevented the British warships from moving up New York Bay to encircle the American position from behind. Washington knew he had to move his army to safety across the river. As if by magic a plan came to him. During the night Washington sent his scouts along the river bank to seek out the British warships. They reported that there were no British warships as far as they could see on the river at that time. Washington knew that if his plan failed the American army would be destroyed.

The rain was still coming down when Washington called a meeting with his officers. Washington's explained that their only chance was to move the army across the mile long East River to Manhattan. He looked around the table at his commanders who all shared the same thought, if the British warships saw any rescue boats they would be in easy range of their canons. The only other choice was to surrender the army to prevent its complete destruction and loss of life. They had come too far to surrender. Washington explained his plan. They would send the army over by boat until they were discovered. Scouts would warn him if they saw any British warships, Lee quickly suggested that the Marblehead Massachusetts Regiment under John Glover that were experienced sailors could man the boats. The rain continued and under a heavy fog, at 9PM on August 29 Grover's men wrapped coats around their oarlocks to prevent the sound of their boats from reaching the British warships and began transporting men across the river. The sky was slowly clearing and the moon was shining brightly. Still, the British sounded no alarm. The evacuation started but it was slow.

Meanwhile Washington moved a small number of troops to his front line positions with orders to move talk and attract attention away from the army behind them going across the river.

They all realized that they would probably never make it to safety, but it was their duty and they would hold as long as they could. They also *knew few would be alive this time the next day if they did not reach the other side. There was not a man did not say a prayer that cold rainy night.*

Suddenly a southwest breeze came up and the boats were able to hoist sails and four times as many soldiers as before were moved to safety. This was still not enough. The first light of dawn found the movement of Washington's nine thousand troops not finished. The boats would need at least three more hours to get the rest of the army to safety.

Both the soldiers in the front positions and those on the beach waiting their turn to board the boats worried that they would be seen or left behind. This situation brought a prayer from the soldiers on both sides of the river and in the boats.

Suddenly, rising out of the wet ground and across the East River, came a dense fog that covered the entire river. The boats moved quickly back and forth across the river using the fog as a shield from the British warships. However, everyone knew that the fog would lift in a short time as the sun appeared on the horizon.

The boats would then be seen preventing the evacuation of the rest of the army. The sailors ignored the sun and moved as fast as they could while the fog protected them. They thought that every trip would be their last. When the fog lifted as it always did when the sun became bright in the sky they would become easy targets for the British warships.

But to everyone's surprise and the answer to their prayers the fog did not lift! When the last boat with General Washington and the frontline soldiers arrived safely on the other side of the channel, the fog began to lift. The entire army was moved to safety across the river. Washington's nine thousand men had been saved from certain capture or death by strange fog that never lifted until they were safe. Some believed that God had answered their prayers.

James Dancer
American History

Dancer handed his paper to Dr. Abston who sat at his desk, leaning back in his chair. Looking at Dancer, he said, "That was a very good report, James, few history books have Washington's escape from Brooklyn Heights. It is time we recognized these occasions," he said as he stood.

"Well, our time is up for today. We had very interesting presentations. We will finish up tomorrow. Class dismissed."

Hound looked at his roomy again as they went out the door, "Thanks a lot for letting me try to follow that."

Dancer smiled at his friend and said, "Well, there is still the War of 1812 when the British tried to burn Washington. The fires were put out by a hurricane and the army was hammered by a tornado forcing them to leave." He continued, "Another is the Battle of Midway in WWII where whose side scout planes spotted the others carriers first would win the battle. We had a put together fleet that would be no match to the giant Japanese fleet of battleships and carriers."

"Well the Americans and Japanese sent out a great number of scout planes to find the enemy fleet first. The Japanese scout plane spotted the American fleet first. When they radioed the position of the American fleet it would be destroyed almost immediately. You know what happened," he said as he stopped to look at Hound who was listening very close.

"No, what happened," Hound asked immediately.

Dancer smiled, "Out of dozens of Japanese scout planes there was the only one radio that went dead that day. Soon after the American scout plane spotted the Japanese fleet and the Americans launched their planes first, sunk several Japanese carriers and won the battle. Again say these are signs that God is always with us."

As Dancer turned, Hound took a deep breath and thought how Dancer was always amazing him. He hoped it would never stop.

Chapter 10

The basketball season practice was to start on October the fifteenth, but before anyone could join the team from tryouts to new players to veterans alike, everyone had to run a six minute mile at six in the morning. At exactly five-thirty the running group met at the gym and started across campus to the Northern football and the college track field that went around it. It was a chilly, sunny October morning, a good day to run the six minute mile.

On the way they had to pass by both the men and women's dorms. And every year a number of the students, especially the girls, opened their dorm windows to cheer them on and wave to them with various bits of clothing. They all waved back and even got some phone numbers on some of the night wear thrown at them. They can expect a phone call shortly.

That is except for the football players, who remembered them waving from the fence as they started football practice in the ninety plus degree heat. Leaning out the windows, some of the football players were rubbing their stomach and opening their mouth knowing that a number of the freshman players and walk-ons, who were not in shape, would vomit their breakfast if they were foolish enough to eat it. Ignoring warnings there always was several bent over the track fence. It was a tradition. The good thing about this is that when it was game time, there were no better supporters than each team for the other.

The team manager, Dennis Sperm

Vaughn, was standing at the starting line. He was called sperm because he was shaped like one, small at the top and large at the bottom, but he took care of everything the team needed from clean practice uniforms to the keeping the team stats. Now he looked at each player, making sure they were not across the line.

While he was doing that veterans from last year were on the inside starting position, with Hound being number one followed by junior Miller sophomores Forest, Darke, Holiday, Keller, Bradley, and Sledd The next in line were the walk-ons Upchurch, Morris and a group of try out players. It was Miller who first noticed the three tall players lined up at the end of the line. "Hey, Hound what are those janitors doing trying out for our team?"

"I don't know but I don't think janitors can finish a mile, do you?" Hound replied, looking at Ellis, Forest and Dancer, trying to keep from smiling.

"O.K., let's just lap those guys and show them that they don't have what it takes to make our team and send them back to mowing and painting where they belong," Miller replied. The rest of the team nodded in agreement, except Hound who looked at Miller.

"On second thought," Hound looking at Miller, "I'll bet you five Huddle Burgers and my turn in sweeping the dorm floor next week that those guys can run a six minute mile." Hound said looking at Miller.

Hound hesitated for a moment, "And if you want to go two to one I bet that they can even beat you."

Now Miller was smiling, then looking at the rest of the varsity players, and thinking here is where I get even with Hound for beating him every time in the teams daily free throw challenge.

"Three janitors beat me! No one had done that in the last two years, and it sure won't be two janitors, you are on," he replied.

"Well," Hound hesitated, "maybe I should think about it."

"It is too late to back out now! Sperm's is a witness. Who wants in on this sure thing?" Miller said looking at the rest of the team.

All of the team knew that Miller was the best runner they had. He had beaten all of them the last two years. They all wanted in except Sperm, Sled and Bradley. They had never seen Hound lose a bet and for some reason didn't they didn't think he would start now.

"Ready, get set, go!" Sperm yelled as he started his stop watch.

The race was two times around the track. At first Miller leapt out ahead as he always did. Then in the second and last lap the three "janitors" made their move. Running as a group, they slowly gained on Bradley who was running as fast as he could on the home stretch. It was only twenty feet from the finish line when as a group they passed Miller to win by over ten feet.

Sperm looked at his stop watch, "Five thirty- five is the winning time, followed by five-thirty-seven. The winners are the janitors followed by Mr. Miller and his sure thing betting group who will be buying Huddle Burgers and sweeping Stateland Hall floors for an extended time."

Then turning and looking at the rest of the team crossing, he shouted out their times and told six runner they try again at six tomorrow morning.

Most of the team was holding their hands on their knees and breathing hard, while the janitors were slowly walking around the track.

Hound looked up and when he was able to breathe, "The Huddle is going to get rich on you guys, and I will really hate to miss my turn sweeping the dorm halls."

Miller, who had caught his breath, shook his head.

Miller looked at the smiling Hound, "O.K. What do you know about these guys? They are not just janitors are they?" he said looking at Hound.

"You will find out at practice this afternoon," Hound said walking with the laughing Sperm, Dancer, Forest and Ellis toward the dorm.

Practice started at three that afternoon. After they had all dressed and gone through several warm up drills, Coach Carty blew his whistle and they all sat down on the lower bleachers.

"I would like for you to meet the new members of the Northern Tennessee Basketball Team. Please stand as I call your name. He nodded at Ellis, who stood up. "This is T. C. Ellis, who played last year in Iowa; he is the first Negro to play in our league. We will not be welcomed in several schools on our schedule. I expect you to be ready for any and all abuse we may meet." He then paused, "I am asking you to endure such treatment because we are a team and because it is the right thing to do. If you have any problems with that now is the time to come forward. We are a team and I expect everyone to be part of it, any questions?"

The players looked at each other, no one stood to object. Then Bradley held his hand up to the surprise of everyone, Carty nodded, and Bradley stood, "Heck, Coach I don't care if he is blue, can he help us win the tournament and go the NCAA Tournament?"

They all laughed and broke the tension over the group. Ellis just smiled and sat down.

Carty continued, nodding for Forest to stand up, "This is James Forest, you might recognize the name, he played for Southern Kentucky State. He was injured and had to set out a year. He is fine now."

Then he nodded to Dancer, "This is James Dancer, he has not played any high school or college basketball. He just got discharged from the 101st after serving two tours in Viet Nam. Before you wonder why I chose him to play for us, wait until after practice."

The team looked at each other and Miller just shook his head in doubt.

"Now, "Carty continued," they will not be eligible to play until the beginning of the second quarter, in the meantime they will practice with us and I expect that you treat them as team mates and friends."

Coach Carty sat down and watched his team run through their drills. He knew the team would watch the new comers every move. Coach

Roberts came over to join him.

"I told them to just take it easy until you tell them to give it all,' Roberts said with a smile on his face.

Carty smiled back, watching the lay-up drill coming to an end, "I think now would be a good time for them to see what these "janitors" can do."

Coach Roberts nodded his head to Ellis who smiled back, said something to Forest and Dancer who both smiled back. The next lay-ups saw Ellis, Forest and Dancer dunk the ball with Dancer using a two handed reverse dunk.

The rest of the team looked in awe, not moving except Hound, who smiled at their startled looks. The practice continued with Ellis, Forest and Dancer standing out. It was during the three on three drills that the players discovered just how good their future team mates could be. It was Forest whose defense gave everyone a difficult time with the exception of Dancer whose drive to the basket and changing the ball from right to his left in midair and hitting a soft layup that made everyone look at each other with amazement and just shook their heads as he stopped quickly and hit a twenty foot jump shot over Forest.

Hound who was at the front of the line, held his hand up, turned and faced the team,"You made up your minds before you even saw them play. As captain of the team I want you to know we will have to press ourselves beyond anything you have ever done. And remember this, it is up to us to win games as a team and they will not be with us for the first quarter. We will have to play harder that you thought you could."

Coach Carty stepped forward, "What Keith says is true. We will demand more from you this year that you ever thought possible. Any time you think you can't do more, do more or quit." All of the team looked at each other. He knew some would not show up for practice tomorrow.

Practices became longer and harder. Everyone was exhausted after the daily sprints touching each line from foul line to half line to the other foul line to the other end line and back to the end line they started on. The first weeks of practice were made up of running and drills. Finally Carty gave them the week end off to see Northern play in the Appalachian Football Tournament.

Northern had won four and lost seven games with a mostly freshman team. Now their final game was with Southern who had won eight and lost three for the Appalachian Football Championship. It had proven to be a disaster for Northern. The game was played at Southern in a very cold and snowy day. Northern had won the game toss and chose defense and had kicked off. On Sothern's return, two of Northern's players had slipped and run into to each other allowing the streaking Southern return player to score. Coach Conner had thrown his clipboard into the air. It got worse.

On the first possession, Northern's all conference tight end, Gary Farley had slipped turned his right ankle and twisted his knee. He would not be able to enter the game again. Northern's all conference receiver Brian

Thompson had his right arm twisted in a collision tackle by Southern's all conference defensive linebacker Michael Staton causing a fumble that Southern recovered and returned for a touchdown. By half time Northern had lost six starters. The half time score was Southern twenty-eight Northern zero.

At the end of the third quarter the score was Southern thirty-five, Northern three. It was then that the snow increased and the bleachers were soon empty except for the cheerleaders dressed it their heavy winter gear and a group of Northern basketball players wearing Northern jackets that yelled loud and jumped high to keep from freezing.

Thorn, had taken a beating, because he was forced to pass on almost all of the last plays because of the score. He had little time because his young line could not protect him from the veteran defensive line of Southern. He walked slowly to the bench after being replaced, holding his battered helmet in one hand and a dirty towel in the other. His nose was still bleeding and his face was cut in different places.

Thorn had been sacked nine times, when Coach Conner had taken him out with eight minutes to go. Conner had come over and wiped the mud and blood from his face with a cold towel. He put both hands on his shoulders for a second, looked him in his eye, and nodded his head "You will do." He turned to one of the managers and shouted, "Get a blanket over here on this man!"

The final score was Southern 49, Northern 17 and the loss of eight clipboards,

three thrown away and five broken in two by
Coach Conner, who finally was forced by his
assistant coaches and players to at least put a
Northern football jacket on over his short sleeve
shirt and whistle. It was then, through the
thick, blowing snow, they all heard the battle cry
of Northern from the group of freezing, cheering
basketball players and cheerleaders who had
stuck with the team.

 It was something the football players
would always remember. The Northern
cheerleaders had all gotten into two college vans
and left. Thorn had shaken hands the Southern
players and coaches, some even looked at him
with respect knowing what he had gone through.
He was last in line and it was starting to snow
even harder, the wind was picking up making
him feel even worse.

 Suddenly someone appeared out of the
snow and put a big arm around him, almost
lifting him off of the ground. He looked up at
Dancer who never said a word. He just looked
Thorn in the eye, nodded his head, gave him
another hug and disappeared into the snow.
Thorn had understood what he had said. It
needed no words.

Chapter 11

The first basketball game was away at Southern Kentucky State. Carty allowed Dancer, Ellis and Forest to travel with the team. He told no one, but he wanted to see how Ellis and the team would react when they ran into problems because of his race. They did not have long to wait.

They arrived at the *Southern Style Restaurant* that Carty had always arranged a pre-game meal for his team. As usual the team was shown to a large private dining room. The plates in front of each chair were filled with roast beef, and gravy mashed potatoes. Each player stood behind their chair waiting for Coach Carty to say Grace as he did at all games. He said grace, with a loud "Amen" and they all pulled back their chair to eat. But they never got a mouth full.

The owner, Max Price, heavy set man with a bald head and southern accent, came into the room, pushing the waitress aside, "Coach Carty, I will not allow a black player to eat at my table in the public. He can eat in the kitchen."

He turned to Ellis, "No offence son, it's just the way it is," being a large overweight man, he started to approach Ellis.

Coach Carty stood up and looking Mr. Price in the face said in a quiet voice, "Don't touch the food. We are going to another place. If it is not good enough for one of us, it is not good enough for any of us."

All of the players pushed their chairs in

and nodded their head in agreement. The players all started for the door, "You can't do this, I want my food paid for," yelled Price.

Price was screaming as they passed him paying no attention to him.

Dancer and Ellis were the last to leave. As Ellis passed Price, Price spit on his jacket, and started to say something, but he never got it out. Dancer was close to Price who suddenly gasped and started holding his stomach. Dancer helped him to a chair and went out the door behind Ellis. As he passed the waitress, he said, "I think he will be all right, after all it was just an upset stomach."

The young red hair freckled waitress, saw what had happened, "I am sure he will be fine; you are right, something just upset his stomach."

Carty had started in the door to make sure Ellis was all right. He saw Price spit on his back. He started back in when he saw Dancer drive a powerful short right handed punch into Price's big stomach and at the same time help him into a chair. He quickly backed out the door before Dancer or Ellis saw him. What he did not know was that Hound had seen it all and stepped back away from Carty who did not see him.

The three station wagon caravan had gone six blocks when a deputy sheriff pulled them over and approached the front car that Dancer was driving with Coach Carty, Ellis, Forest, Hound, Sperm and the team's uniforms.

The young deputy, wearing sun glasses, looked at Dancer driver's license. He gave it back to him and said, "The reason I stopped you is because Mr. Price, owner of *Southern Style Restaurant* called about a basketball team that left his restaurant without paying for food. He raised his head and looked at the tall group of men whose sport coats had the Northern Tennessee logo on them and then added, "A tall Northern Tennessee player struck him in the stomach." He looked at Dancer.

"Donna, the waitress, my wife, said he deserved it for spitting on your black player," he said this while looking at Ellis.

Dancer, looked at the deputy, "Your wife was right, I did it and I would do it again. If there is any problem blame me not the team, officer. "

The deputy looked at him for a minute, "I would do the same," he said holding out his hand that had the tattoo, Eagle in red U.S.A ALL THE WAY and under the eagle was his name ROGERS in blue.

"We belong to the same brotherhood. My wife saw it on your arm and made sure I was the one that stopped you."

He then pointed down the street, "Go down two blocks and on your right, and stop at the *Down Town Restaurant.* Ask for Jeff, the owner, he has one of these on his hand too. He also has the best food and prices" He turned as he was leaving, "Good luck tonight."

Coach Carty, Ellis and Dancer went into the restaurant and asked to see Jeff. The waitress quickly turned and went into the back. A few minutes later a wide shouldered man dressed in a white cook's uniform came out of the back and approached Carty and Dancer.

With a smile he shook Carty's hand, Ellis's and then Dancer's holding it for a minute. "Is this the hand that put fat Price on his seat?" he chuckled, "Deputy Rogers called ahead and told me about what happened. He deserved it and more."

He held out his left hand and brought Dancer's hand up, the tattoos were identical. "There is only one place to get one of these and few of the people that have one are alive.

"Coach bring your team in. We are honored to serve them, and don't worry about it being crowded, it is just three and the dinner crowd don't start getting here until after five."

Soon Carty had a method of finding a place to eat for the team. He would go in to check the restaurant out. If he came out with a red face, it was a no go and if he came out with a smile, the team unloaded.

With Hound leading the way, Northern Tennessee was 3 wins and 5 losses just before the Christmas break. They had established a rule that was not in any of the play books. It started the first game with Albany Baptist when Ellis was shooting a lay-up and two players hit him hard in the back and he skidded to the wall.

While he was being helped up by Hound and Miller, Forest watched as the two player's number thirty one and forty five both tall, strong, forwards being cheered by the crowd for their effort to hurt Ellis. Hound looked a Forest. Both knew one of them was going to pay for what just happened. It would just a matter of time. It was just a matter of who got the first opportunity Hound or Forest. It came to Forest.

The next play down on the other end, number thirty-one had driven around Hound and was going in for an easy lay-up when Forest cut in front of him blocked his shot by slapping the ball as hard as he could back into his face. He fell and rolled to the floor with blood coming from his nose and mouth.

As they lined up for him to shoot the two free throws, the referee, a tall black haired, athletic person, who dressed in his stripped uniform looked more like a football player than a basketball referee, came over to stand by Forest, under the goal foul line, waiting on number thirty-one's first shot. He looked at Forest and said in a quiet tone, "I saw what they did to your Negro center and I understand that payback was due. However, if it happens again to either side, I will throw them out of the game. Do you understand?" he said.

Forest nodded his head in agreement, "Yes, sir, it will not happen again unless they try to hurt Ellis."

Thirty-one hit his first shot. The referee stepped back off the floor as the other referee handed the ball to thirty-one for his second shot.

"I'll remember that, you remember this from now on there will be no warning. You or anyone one else on either side does anything like that again they will be removed from the game."

Evidentially the word spread because there were few incidences of attacking Ellis on purpose. When it happened the referee threw the player out of the game.

Chapter 12

There was no more intentional fouls. And
Carty was glad to give the team time to heal
during the Christmas break. It was Christmas
Eve at Northern Tennessee State. And it looked
like Christmas, the ground and trees were
covered with new fallen snow and the streetlight,
the Christmas lights from the dormitory
Christmas trees added to the beauty.

There was just one thing wrong, thought
James Dancer as he looked through his dorm
room window at the falling snow and Christmas
lights, he was lonely. Hound, Ellis, Forest and
other members of the team had invited him to
share Christmas with their families, but he
thought he would be intruding. He had no car
to drive and besides that the roads in the
mountains around his Appalachian home would
make it impossible for him to reach and return
for the Holiday Tournaments they would play in.
His mother Nada had called and said her roads
were completely closed and wished him a Merry
Christmas and that they would get together later
in the year.

The hall phone rang he quickly picked up
the phone. "Fisher Hall," Dancer replied and
without pausing, "Merry Christmas."

"Merry Christmas to you James," said the
voice from the other end of the line, "How are
you this snowy Christmas eve night?"

"Fine, Mrs. Coach," Dancer replied
recognizing his coaches wife voice.

"James the reason I called is to invite you
over to trim the tree and to have a Christmas

Eve dinner with Michael and I," and before he could reply, she said, "we know how lonely it is in the dorm at Christmas and you have probably had enough of the *Huddle* food for a while."

For a moment Dancer didn't know what to say. She was right about the food. His friend, Lewis, was the best short order cook around but even he got tired of the famous Huddle Burger. But at the same time, he did not want to intrude on a special family day like Christmas. Before he could think of a suitable refusal, Mrs. Carty spoke on the line.

"James, our children Michael and Dan are both in Viet Nam. It is not the same without someone we care about sharing Christmas with us," pausing she continued, "we will expect you in an hour. Be prompt or you will run extra laps," she laughed.

Suddenly he felt good, "Don't worry I won't be late and thank you for thinking of me."

"Remember be here at six, "she said hanging up.

This was much better than staying in his dorm and watching the black and white TV in the lobby. He had seen enough and heard enough of the Christmas stories and carols. He wanted a reason to get out and here it was.

He hurriedly took a shower and dressed. Putting on his boots he started walking at a brisk pace through the snow toward Coach Carty's house. The house was about a mile from the dorm on a side street across from the gym.

Dancer loved walking in the new fallen snow. It reminded him of when he and his mother, Nada. They tried to find the perfect tree

185

for the Troublesome Creek General Store. His younger sister Star was waiting anxiously for them to return as well as Ma and the rest of the neighbors that always congregated at the store in snowy weather.

Up and down the mountainside they would trudge, leaving foot prints in a sea of white, while keeping a vigilant eye out for the tree they would drag home. Sometimes they would say nothing for length of time, each lost in their own thoughts. Other times they would just stop a just look at the majestic sight of woods, hills and mountains covered with snow.

Once, two small rabbits, their white coats making them almost invisible in the snow, crossed their path. His mother made a strange sound like the wind, and they stopped right in front of them.

"Ho little ones," she said as she reached down and softly petted them behind their long ears, "it is a time of peace. Now go and share this with your families." They looked up at her and moved their little noses and hopped off into the trees.

Another time they saw three deer, one a large ten point buck and two smaller does. As they approached, his mother looked at the large buck and just nodded her head. They just stood there, their deep, thick, tan coats covered with new fallen show, watching with their big brown eyes, as he and his mother walked by, not three feet away. It was as if they knew that on this special time shared by all living souls, a time of peace.

He had just reached the silent, dark

student center when he saw Officer Bixby making his rounds, checking the doors to see that they were locked. He glanced up and saw Dancer walking toward him.

"Dancer, what are you doing out on Christmas Eve?" he said locking the door.

"I am on my way to Coach Carty's house for Christmas Eve dinner." Dancer replied cheerfully, "Mrs. Carty called and invited me over this evening."

"Good for you. Dancer, Coach Carty and his wife are fine people, I have known them for years," Bixby replied turning to go and over his shoulder said, "Have a Merry Christmas, Dancer. The Missus and I are expecting our daughter Peggy and her family to be here around 8:00 from Alabama. I really want a chance to spoil my grandson," and turning and waving said, "Take care James."

"Merry Christmas to you Mr. Bixby," Dancer replied picking up his pace in the snow. If he was at home, he thought, the store would be decorated with a Christmas tree and Ma, Scratch. President Truman, Cat and other people from the mountains would bring what every they could to share around the wood stove telling Christmas stories and eating home baked cakes, pies and drinking hot apple cider.

Although he had seen no snow in Nam, he still thought about being home for Christmas for years. Well, at least no one was trying to shoot him or trying to blow him up or.....enough of the past he said to himself shaking his head violently. He was going to have dinner with a family he could share Christmas Eve with. It was enough.

It was dark, when Dancer stopped to look at the gaily decorated door of Coach Carty. Under the streetlight car he saw the coach's car an old Ford Fairlane as the coach like to call it covered with snow. Old, he shrugged, it is a lot better than what I have which is none.

Just as soon as he knocked, Coach Carty opened the door, "Come in Dancer," he said with a big smile, "glad you could make it, hang your coat up and let's go to the kitchen and see what going on. Jill has been cooking all afternoon and if you and I don't eat our weight in fried chicken, biscuits and apple pie, she is going to be upset," he said with mock seriousness.

Dancer hesitated a moment in the living room where the tree waited to be decorated. He closed his eyes and smelled the pine and the wonderful holiday odor of the kitchen. It brought back memories of his Christmas with his mother and the gang at the Troublesome Creek General Store. Every Christmas it was like this from the ones he had in Nam to this one. He opened his eyes and looked away.

Coach Carty had stopped also. He knew the thoughts going through this lonely boy's head of some happy Christmas Eve past that was now gone forever. He saw the tears starting to form in the comer of Dancer's eyes. "Better wash up in the bathroom on the right, I'll go on in and see how table looks. Jill will need me to help with the setting of the table," he said loudly going toward the kitchen, "come on in when you finish."

Carty knew Dancer was blinking his eyes

and pretending to have something in them that caused the tears. He washed them from his face in the bathroom sink. Somehow Carty always knew how he felt. It was strange he thought. Well, he did not want to think about it anymore. No more past for a while any way. He dried off and went toward the kitchen. He had come to share Christmas Eve with this family and he was going to do it. No more unhappy thoughts of the past tonight if he could help it.

He ducked under the mistletoe that hung from the top of the door facing and stepped into the kitchen. He had never seen a table so full of food. Not just the fried chicken but everything else the coach had said was there and more. There were sweet potatoes, brown gravy, and more. The centerpiece was a small Christmas tree with tiny presents around it. He just stood there and gaped taken in by the Christmas surroundings.

Meanwhile up stairs Courtney was turning and looking at herself in the mirror for at least the seventh time. She and her aunt had finally selected her outfit from at least two dozen others. At five ten and one hundred thirty five pounds she did have a good figure she thought. Courtney's measurements were thirty-seven, thirty-two, and thirty-six which some considered perfect by some.

Her best friend, Kit Simpson Northern Cheerleader Captain, measurements were the same except she was five-eight. Running cross country in the fall and playing tennis in the spring at UT had helped her keep a good figure. She also lifted weights with her friends in her PE class. She hoped that her figure was good enough to make Dancer pay close attention to her tonight. This is the first time she would actually meet Dancer face to face. Courtney really wanted it to be special time for both of them.

Courtney was looking in the mirror one last time and thought of when she first saw Dancer. It was in the summer and she had come to Northern Tennessee State College to have lunch with her close friend Kit Simpson, captain of the Northern Tennessee Cheerleaders. They had been friends and cheerleaders all though high school. Now Kit was going to college here and she was going to the University of Tennessee where her parents taught.

Courtney had arrived early and decided to visit her Uncle Michael Carty, the basketball coach at Northern. She was just coming from the restroom when Hound and a young, tall, dark, clean cut soldier one hand on an army duffel bag over one shoulder and carrying his army cap with the other, came out of her uncle's office.

In the door frozen in time Courtney was watching him laughing with Hound passing her as they went out the door. How easily he laughed, he was so handsome and tall. He was taller that Hound and Hound was not short. For a moment she had stopped breathing. She tried to shake it off and reminded herself she was engaged to Marvin Smith. She shook her head to clear it. Then she had gone directly to Carty's office.

When she came through the office door

Shirley, Carty's secretary, had sat up with a happy look. She came around the desk and hugged Courtney. Then she stepped back and remarked on how she had grown into a beautiful young woman. Shirley had known her parents when they had taught at Northern and had watched Courtney grow up. Often she had taken her to lunch. Courtney has never forgotten the next surprising statements from Shirley.

Shirley then said, "I saw you looking at Hound and our newest recruit."

Then in her-listen-to-me voice she said, "His name is James Dancer, he has just been discharged from the army and is going to play basketball for us. Short, rich and fat Marvin will never see the day that he will compare with Dancer and he is not for you. Dancer is the man for you. He was recommended to us by Coach Fisher as both a basketball player and a man."

Shirley paused and hugged Courtney again, "And when you get to know him you will find out that what I say is true."

Before she could say anything Shirley knocked her patented three knocks and opened the door for Courtney to be hugged again by her uncle. They had visited for a while and as she left the office she turned to look at Shirley who smiled, "Don't forget what I said and say hello to your family. Next time, we will have to have lunch together like we use to," and smiling said, "and you can tell me if I was wrong or right."

She left and wondered how Shirley knew what she was thinking. But on the other hand she was like that and could read Courtney like a book. Shirley always, always give her advice whether she ask for it or not. She had been right most of the time and just might be right this time Courtney thought.

After that visit she found out that Kit would be gone for the day and decided to see her Aunt Jill. She needed her for her plan. They had talked about school and her engagement to Marvin Smith. Jill noticed a distracted look when the conversation had turned to that.

It was then that Courtney said she missed going to basketball games and she had missed talking to her friend Kit today. Would it be all right is she came from UT, went to some of the games with her and stay overnight with them. Jill was thrilled to have Courtney with her and told her she looked forward to seeing her. Jill had no one to go to the games with until now.

They had gone to a few basketball games before Jill discovered why Courtney had gotten a sudden interest in basketball games. She noticed that at each game, Courtney at times, was staring at the bench not the game. Sitting at the end was a tall, dark handsome young man in a white shirt, blue tie and dark blue slacks. As he stood up during a time out she saw how tall he was. Jill had smiled, took Courtney's hand and looked her favorite niece in the eye and nodded toward bench where Dancer sat. She never could hide anything from her aunt. Her face always turned a little red, now she had to tell the truth. She did, she nodded yes.

Now at last her aunt had arranged this meeting. After months of planning she would finally meet Dancer. Why she was so nervous she did not know. It certainly wasn't over

Marvin. As usual Marvin had called to say he would be busy for the upcoming weeks and he would see her as much as possible which meant he would be at the country club playing card all night and just hanging around the club all day with the rich.

Most of their dates had consisted of sitting at a table at the club listening to how he had found to way to make money on the stock market and telling his success to whoever would sit down and listen. Their engagement had been arranged by their parents. His parents were good friends with hers and after all he was rich. What could she say? There was no one else in her life. No one she even considered until now.

Through the upstairs window, Courtney had watched Dancer coming across the snow to the door. Again she thought he was so tall, handsome and moving like a cat through the snow. Her heart was doing that tricky stuff again. He was here, why was she waiting. Courtney took a deep breath and went down the stairs to the dining room.

"Before you sit down, James," Mrs. Carty said as she and her husband pulled their chairs away from the table, "we were waiting for a late arrival to join us. She is putting her things away in the upstairs bed room," and she added, "you have probably never met our niece, Courtney have you? Her parents had to attend a seminar in England during the Christmas break. They teach at UT in Knoxville. Rather than have Courtney spend Christmas alone in an empty house, we invited her here."

"No ma'am," he replied, "I have never had

the pleasure..." he stopped in the middle of the word. For standing in the doorway, was one of the most beautiful girls Dancer had ever seen. She was tall, her blond hair was in a ponytail that draped over the shoulders of the white and orange Tennessee spelled out on the front of the sweatshirt she was wearing. The jeans were worn but comfortable looking and neither one could hide the body that was underneath them. She was looking at Dancer with a shy smile and dark green eyes that seemed to look right into his thoughts. For once in his life Dancer had no immediate reaction to this strange feeling that had come over him, numbing his senses. He just stood there looking at Courtney.

Carty cleared his thought, "Courtney Ryan, this is James Dancer. James this is Courtney."

Courtney extended her hand, "James, I am glad to finally meet you, but I feel like I know you already. Uncle Michael and Aunt Jill have told me all about you."

Dancer regained his posture. "You probably have not heard anything except how Ellis, Forest and I complain about not be able to play until the second quarter," Dancer replied as quickly as his frozen senses let him, "I hope he says better things about me than he does in practice." They all laughed at that remark.

"Everyone sit down, and join hands," Mrs. Carty said as they moved to sit around the bountiful table, "Michael, please bless the food and thank the good Lord for all the blessings that he has given us this year."

Dancer had been waved to sit beside

Courtney and grasped the extended hand. As they bowed their heads for the prayer, he thought what a small hand but how warm it was. It felt like it had belonged there now and forever. His thoughts were of her there in the doorway, looking at him and him at her. It had taken his breath away. Stop it he thought he shouldn't...

"Amen," Carty said interrupting his thoughts, "now pass the biscuits," he said with a fork in one hand and a knife in the other, "I've smelled this all day, and someone has been keeping me from sampling the food," with a mock glare at his wife, who replied with a smile and a nod of her head.

"Now, now Courtney and I have been trying to do our best for you men and this is the thanks we get," looking at Courtney, "next time we will let them fix the meal and we will do what they do."

"Which is watch ballgames on TV and keep trying to steal the chicken before you serve it, I saw Uncle Michael hide a drumstick under a napkin he wiped his hands with," Courtney joined in with a laugh.

Carty looked across the table, "You sneak!" speaking with a mouthful of biscuits and gravy, "I thought I got away with it."

Everyone laughed at the exchange and it set the tone for the evening. The rest of the meal was spent eating and laughing at stories Carty and his wife told. Courtney and Dancer were content to listen and join in whenever they could

Finally after everyone had eaten what they could, they just sat there for a moment. "This is the best meal I have eaten in years," Dancer finally said finishing a large piece of apple pie, "Mrs. Carty, you and Courtney really did a job."

"I got here just a short time before you did. Aunt Jill deserves all the credit. She and mom always could fix the best meals for the holidays. Sometimes our house had over twenty relatives and friends drop in during the holidays," Courtney replied looking Dancer with her green eyes.

"You and Courtney start decorating the tree, James, while we clean up a little," nodding to her husband, who sat there with a look of contentment on his face, "we will join you in a minute or so."

"We need you to put the star on top of the tree, James," Courtney said taking his arm and leading him toward the living room, "no one else here is tall enough to do it."

When they had left the room, Carty looked at his wife shaking his head with a little smile, "I wonder how Courtney knew Dancer would be here for dinner tonight? Although, I appreciate her driving here from Knoxville, just to spend Christmas with us, I feel like there are sinister forces at work here."

"Hush, now," Mrs. Carty said turning to her husband, "all I did was mention the fact that we were going to invite him to dinner, when she called last night to wish us a Merry Christmas. I had no idea that she would drive all the way up here just to spend Christmas with us," she finished with a mock gesture.

"Besides she deserves someone better than that fat faced I am richer than you Marvin," she replied as she turned hiding her smile.

To that, Carty did not say a word, he just looked at his wife and rolled his eyes to the sky and began helping her clean the table.

Meanwhile Dancer and Courtney sat on the sofa and talked and talked. He found out she played on the UT woman's tennis team and ran cross country. She also worked as a student assistant in the chemistry lab where her father taught. She wanted to be an elementary teacher which did not set well with her parents who had aspirations of her becoming a doctor or a university professor.

"I think it's important to pursue the things that you feel comfortable with and really want to do," she said to Dancer who was leaning back on the sofa, with his long arms stretched over the back.

"I know money is important, but I think it should not determine your life. Besides I have been a volunteer at the day care center on the campus for the professors' children and I really love being around the little fellows."

"And I'll bet they love being around you," shaking his head with agreement, "my mother always said that a child could tell how you felt about them just by reading your eyes and you have beautiful eyes."

At that remark she jumped to her feet, "We better start on the tree or it will be Christmas morning before we are through."

So they began by Dancer putting the star on top of the tree. Before long, the other ornaments and decorations made the tree glow in the street light from the window. They were about ready to turn on the lights for the first time, when Mrs. Carty brought hot chocolate and fresh baked cookies in on a tray.

"You all have worked so hard, it is time to rest," she said placing the tray on the coffee table in front of the sofa and motioning them to sit down.

Looking at couple she said, "Please wait until Michael gets here before you turn on the lights. He is just finishing taking the garbage out."

The back door slammed and they heard the stomping of Carty's boots from the kitchen. "The snow is really coming down now. I am glad everyone is in here warm, safe tonight and doesn't have to drive anywhere."

He appeared at the door and was taking his coat off that was flaked with snow, "Have I missed anything?" He said looking first at Dancer and then at Courtney.

Turning a little red, Courtney replied, "We have been waiting on you, Uncle Michael," and turning to Dancer, she said, "plug in the lights, James."

He did so and the darkened living room was transformed into a light spectacular that all just looked at with appreciation and wonder. Everyone agreed that was one of the best trees they had ever seen and began talking about Christmas's past and turned on the TV. They watched and listened to the Christmas carols and all felt at peace with the world. Finally after the late news tracked Santa' sleigh on the radar heading for them, it was time for Dancer to go.

Dancer stood up, "This is the best

Christmas that I have had in years. I don't know what to say except thank you for the fine meal and sharing your Christmas Eve with me. I will never forget it." He said while putting on his coat.

In the meantime Mrs. Carty was moving her husband up the stairs to their bedroom, "Come back tomorrow James, we have a surprise for you. Courtney and I will serve lunch at eleven. We need you to share Christmas Day with us."

"Good night Dancer," Carty said as he and his wife disappeared up the stairs.

"Good night and Merry Christmas," Dancer replied as he started for the door. Dancer and Courtney stood at the door, looking at the glowing tree. Each finding it difficult to say or move in fear that this would end the special moment they were sharing.

Finally Dancer grasped the door knob and turned to Courtney who had buried her head into his shoulder. As she looked up, the light from the tree made her hair glow and she held his arm with both hands. James Dancer had never felt the way he felt now and about anything or anyone. It was a feeling that he never wanted to end.

"James, you know everything about me and I know little about you," she said looking up into his face, his dark complexion and hair reflected little light, but his dark eyes seem to glow she thought and read what was in her heart.

"I will save it for tomorrow," Dancer said as he stepped out.

As Dancer turned to say good night, Courtney gave him quick kiss on the lips and said, "Mistletoe," and with a smile he could not fathom, "don't be late or Santa will leave you a box of coal," she said closing the door behind him.

Outside in the snow, he just stood there staring at the decorated door. He tried to get his thoughts and emotions in order. He did not say anything. Why? And finally, she had kissed him and he had just stood there. Why was standing here in the snow in front of a closed door on Christmas Eve? He snapped out of it and started walking toward Fisher Hall.

He did not see the beautiful face framed by long blond tresses in the upstairs bedroom window with tearful eyes watching him walk away in the snow. No matter how she felt she was engaged to be married. What could she do?

Dancer walked slowly back to the lonely room in the basement of Fisher Hall. He had never experienced anything like this in his life. He was happy and frightened at the same time. Frightened? How could that be after what he had seen and been thorough in Nam?

Then he realized that he was not scared of what was happening to him, but he was scared of his feelings. For the first time in his life, James Dancer discovered that his future revolved not around life and death as before, but around a tall blonde girl in a Tennessee sweat shirt that he had not known existed until tonight

He decided, as he approached Fisher Hall, all that the feeling he had was one that he had always looked for without realizing it, but never found. He had found it now, and suddenly he was happier than he had ever been. The only problem is he did not have Courtney a gift for tomorrow. As he stepped through the door he heard the phone in the hall ringing.

"Fisher Hall and Merry Christmas," he smiled as he spoke into the phone.

And he heard a familiar voice say, "Merry Christmas to you too, my brother."

"Star," he screamed, "how are you, Dan, Little Dan and Liza doing this Christmas."

"You don't have to scream James," she laughed, "that is what telephones are for. Everyone here is fine; Dan and I are sitting by the fire, Eliza and little Dan are in bed after a battle to get them there. They are so excited about what they will find under the tree. Dan just said that we might not go to bed until daylight or until they get up, whichever one comes first."

"Did you get the Christmas card I sent? Sorry about it just being a card. I know it's not much. But you know how I feel about you and your family. I just haven't had the time before Christmas to shop much," he said with regret in his voice.

"Yes, we got the card and calling the two hundred dollars you sent not much is so wrong." She spoke slowly. "It bought a sweater for Eliza, a leather jacket for little Dan and boots for Dan We still had enough left over to get our old Jeep running before the new snow."

Dancer was silent for a moment. Star had left herself out, she always did. Indian training, a Spirit Woman like a chief or a leader always looked at the needs of their family before themselves. Their mother the Keeper of Secrets was that way.

Star interrupted his memories, "I called for another reason too James, give the girl you are in love with the Azar Necklace for Christmas. It will protect her during things to come."

Dancer was taken back. His sister, like his mother, had the gift. His mother could see it "like watching a TV show," she told him once. Star on the other hand, had less power, but still was accurate most of the time. Their mother did allow her to tell anyone about it for fear their neighbors would think them witches or worse

"I can hear your soul singing all the way back here in North Carolina. Well, I think it is time to get the cookies and milk out for Santa and try to get some sleep while we can. You need to go to bed, James, you will have a busy day tomorrow," she said, "and may the Great Spirit watch over you."

"And over you," Dancer answered and before he could ask her any more about the prediction she hung up. There were so many questions he wanted to ask. How was Courtney in danger? The danger came from what and who? When and where will it happen? Unlike her mother Star's vision revealed a little at a time to her.

He could see Star's little smile as she put the phone down. She always did that to him when she saw something about to happen to him. It was her way.

Chapter 13

Back in his room, Dancer pulled a heavy oak chest out from under his bed. It was covered different Indian drawings Opening the lock he reached inside and brought out a smaller box. It was hand carved and polished walnut. The lid and the sides were carved scenes of wolves. Opening carefully, he brought out a black silk wrapped golden necklace and holding it to the light, he looked at it carefully. The necklace had a round black stone surrounded by gold in the middle. The stone looked ordinary to the casual observer but looking carefully and holding it up to the light you could see the face of the legendary Azar, the red eyed White Wolf of Death.

When summoned he destroyed any and all threats to the wearer. Azar stories were passed on for centuries. Some said that it was just that a story meant to frighten youngsters on Old Christmas nights. But Dancer knew better, he had promised Azar to go hunting with him and he looked forward to it. Then he remembered how he had first met Azar.

Years ago, he and his mother were deep in the woods on day selecting different herbs and plants for her to brew her different healing drugs. She motioned him to sit down on a log by a stream. She asked if he had ever heard the stories of Azar, the White Wolf of Death. He said he had but really did not believe them. She looked at him and said, "Then my son, it is time you met Azar."

Nada pulled out the golden necklace and

said, "Look at the black stone. What do you see?"

Dancer looked puzzled and said, "I see nothing."

Nada smiled, "Now my son, hold it up to the light and tell me what you see."

Dancer did. "I see a white wolf with red eyes," he said in an amazed voice, is that Azar?"

Without replying his mother held the black stone next to her heart and said, "Come Azar, you must meet someone."

There was thunder and a flash of light. Coming from out of the smoke was the biggest wolf Dancer had ever seen. He started to get up, but his mother said, "Sit still. He has been summoned to meet you."

Dancer never forgot the giant white wolf with red eyes that seem to glow approaching them as they sat on the log. As he got close his mother stood up and held her hands out. The wolf leaped the final ten feet and landed at his mother's feet licking her hand and wagging his tail.

She held is head in both hands and rubbed his ears and said, "This is my son Dancer. I will be giving him the necklace in which you dwell. In time he will give it to a girl that has captured his heart. She will call on you to protect her from evil."

She turned to Dancer, who sat looking in wonderment at the giant white wolf with red eyes. He was thinking all of the legends of the White Wolf of Death he had heard and dismissed as a fairy story. He knew now the stories told by the Ancient Ones were actually true.

"Stand and meet Azar," his mother said as Dancer stood looking down at the wolf whose head came way above his belt. He extended his hand and watched as the wolf licked it. Then it looked at him.

"You have always asked about the white wolf with red eyes that appears on your right palm whenever you ask. It is the sign of Azar that you can use to call him to you for any reason. Remember those who wear the necklace and their loved ones will always be protected by him. Now it is time for your new friend to go," and with a final pat on his head, Nada said, "Home Azar."

There was a flash and he was gone.

Now Dancer carefully wrapped the necklace in some Christmas wrapping he found in the hall that was left over from the teams Christmas party. He felt good now because Courtney had a Christmas gift, a gift that would protect her from what he did not know.

Dancer was up early the next morning, it fact he didn't sleep much at all. He kept thinking of Courtney and how he held her under the Mistletoe He kept trying to forget the moment but to no avail. Well, he decided, I am acting like a love struck eighth grader. He quickly showered, shaved, dressed, and wrapped Courtney's gift again.

As Dancer walked he saw that College Hill was already full of sled riders and snow ball fights. He reached the door, checked his watch, took a deep breath and before he could ring the bell, Courtney came around the corner pulling a large toboggan. She was wearing jeans, black boots an old Northern Tennessee jacket that her uncle had insisted she wear, a red scarf that her aunt insisted she wear and a bright orange Tennessee toboggan that she insisted on wearing. Again Dancer was speechless he just stared at the girl that had been on his mind all night.

"Uncle Michael and Aunt Jill wanted us to go sledding on College Hill before we open the presents," pausing and smiling, she looked up though her ever present sun glasses, "that is if you are not afraid."

Dancer, who was afraid to say anything because it would probably sound stupid just smiled and took the long toboggan and reached for her hand. They started walking up College Hill. It was covered with snow and people dressed up in their winter attire. Some families riding sleds and toboggans down the long slope yelling and laughing as they either made it to the bottom or overturned half way down.

There was, as there always is, mischievous group of boys that threw snowball at each other and girls who squalled with excitement. It was a beautiful sunny day with a blue sky and everyone having a good time.

Finally they made their way through the crowd to the top. A snowball came close to Dancer's head and as he turned he saw an eighth grade boy he knew as Tommy Smith. "Sorry Mr. Dancer," he stopped in mid swing with another snowball and said, "I did not recognize you."

As he said it, he turned to the rest of the gang of boys throwing snowballs at any one in range, "Hey, don't throw at these people, it's Dancer and his girl."

They were immediately surrounded by a gang of young boys and girls who asked so many questions at the same time, Courtney had a hard time understanding them.

"Can you, Hound and Ellis practice with us Saturday?"

"Can you get us into the game with Vandy?"

"Is this your girl, she is pretty for a Tennessee fan?"

"When are you going to play?"

Before he could answer, "Leave Mr. Dancer alone," an older lady said looking at the group, "let him and his friend enjoy the hill without you pestering him. Now go play and stop throwing snowballs at everyone. Just throw them at the ones that can throw back."

"But Mrs. Farley that is no fun," Tommy Morison said, just before a snowball hit him in the back. He turned immediately to see a brightly blue clad, girl laughing and escaping on a sled down the hill.

"I'll get you for that Mary Ann," he yelled as he raced after her down the hill. The others laughed and piled on half of a large red, round aluminum Coke sign. Over the hill they went yelling, spinning, falling and rolling in the snow.

"I am sorry for this James," she said looking more at Courtney than him. "It's just that most of them really have no one to look up to and who takes time to play with them."

Then looking at Dancer, she said, "And you have no idea what it means for them to go to see Northern play. If it wasn't for you, your friends and Coach Carty, a lot of them would have dropped out of school. The A Play Program is really helping our seventh and eighth teachers reward them for good class work."

She turned to look over the hill, "I have to go round them up for the trip to the Huddle for lunch. They just love those burgers that Lewis fixes for them and I love them too. Have a good day."

Courtney looked at Dancer, "You are full of surprises James Dancer. Do you have any more that I need to know about?" turning her head with a quizzical look and raising her sun glasses.

Dancer shrugged his shoulders, "I will always try to have a few for you," pushing the toboggan   toward the takeoff point," now let's go for a ride."

Dancer got in the toboggan first, and Courtney sat, in front leaning back against him. He hesitated for a moment, taking in the closeness of her. I could sit like this forever he thought. Then a yell behind him to go or move snapped him out of it. He used his legs to move forward. When they started to move, he wrapped arms around her and put his feet on each side of the toboggan and away they went.

As they raced down the hill, faster and faster snow began to come over the front of the toboggan hitting Dancer and Courtney in the face. They had almost made it to the bottom when they encountered a snow covered fence post and over they went while the toboggan continued moving and hit a car in the front tire.

The driver stopped and hurried around the car. "Are you to two all right?" he said as she looked at them.

Dancer pulled the hood back from his coat, "I think we are fine, Lewis," he said with a smile.

Lewis stepped back, "Dancer, you rascal, I was in a hurry to get the grilled fired up to feed our hungry group of A Play students," he said as he stepped forward to help Courtney to her feet. Courtney bent over and to shake snow out of the back of her neck and hair.

At the same time, Tommy Smith came over. "Why did you hold your girl's hood up? It sure collected a lot of snow, I am going to do that to Mary Ann the next time we ride down the hill," he said with a laugh and ran to join the others who were laughing and pulling their hoods up, even Mrs. Farley.

Courtney stared at Dancer for a moment then said, "James Dancer, no wonder I had snow running down my back, let's see how you like it," as she scooped up two hands full of snow and proceeded to push it down Dancer neck.

"This is just another little surprise," Dancer said, as he and Lewis both were laughing so hard they almost cried.

Courtney lost her balance, started to fall and grabbed Lewis who fell beside Dancer. Then all of them laughed until they could laugh no more. Even Ms. Farley looked at the scene, shook her head and moved the children up the hill.

Dancer introduced Lewis who had

recovered and invited them to the Huddle for lunch.

"Another time Lewis, we are going to ride down the hill some more and go to Coach Carty's house for Christmas."

He shook Dancer's hand and hugged Courtney and went to his car. "Glad to meet you Courtney, come by any time," he said as he rolled the window up as he was leaving.

When they reached the Carty house, Dancer stopped and sat down on the porch to remove his boots and Courtney went to put the toboggan up. He had just finished and changed from boots to shoes when a snowball hit him in the back. Turning he saw Courtney at the corner of the house, rolling another snowball, laughing as she rose up to throw it.

"Ambushed me on Christmas day, you will pay," shouted Dancer as he threw a large snowball at Courtney, who was laughing too hard to dodge it. But she tried and fell back toward the side walk. Before she hit the walk, Dancer raced across the yard and grabbing her, put himself between the sidewalk and her.

Dancer and Courtney, in their heavy winter gear, had landed on the pile of snow from the shoveled walk. Instead of sitting up and helping Courtney to her feet, they lay there with her on top of him. She turned to face him.

"Are you hurt?" Dancer managed to say after a long moment.

Courtney said nothing. She did not have too. Dancer was lost in her green eyes. And he held his close and kissed her softly on the lips and she responded by closing her eyes and kissing him back, only harder. That moment, if the good Lord allowed him to live a hundred more years, would never be lived again. His heart and soul merged with the beautiful girl he held close. There would simply never be another moment like this.

Inside Carty and Jill were watching them. Then they looked at each other and Jill smiled with a triumphant look. She went into the kitchen while, Carty hesitated at the door, he remembered the look each had for the other under the Christmas lights. A magic moment, like the one had when he first met Jill. Courtney was already engaged and it could be a problem. Still, he thought as he reached for the door knob, it would not be bad having Dancer in the family. He and Dancer shared a past that few men had and he had turned out all right.

Carty, with pipe in one hand and door knob in the other opened the door and announced, "Time to come in and open the gifts. I hope I haven't interrupted anything."

Courtney sprang up. "Of course not Uncle Michael, James just kept me from a bad fall is all, I am going to help Aunt Jill in the kitchen," she said as she hurried into the house passed him and into the waiting arms of her aunt.

"Come over by the stove, dear and let's get those wet gloves, socks, and jacket off, and then you can go in the bedroom and change into something dry," her aunt replied with a motherly tone

Meanwhile, Dancer had followed Carty into the living room and was warming his hands by the fire place. "Coach before we open gifts, I

211

only have a gift for Courtney, is there any way I can make it up to you and Mrs. Carty? You have been so good to me I am very sorry," he said with his head down.

Carty stepped forward and put his hands around Dancer's shoulder, "James it would not have really been Christmas with just Jill and I. You and Courtney coming here made it something that Jill and I can always cherish. It is a gift that can only come from sharing Christmas with others that you care about. It is us, who should be asking you to forgive us for not getting you anything for Christmas."

Pointing toward the pile of colorful Christmas gifts under the glowing tree, he said, "Put Courtney's gift there in the middle. The rest of the gifts are for our family who will not get here for at least another day because of the snow storm."

As Dancer placed the gift, Carty turned toward the kitchen and called out, "Jill, Courtney, time to open the gifts,"

They sat down and Jill handed out the gifts. The first opened was a new watch for Carty. As Jill handed it to him she said, "Something you need to look at before you get upset at the referees." She smiled as he looked at the new watch, "Your older one can't take much more of the beatings you give it when you disagree with the referee's."

Carty saw Dancer hold his head down to keep from laughing out loud. Courtney tried to do the same but could not help herself and burst into laughter. This caused Dancer to do the same and finally everyone, including Carty did the same.

Carty turned as he put the new watch on and announced, "I appreciate the concern that everyone here has about me. I am going to make a new year's resolution not to get more than one technical every other game."

Courtney, who was still laughing, pointed to Carty, "I saw your fingers crossed behind your back with your other hand as you said that."

"Courtney, you always catch me when I try to get away with something, this proves my point you are a sneak," Carty replied as he shook his head.

Everyone laughed again. As the other gifts were opened, Carty got a new socks, Jill got new bracelet and sweater. Courtney got a new Northern Tennessee Sweater and scarf. Carty said he wanted his favorite niece to wear something besides orange UT all of the time.

Courtney took the Christmas wrapping off of the necklace box. Everyone stared with wonder at the carved walnut box. She finally opened Dancer's gift. "Oh, it's beautiful," she said as he held a golden necklace with a gold mounted black stone up for everyone to see.

"But it is too much, I know it must have been very expensive," she said as she started to hand it back to Dancer.

"No, it cost nothing, it came from my family, please accept it," Dancer held his hand up.

She hesitated, "If that is your wish," as she placed in around her neck, stood up and modeled it as she turned for everyone to see.

Jill got up and hugged Courtney, "It is

beautiful. Now if you hurry you all will have time go to College Hill and ride our toboggan again. It is a beautiful day."

They watched Dancer and Courtney laughing and walking hand in hand, pulling the toboggan behind toward College Hill. Jill turned to Carty, "They remind me of the day someone hit me in me back with a snowball."

"It took me three times before I hit you," Carty replied holding her close.

Without looking Jill whispered, "I know I saw the other two that you threw miss. I slowed down to let you get closer."

Carty said nothing but held her tight and thought this is the woman that I hope I live to long enough to let her know how much I love and need her.

Meanwhile Courtney and Dancer did not ride the toboggan anymore that day. They had just walked hand in hand and talked about everything. Before they knew it, the slope was clear of people ridding sled. It became cold and it was getting dark. Dancer walked her back to the Carty home and at the door as they parted Courtney gave him a light kiss as he held her close.

Dancer turned to leave, "This was the best Christmas I have ever had."

"Mine too," echoed Courtney and then holding both hands they just looked at each other for a few minutes. They looked at each other for a moment then he turned started back to his dorm.

Inside Carty and Jill discussed the Christmas with Courtney comparing gifts and how much fun they had this Christmas. Finally Courtney excused herself and went upstairs to her bed. She was tired, but Dancer's handsome face and the way he held her kept coming into her thoughts before she finally went to sleep.

Courtney was supposed to go home to Knoxville the following morning after Coach Carty, Dancer and the Northern Tennessee Basketball Team left for Washington to play in the Quantico Invitational Tournament at the Marine base there.

Her parents would arrive from England on a late flight at eleven thirty that night in Knoxville. Instead of driving directly home, for some reason she wanted to take time to think. Aunt Jill had listened to her feelings and to Courtney's relief had understood exactly how she felt. Suddenly she felt a strange happiness just thinking about Dancer.

It had started when Courtney went upstairs into her room to pack. As she turned around and she saw that her aunt was in the doorway. "You seemed bothered by something Courtney," her aunt had said as she came into the bedroom and sat down on the bed, "is anything wrong?"

"No, Aunt Jill, there is nothing wrong." As she sat down on the bed beside her aunt, she said, "It's just, I just I have a lot on my mind with the new semester starting soon, getting back to Knoxville in time to meet mom and dad at the airport tonight and," she stopped for a second and looked at her aunt, "my engagement."

"And James Dancer," her aunt smiled as

she put her arm around her favorite niece and asked," is he on your mind?"

"Oh you know he is! Why does life have to be so complicated?" she asked as she put her head in her aunt's lap as they sat on the bed. "Why do things not happen when they should?"

"You did not tell James about your engagement?" she asked while gently stroking the blond head with hair that fell across her lap and onto the bed.

"No, I just couldn't. I wanted to time and time again but the words would not come out," she spoke softly, "what is wrong with me?"

"You are very fortunate, you have found someone to love," pretending not to notice the tears that she felt on her hand as she rubbed the hair away from Courtney's eyes, "not just the word love that is used so freely by everyone but something that makes that special couple have a special bond that only they can feel and give to each other."

"Like you and Uncle Michael share," she said turning her tear stained face to her aunt, "I saw the way you looked at each other before he left. Is it like that?"

Before answering, Jill had found herself thinking of the young cheerleader that had wanted so bad to meet the handsome soldier that had caused her to lose sleep for days by just thoughts about him. She had seen him around the campus hangouts but every time she had tried to meet him a group of her friends and gathered around her.

The snow always reminded her of the snowball that had hit her and how she had planned the perfect fall in front of him. She had seen him going to the gym for practice every day at the same time.

That day she made sure she was dressed up in her cheerleading outfit and that she would be just in front of him. The snowball had saved her from faking a fall in front of him. She still remembers how strong he was picking her up and carrying her to the gym. She had pretended to be light headed so that she could bury her head into his wide chest. Just before he had sat her down, they had looked into each other's eyes. That was it.

There had never been anyone else for her and anyone else for him after that. Courtney deserves to share this with Dancer she thought.

"Yes, it is like that," she said getting up and helping Courtney to her feet.

"Now dry those eyes and I'll fix us some hot chocolate before you leave and we girls can plot how to snare one James Dancer, I still know a few tricks."

"But Aunt Jill what can I do about Marvin? I am still engaged and mother and dad want me to marry in June," almost whispering with anguish in her voice.

Taking both of Courtney's hands in hers she looked her in the eye and in a comforting voice, "Bosh, my sister and your father want what is best for you and what is best for you is James Dancer. They just don't know it yet. But we will figure out a way, don't worry."

Courtney then hugged her aunt and with a laugh followed her down the stairs into the kitchen to plot further before she left. As she went down the stairs the words from Shirley, the secretary at Carty's office rang in her ears. Dancer is the one for you.

She and her Aunt Jill spent two cups of hot chocolate each talking about Dancer and discovered neither of them knew much about him. Courtney said goodbye to her aunt, but instead of going back to directly to UT, she decided to walk around for a while and get her thoughts in order.

After all, it was a beautiful sunny day. Courtney was lost in thought when she stopped at a corner of the street as an old truck came by and splashed ice and slush upon her shoes and feet. Looking down at her cold, wet feet she knew she needed a place to dry them off. Before she knew it she was in front of the Huddle. The smell of the onion covered, pounded out hamburgers suddenly made her hungry.

As she sat at the counter a waitress came up and gave her a menu. Courtney ordered the famous Huddle Combo consisting of a Huddle Burger, fries and coke. As it was brought to her she noticed the waitress for the first time. She was a tall, friendly smiling dark woman who constantly ran from one end of the counter to the other shouting orders as she went.

Chapter 14

Then she saw Lewis at the grill shaking his head as the waitress shouted out the orders. When he looked up, saw Courtney he came limping around the corner of the grill he was manning. "Courtney it is so good to see you again," Lewis said, pointing to a tall woman dress in white with a greasy apron, that was refilling coffee to those in front of the counter and they watched as she began taking orders from the ones at the back tables, "that wild woman is Dora my wife."

Then pausing, "Excuse me for not minding my own business, you and my friend Dancer looked like you were having such a good time today."

Courtney smiled," Yes, it was fun, do you know James Dancer well?"

Suddenly Dora was there, smiling at Courtney. "I should say so Miss..."

Courtney shook her extended hand, "My name is Courtney. You are the first people that actually know James. I just wanted to know more about him than he will tell me."

Dora looked at her husband, "This girl wants to know about her man."

Then, glancing at Courtney who was a little red faced, Dora smiled and said, "Honey, don't you fret, my Lewis and James Dancer are brothers."

Then looking at her husband, "You and Courtney go in the back at our conference table, where you can talk in private. I'll take care of the counter and grill."

Limping, Lewis led Courtney through the double doors into the kitchen, where an older woman was at work washing dishes at the large sink. She didn't even glance up.

"Here we are." Lewis said guiding Courtney toward a small square table with a red and white checkered boarded top. Across the table were two short old wooden stools. It was in back of the kitchen in front of a small white painted window.

As they sat down, Lewis looked across at Courtney with his eyes twinkling, "She calls it our conference table, and I call it my getting orders place."

Courtney smiled. "She seems like a fine person and that she cares for you very much."

Lewis looked seriously at her and said, "She is my foundation of life, without her I would have not made it through Nam or be here today. But that is enough about me; you want to know about James."

"I just am curious about him. He talks a lot but never anything about his family or his time in Viet Nam. He just changes the subject or goes silent for a while. I guess I am just a little worried about him Lewis."

"I can tell you about Nam and the first time James Dancer saved my life," Lewis said looking at the white window.

"It was in a bar in Saigon, you know, a place where everybody goes to and anything goes for a price. I was just starting out when two big white dudes in army uniforms stopped me.

While Lewis told the story to Courtney, in his mind it was a replay, everything was again real. "Niggers are not allowed on the streets at night. It's too hard to see them and they might get run over," the one with the broad shoulders and scar on his cheek said.

"Yeah," said the thinner one, "they might get run over."

"Yeah, two or three times," the scar face man said.

"Well, I just couldn't stand that and I knew what was coming," he said looking out the dirty window, "so I hit the run-over –man in the mouth as hard as I could. I figured I would get one or maybe two good shots in before they hurt me real bad."

"Sure enough, the big fat guy hit me in the head with a bottle, I didn't remember much after that," he said looking at Courtney, "the rest was told to me by some of the men at the bar I saw later."

"It seems that about that time Dancer came through the door and proceeded to make them understand that they should not be picking on a poor little black boy," half smiling now, "in fact as he was helping me up and out the door, I stumbled over the feet of Mr. Bottle Man."

He took a deep drag from his cigarette, "Dancer laid them both out and he did not even have a scratch on him. He made sure that I was all right and left me. I did not even get a chance to thank him."

Pausing, he looked directly at Courtney and said "That was the first time he saved my life."

He stood up and began to walk in a small

circle around the room," I didn't see him anyone for about a year, and then he dropped in on us from a Huey, a helicopter. At that time we were in country," he said, looking at Courtney," in the middle of the jungle,"

"We had been there for three days. The captain had to go back to headquarters to receive new orders and that left Lieutenant Makin in charge."

"Now Makin hated two things in his life," he said as he looked at her," one was a black man like me and the other was a tall man like Dancer. That was why I had been point man for three days. "

Looking at the floor, Lewis replied bitterly, "He was hoping that Dancer would be killed and then find a way to make me be next."

Pausing, he said, "You see the man going ahead at point that time in the war, was the first to die if he walked us into an ambush, but Dancer was like a ghost in the jungle. In fact he was called the Jungle Ghost by the VC who even had a reward out on him."

"Makin was a little over five feet tall and grew up on his daddy's cotton plantation in Georgia," Lewis was looking at his feet as he said this, but looked up at her when he said, "he was a little man with a big hate."

"Anyway to make a long story short, the next day I was bringing up the rear when Dancer came out of nowhere and reported to Makin. He had been the point and had found danger. Makin was screaming at Dancer.

Makin ordered a guard come up on Dancer because he was going to send him back to Saigon for a court martial. He had disobeyed an order to not come back until relieved."

He sat back down and put out his cigarette and told her, "Dancer had come back to tell them that we would be ambushed if we went in a straight line toward the point marked on the map. He said we should go back and circle around to the right."

Even as he talked to Courtney who watched him as his eyes looked beyond the dinner's walls into the past, the scene came back into his mind like it was yesterday.

"As I passed he said watch out Lewis, the ambush will come in a clearing about three clicks away. You will be caught cross fire from three directions and they probably have it zeroed in with mortars, too. At the first sign, have the men fall back into the creek bed on your left. It is your only chance," he said with a sad look on his face, but a hearty, "good luck."

"Thirty minutes later, I noticed a creek bed and a small clearing ahead. I drifted toward the creek. Before I could say anything there was a chatter of machine gun fire coming from everywhere. A man on my right was cut in two and others around me flattened themselves out."

"I shouted: Get in the creek! Hugging the creek bank, we began to return fire the best we could. But everyone knew it was just a matter of time before we were wiped out."

"I saw Making with a map and he was giving coordinates over the radio. He looked up at me, smiled and ran into the jungle. When the first mortar round hit, we knew what he had done. He had called in a mortar strike on both the VC and our positions. The jungle was alive with falling trees and screaming men," Lewis said bowing his head and starting to shake.

He paused and looked up, "Out of the jungle came Dancer and his guard, Pvt. Jerry Cook, who all we called Big Texas because he was a real big man from Texas and he always wanted everyone to know where he was from. Before the day was over he was even bigger to us. Big Texas and Dancer jumped into the creek bed by me."

He smiled and said, "I will always remember what Big Texas said: Well, me and Dancer heard the shooten and thought that we might as well come and join the party, and he lifted the heavy M-60 machine gun like it was a toy."

"Then Dancer looked at Texas, who was a man who never said much or complained. He was known as the kind of man that you wanted to be at your side when it was a life or death situation, a situation like the one we were in."

He turned to look at Courtney and continued: "They had a special bond those two. It started one day when we were eating chow in the middle of the jungle. Everyone was quiet. Dancer sat next to me and across from Texas. He suddenly he just put his chow down and without a word reached behind his neck with his right hand and threw a knife across at Texas. It was so fast no one had a chance to move."

Lewis grinned and lowered his voice, "Well, Texas came off the ground, reached into his boot and pulled out his Texas Bowie Knife that he always showed and carried that was about a foot long. He took a step toward Dancer who was holding his rations in one hand and a fork in the other. He just looked up at Texas and pointed his fork toward the tree where Texas had been sitting. There was the head of the biggest snake I had ever seen. It was pinned to the tree with Dancer's knife. It had come out of a crack in the tree."

He looked at Courtney and pointed to the wall on the other side of the room, "It was that far away and he did it so quick. I always wondered how he did stuff like that."

Lewis continued, "I can still see Texas when he looked at the snake and looked back at Dancer. He went over and pulled Dancer's knife out of the tree, wiped it clean and handed it back to Dancer. He flipped in over so that Dancer would get the handle. Dancer nodded his head and kept on eating."

That was the story he had told Courtney.

Lewis then had thought of the real story of what had happened. It was just another strange, unbelievable, thing Lewis had learned, but told no one about his friend Dancer. The strange knife was one of them. When the knife was going through the air, it had turned red. No one saw it but Lewis.

Then afterwards when Tex had turned to give Dancer back his knife Dancer had yelled at Tex to leave the knife alone. Texas had paid no attention and grabbed the handle to pull the knife out. He had yelled and held his hand. It was burned. Dance had come over and took the knife out and said he was sorry about his burned hand.

Texas has not said a word, he had just looked at Dancer and shook his head and sat down.

Lewis had looked at the strange knife as Dancer put it back in its sheath behind his neck. He had noticed that even though the blade had been wiped clean of the snakes blood there was still died blood at the base of the blade. It had been used before. Lewis had a good idea of where the blood had come from.

Another strange thing that Lewis noticed as the patrol was going back into the jungle was that the tree that Dancer had thrown the knife into was turning brown and dying. Lewis just added this as another strange happening you grew used to when you hung around Dancer very long. But you never could see them coming.

Leaving those thoughts and going back to his story, Lewis sat down and looked at Courtney, asking, "Do you know what Dancer said?"

Courtney was listening to Lewis and found it hard to imagine what they were going through. She was batting her eyes to keep the tears from showing. She just shook her head, "No."

"Without waiting Dancer took up his AR-15 and said I can't think of better men to go to this party with. It's time to make a move; too many of our people are dying. He then asked me if I could come along and cover Tex. He knew I was hit, but how could I not take my part with these two"

"Instead of marching into the fire fight in the clearing, we crawled around and up a small hill that looked down at two of the machinegun positions. The third nest was across the field and above us. Dancer said from here you can take out the ones on the middle and right. He would get the other one across the field."

Lewis took a deep breath, "He said Count to twenty and open fire. I watched Texas set up his machine gun and then turn to say to something to Dancer, but he was gone. Dancer was always like that; you would be talking to him and before you knew it he disappeared. He could not give Dancer much time before he had to take out the two machineguns that were putting heavy fire on our platoon. When Big Texas fired he knew that his position would draw deadly fire from the third machinegun that was above us."

Lewis stopped walking for a moment and looked up, "I saw Big Texas look up and say a prayer as he fired at the first machinegun position taking it out. Before anyone knew what had happened, he changed fire on the other machinegun in the middle."

"I watched the third machine gunner turn his gun around to fire on us. They were above us and we did not have a chance. But before they could fire their position exploded."

He shook his head, "I did not see Dancer, but I knew he took out that machine gun."

Lewis took a deep breath and continued, "The VC were not dumb. The mortar explosions were continuing on our platoon's and the VC positions. Losing the machineguns and with mortar fire raining down on them, the VC were moving back into the jungle. We would have done same but most of us were wounded and could not move. We were waiting of the one with our name on it."

He stood up and held his shoulders back and said in a proud voice while looking at Courtney, "That is when Dancer proved he was the man I thought he was. He ran into the smoking, deadly kill area. It was too smoky to see who, but he didn't care, he just lifted the living men up and carried them to a small clearing and went back into the area still being shelled. When Dancer reached me, I was about out, everything was getting dark, he lifted me and carried me toward the jungle when an explosion behind us turned everything dark. I knew it had hit Tex who was trying to get to us."

Lewis sat at the table, looked down, closed his eyes and held his head with both hands. Courtney came over and put her arm around him. With his eyes closed, Lewis's mind was replaying just what happened after that. For the first time it was like watching color movie, except he was the leading man.

Remembering that when Lewis opened his eyes next, all he could see was the sunlight peeking through the almost dense overhead ceiling of trees and vines above his head. Then a jolt of pain came in waves coursing through both of his legs. An involuntary groan escaped his lips.

The next thing he knew, Dancer was holding his head and pouring water over his face and then pressed the canteen to his lips. He drank greedily almost forgetting the pain.

"Hold it Lewis, "he said as the pulled the canteen away from his mouth," too much will make you sick." Dancer gently lowered his friend's head onto the jungle's turf.

"Don't move, I stopped the bleeding in your leg, we need to find a radio to call in help," then looking at the group he shouted, "If we don't get a radio more of us will die! I have seen enough death today,"

Moving away he told me, "I will give you more water later, right now I have to attend to the others. Don't move! You have two wounds in that leg. If you do, you will start bleeding again."

The pain had turned into a steady throb now and he felt better. He sat up and looked. He was surprised beyond words. There in a circle around a small fire he counted eight wounded men. He recognized five of them from Charlie Company. Next to him was Texas, but he was unconscious and Lewis saw the blood coming through the bandage Dancer had put on both of his legs. He had been hit hard by a mortar exploding almost under him.

It was the other three next to him on his right that caused him to blink twice and look carefully three times. They were North Vietnamese; two were still dressed in their jungle fatigues lying protectively on both sides of the third younger man who was wearing a black uniform that he did not recognize. He did recognize the Cobra patch on his shoulder.

This is not good he thought, the dreaded Black Cobras. He had heard about them since he arrived in Vietnam. They were the Special Forces of the North Vietnamese, operating throughout the border between North and South protecting supply routes and discouraging any attempt to enter the North. Their reputation was that they were tough fighters that gave no quarter and ask for none.

As Dancer approached the group, the man on the right tried to rise but fell back. The older soldier on the left followed Dancer with his dark eyes.

"Time I changed the bandage on your young friend here," he said as he reached for the bloody bandage on the young man's head.

He was stopped by the older man's hand on his arm. They stared at each other for a full minute. Then the older man seemed satisfied and let go of Dancers arm. Dancer quickly changed the bandage and gave the young man a drink of water. As the he lay back down, he nodded to the older soldier, who also lay back down.

"I'll see you court marshaled for this Dancer," a screaming voice yelled, "giving aid to the enemy."

It was then that Lewis saw Lieutenant Makin. He did not get away fast enough. Evidentially the lieutenant was not hurt as bad as the other in the group surrounding the camp fire, because he was on his feet with the aid of a make shift crutch of a dead tree branch.

Dancer who was treating a man with heavily bandaged chest injury did not look up. He replied in a loud voice, "Lieutenant, sit back down and relax before you open your wound. I am having a hard enough time stretching the limited medical supplies now. I don't need any kind of disturbance from you. Every man here is critical."

"Damn you, lieutenant, you're the one who is going to get court marshaled," the man Dancer was treating spoke up, "You called in that mortar strike on us after Dancer told you we would run into an ambush going your way."

Makin produced a forty-five automatic and pointed at Dancer. "Not if everyone here is dead. I'll be a hero, a last survivor. I am going to enjoy this Dancer."

Lewis was never sure of what happened next. Dancer spun, falling face first into the ground and just as Makin fired his head exploded.

Suddenly jungle around the group came alive. Men in cameo suits with jungle brush attached to helmets and cameo smeared faces appeared around Lewis and the wounded men. Each had an AK-47 pointed at American wounded.

Lewis sat up and looked at Dancer. It was then he saw all of the blood on his friends back. He did not move. Lewis lay back down and thought he was dead.

It was then a soldier stepped out of the brush into the clearing. He was dressed like the others except in his hand he held what looked to Lewis to be an old western forty-five Colt. As he approached the wounded Cobras, all that could rise stood at attention. He waved them down and quickly ran to the young man on the stretcher just as a group of medics that had followed him began treat each of the wounded Cobras. He held the young boy's head in his hand and wiped his face with a wet cloth.

Lewis could not hear what the young

soldier's guardian said to the leader but he pointed to Dancer. The man snapped out a command and immediately two medics ran to Dancer and began treating his wounds. It was then that one of them became excited and held up a feather. Lewis recognized it as the one Dancer had always wore on his green jungle cap. All of the Cobras that were not guarding the American wounded, gathered around Dancer.

The leader snapped out another command; the men around Dancer saluted and went back to their post in the jungle. It was then that the leader approached Lewis.

What happened next amazed Lewis. He held out his hand and said, "I am Robert Parker, University of Tennessee class of 1957. I came home when I heard about the war growing around our village. We protect our village. They have been trying to move us to a village that they have turned into a fort. Generations have lived in our village. That is why we were watching you before the attack. We thought you were coming to move us."

"But," raising his shoulders, "I have never seen a patrol call fire on itself before."

"My sergeant tells me the man there," pointing at Dancer," saved my son's life, and," looking at Lewis, "he has also saved your life and the lives of the others."

He took a deep breath and dropped to one knee, "You probably want to know why they were so excited. My friends in the North have tried several times to ambush Americans in this jungle. But all have failed until today. And each time they failed, they found a feather like this," holding Dancer's feather in his hand.

He turned to look at Dancer who had not moved, for he was surrounded by medics and curious men. "He is a legend. They called him the Jungle Ghost, and the North Vietnamese have a price on his head."

"How did this happen today," he said putting the feather in his pocket.

Lewis explained what happened. Parker listened intently. Then he stood up and gave a command. One of the medics treating Dancer came and gave a short report, then returned to help get the wounded Cobras ready to move into the jungle.

"His name is James Dancer you say. I have his dog tag number and will be back in the states when this is over to look him up. He will survive if he gets medical attention soon. We gave your radio we found to one of your men to call in a helicopter to move you to the rear as soon as possible. Tell him I am in his debt and I will repay it someday when I do I will give him back his feather."

He turned to leave when he saw Lewis looking at the cowboy holster and Western Colt forty-five he wore. Parker smiled, "I always liked American cowboys," and drawing it out of the holster in a smooth motion," it came in handy today for it spoke its language of death to that lieutenant who was going kill everyone."

Lewis remembering, closed his eyes for a short time and when he opened them all of the Cobras had disappeared. Soon he heard the helicopter approaching their clearing and all of the wounded were taken to the nearest hospital.

While in the hospital, Lewis and the others were interviewed on what had happened in the ambush. Each one had made sure that they had the same story. Dancer had saved them all and deserved a medal. Dancer was not with them because his injury was too serious and he had been sent to Japan for treatment. There was no mention of the Cobras. Although Lewis did not see Dancer until he walked into the Huddle with some army friends a year ago, it was then that he found out that Dancer had received the Silver Star.

Lewis raised his head, rubbed his eyes with his hand to keep the tears from falling and looked at Courtney. She had watched Lewis as he had finished the story and felt his pain. She reached for his hands and held them while she looked at his eyes where she could see the pain coming out from his memories.

Lewis looked across at Courtney, with concern in his eyes, "Sorry about that, but now you see why I feel the way I do about Dancer."

He needs you to see him through and put the past he dreams of behind him."

Courtney said good bye to Lewis and Dora promising to come back with Dancer in the future. Now she did not even feel her wet and cold feet. She now knew what she must do. She had someone who needed her and yes, she loved him. She said that to herself several times. The last time she even sang it. Courtney was the happiest girl in the world. Now if only Dancer felt the same.

Chapter 15

Carty was awakened by the phone. While answering, he glanced at the clock. It was three in the morning.

"Coach, this is Hound, they just took Dancer to the hospital, and we are on the way there.

"I am on my way," Coach Carty said, slamming the phone down. He hurriedly explained the situation to Jill as he went out the door.

Jill watched him go and her thoughts turned to Dancer. The tall, dark handsome young man who had a smile and a grin that turned every girls head. He always said," Yes sir," to Coach Carty and called her "Mrs. Coach." He must be going through the same problems that her husband had gone through.

She closed her eyes and whispered a prayer, "Please God, he has been through enough, grant him a time of healing and peace like you did the man I love." She hesitated only a minute and picked up the phone to call Courtney.

A few minutes later, arriving at the hospital, Carty was met by Hound, Ellis and Forest in the waiting room.

Hound explained, "Coach, Dancer was shaking my shoulder when I woke up and said he needed to go to the hospital because his legs were becoming numb. He started to fall but I caught him. I yelled for T.C. and Forest. They came in a hurry. We started to help him up but he said just to l let him lay on the   floor on his

235

back and told us not to move him. He said he knew what it was. I called the hospital and they sent an ambulance then I called you. He is our friend, coach, and we are really worried about him," he said looking at Coach Carty.

"He was really hurting coach," T.C. added, "he was trying to smile but he was sweating and looked awfully pale."

Forest added, "Coach, I think it is something serious. We all know enough about him to know if he is hurting that bad, it has to be serious."

Just then at the door opened to a stocky, white uniformed man with gray eyes and a worried look on his face. "Who knows the young tall man the ambulance has just brought in to the emergency room?" he said in a loud voice.

"I need all the information I can get about him and I need it now, he tried to talk but was in too much pain, we gave him a sedative for the pain but it put him out" he said looking at the group standing in the middle of the floor.

Coach Carty stepped forward, "I am Basketball Coach Michael Carty from Northern Tennessee State College, his name is James Dancer, he plays basketball on the college team. He was discharged from the 101st Airborne. The only relative I know of is his mother, but I don't know how to reach her. "

"I am Doctor Hay, he was able to tell us his back injury caused numbness in his legs," then looking at each one, "and I know why."

Dr. Hay continued, "Have any of you seen him with his shirt off?"

The group looked at each other. It was

Ellis who said, "He always took a shower by himself."

Forest joined in "We all thought it was strange that he always waited until we left and then he took a shower and always came out with a shirt on."

It was Hound's turn, "We thought it was because he was shy."

Dr. Hay was rubbing his eyes with his hand, "I wish it was simple as that, "he replied with low voice. " I did three tours in Viet Nam during the war and I have seen such wounds before, "then adding, "but few men survived them."

He looked at each of group, "That boy has been hit in the back by shrapnel from a mortar round. Some doctor did a great job getting all of the shrapnel out of his back from the looks of the scars it must have been great deal."

Pausing and looking at Carty, "However, being a battle field surgeon I know, he did not have the time or the equipment to do a though job. The piece he missed is causing all of the trouble. "

Then turning," We will have more x-rays with the hour and I will get back to you as soon I read them. In the meantime try to contact his mother."

Hesitating he turned again, "Praying for him would be good thing to do."

The group looked at each other and without a word sat down. Each said a silent prayer for their friend. They all knew without looking up that each was doing the same.

Carty was thinking about calling Coach

Fisher in the morning and having him try to find a way to contact Dancer's mother when Dr. Hay rushed through the door again holding x-rays.

With concern on his face, he looked at the group as they rose to their feet. "Not good news I'm afraid. He has a small piece of steel next to his spine. It is putting pressure on nerves causing pain and paralysis. What makes it worse is it is almost impossible to remove without the possibility of causing complete paralysis in his legs for life. But on the other hand, it is moving and will cut the nerves if we don't operate immediately. That is why I need permission from his parents, now, if we want to save that boy's legs."

He quickly turned and went back through the door, "I'll be getting the operating room ready now please find his mother as soon as possible."

Then the door swung open, in it stood the biggest man Carty had ever seen. He must be almost seven feet tall, with long dark skin face with a scar on his right cheek, black hair over his shoulders and black eyes that seemed to almost glow. He was dressed in what seemed to be buck skin pants and shirt both decorated in red and white beads. On his feet were leather moccasins with the same ornate beads. He looked at the group carefully and when satisfied he stepped aside.

Again the group was taken back. Into the room came a tall, attractive slender dark skinned woman with black braided hair and dark eyes that slowly looked at each person in the room. She was wrapped in a beautiful deer skin coat.

She stepped forward standing before Carty she said "I am Nada, James Dancer's mother. I am here because he is in danger."

She extended her hand to Carty, who replied "Dancer has spoken of you often and has great affection for you and your wife Jill"

Though he was startled, Carty extended his hand, "I am glad finally to meet you, Dancer spoke of you often, too." Then in a serious tone, "He is in very serious condition. He..."

It was then that Dr. Hay came through the door a new x-ray in his hand. After introductions, he looked directly at Nada, "Your son has a piece of steel against his spine that will paralyze him unless we operate on him within the hour, and the problem is his nerves cause movement that we can't control. During the operation if he moves the shrapnel will cut through his nerves causing him to be paralyzed the rest of his life."

Nada looked at Dr. Hay, "Then operate doctor; he will not move if I can sit in the operating room."

Dr. Hay looked at her a long minute and made a decision and asking no questions, "Come then, we have no time to lose."

As she started to follow the doctor as he hurried down the hall while looking at the x-ray. She hesitated at the door and said looking at the giant, "Kana, I must go, protect all and listen to him," pointing at Carty, "do you understand?"

The giant nodded his head and Carty motioned him to sit in a chair nearest Forest. Kana sat down, placed a large hand on each knee, straightened his back up and closed both eyes. Everyone looked at the giant, Carty thought of the statues of Egyptian gods he had seen in books. Another thought that everyone shared was that he was a very dangerous man if he wanted to be.

Dr. Hay had readied the operating room before he left. By the time he was ready, Dancer had been prepared for the operation. Everyone around the operating table looked at Nada as she placed a mask on her face and was directed by Dr. Hay to a corner in the operating room.

After sitting down she nodded her head and began a low chant. Before anyone could speak, Dr. Hay nodded his head and began to move closer to the face down Dancer whose body jerked with uncontrollable movement. Just before the used his scalpel he took a deep breath and looked at Nada, who without interrupting her chant nodded her head yes. He hesitated for a moment, said a quick prayer and began the operation.

The hospital outside door opened, Jill and Courtney entered and both were met with a hug from Carty. Jill had called Courtney at UT and had waited for her to arrive to come to the hospital. Carty answered all of their questions about Dancer, Dr. Hay, Nada and the giant who sat silent, showing no emotion and staring straight ahead.

They joined the group and waited, Courtney sat on one side and leaned against Carty's shoulder while on the other side, Jill held his hand. Each knew that it was going to be a long night.

An hour later two men pushed open door. One a hawk face man the other a heavy sat man with tattoos on his large arms. Both had dirty, greasy, brown hair below their shoulders. They stopped in the middle of the group and looked around until their eyes fell on Ellis.

The hawk faced man looking at the other said "I told you Willie, there was a black nigger in our hospital. Can you imagine that?"

"Don't you worry none Billy Jack, after we take him outside he will need a hospital," answered Willie.

Then each pulled a large knife. Before anyone could do anything about it, Willie grabbed Courtney by the arm and put his knife close to her throat. He then looked at Carty and the rest there said, "If you want to see her live don't get in our way and that goes for you too Tonto," Billy Jack said, as he kicked Kana in the ankle.

What happened next no one was quite sure of. The giant exploded from his chair, grabbed Willie by the knife arm he had around Courtney and threw him like a rag into Billy Jack with such force that both skidded across the tile floor and went down in a heap of arms and legs after bouncing off the block wall.

They were dazed when Kana grabbed each by the neck with giant hands and brought their heads together with a loud crack. Before they fell he grabbed each by their long hair and threw both of them outside on the side walk, where each one did not move.

He came back in stopped and looked at Courtney. For the first time Courtney saw concern in his eyes about her. For some reason she placed a hand on his shoulder and said, "I am all right; we are all fine thanks to you."

He gave a little nod and returned to his chair and again placed his hands on his knees, closed both eyes and was peacefully at rest again

The hospital night watchman came through the door, looked first at the sleeping giant, and shook his head. Then looking at Courtney, he asked, "Are you all right miss? Those two are have caused a lot of trouble and been in and out of jail for years."

Then looking at the pile of hands and legs stacked on the side wall that began to move slowly, he said, "I called the local police to come and get them."

Courtney said she was fine. Then as he left the room, he chuckled and they heard him say as the door closed, "Tonto did not need the masked man tonight."

Finally at three in the morning, Dr. Hay came through the doors, meeting the entire group before he got two steps into the waiting room. He was shaking his head, "I never would have believed it possible, but the operation was a success," he held out a quarter sized piece of white jagged metal, "he never moved during the entire operation. "

Then turning to Nada coming through the doors behind him with an exhausted look on her face, "Somehow she took his pain, I saw her shake with pain during the operation just like Dancer would have done."

Then turning to her, he said, "In all of my

medical years I have never seen anything like it," then turning to Carty, Courtney and the rest of the group, he explained, "He will not be able to see anyone for at least twelve hours. Go home and get some rest, I will keep the desk nurse advised of his condition. Call and check on him tomorrow."

Then turning to leave, he stopped and turned, "Your prayers were answered and we were helped by a force his mother possesses that I am sure that in all of my medical years I will never understand."

They all thanked Nada and Kana. All could see the stress she had gone through as she hugged each one. As she hugged Courtney she whispered something to her and Courtney smiled and nodded. She did the same. Kana shook hands with each one nodding his head as he did so. Then he put a big arm around Nada and helped her out the door to waiting car. Who was driving they could not tell as it drove away.

Courtney went home with Jill. Carty drove the rest of the team back to the college because he was afraid they were too tired to drive safely. All were silent until they reached the dorm.

As each thanked Carty for the ride as they left the car, Hound stopped and turned to Carty, "One thing coach, remind me to never call Kana, Tonto."

Even as tired as they were, they all laughed, slapping Hound on the back as they went toward their dark dorm. Carty was still smiling as he pulled into the driveway at his home.

Meanwhile the police had taken Willie and Billy Jack to the emergency room. And after being treated for concussions and other cuts and nicks they were taken to the jail, where the police asked what gang had attacked them. After all who would believe the tale about a giant Indian named Kana?

Chapter 16

The next day, Carty and the rest of the team visited Dancer in the hospital. Dr. Hay told them not to mention anything about the incident last night and about his mother. He would do that when the time was proper. As Carty led the team down the hall the nurses and other patients stopped what they were doing and looked in amazement as they walked by.

Few had seen a group of young men that tall and especially a black person walk down the main hall of the hospital. And few had seen a group as polite as they smiled and greeted every one they passed. The word soon spread throughout the hospital that the Northern Tennessee Basketball team was a group of fine young men, even the Negro that they called Ellis who wore a red tie and white shirt always smiled as he greeted to everyone he passed in the hall.

As they crowded into the small room, the other two patients sat up and stared, Joe was an older man, with both legs in casts due to a car accident, the other patient, Ted, a younger man who had his right arm and leg in casts from a hit and run accident. Before they arrived, Nurse Ann, a short, middle aged brown haired nurse, had told them of the visitors and what to expect.

Dancer was pale, lying on his side with different tubes running into his arm, but he managed a smile. "Sorry I'm missing the weight lifting and the running. I know you will miss me. But I decided to take a little time off," he said as Nurse Ann checked the different medications running into his body.

It was Hound who replied with a smile, "Don't you worry Big D. We are saving the two a day practice coming up during the next two weekends just for you. I never saw someone work so hard to find a way to miss practice."

Carty and the team spent the next thirty minutes talking and laughing about things at the college and the practices, when Dr. Hay came in.

"Glad to see you again, coach" he said as he shook hands with Carty, but upon reading the chart the nurse handed him, and looking at Dancer, he said, "He will be just fine in about six weeks; that is if everything goes to schedule. But now I am afraid you will have to leave, I have to change the bandages and see how the wound is looking."

But Carty saw the worried look on Dr. Hay's face even as he spoke. Taking Carty aside, Dr. Hay explained what was about to happen. When Dancer had recovered enough, probably in about two or three days, he would give Dancer a simple test to see if he would ever walk again. He promised that he would call him as soon as the results of that test were confirmed.

Nurse Ann and the other patients, Joe and Ted, had learned to like the tall, dark young man who went out of his way to listen to their stories and tell them some of his own. But after he had gone to sleep, they often whispered about the upcoming test; they had learned about; that was coming soon to determine his ever walking again.

On the fifth day, early in the morning

before breakfast, Dr. Hay and Nurse Ann went to work on Dancer's wound. They realized that the results of the test in the next few minutes would determine if Dancer would ever walk again. After they had changed the bandage, Dr. Hay turned to Dancer and said, "If you feel anything wiggle your toes."

The moment of truth had come.

Although Dancer could not see it, Dr. Hay, Nurse Ann, Joe and Ted were saying a silent prayer for the young man lying on the bed before them. Dr. Hay took a deep breath and ran an end of a small spoon across the bottom of Dancer's feet. First the right, where his toes moved...Dr. Hay took another deep breath, said another silent quick prayer, and used the spoon again. When it moved across the bottom of Dancer's left foot, his toes moved.

Nurse Ann looked across at Dr. Hay with happiness in her eyes and a smile on her face. She came around the table and hugged him. Dr. Hay let out a deep breath, looked at her and shook his head. Elsewhere in the room, Joe and Ted were celebrating and giving each other high fives. Each had to be cautioned not to move much, for Nurse Ann meant to hug each of them.

Dr. Hay, in the meantime, came around the bed and looked at Dancer with a smile on his face and shaking his head, said, "Dancer you have beat the odds both on living and ever walking again. I just did not know what damage had already been done to your legs nerves before the operation until just now. You will be on the basketball court before you know it. Now rest and I will see you again later."

He quickly called Carty with the news. The coach was silent for a second and then said "I don't know how to thank you enough doctor."

Dr. Hay hesitated for a moment and said, "Don't just thank me; thank the strange powers that were above and beyond our understanding that wherewith us all that night."

Coach Carty called Ma Thomas at the Troublesome Creek General Store. He had called her earlier and explained what Dr. Hay had told him. He promised he would call her back as soon as he found out anything. He told her the good news and he could hear the cheers and yells coming from the gathering in the store.

Coach Fisher was there too, and taking the phone from Ma said he appreciated all Carty had done for Dancer. Carty said he was the one who should be thanking him for sending Dancer to Northern and working with him all of those years. And especially for the "he will make a difference," remark. Both he and Fisher laughed together, because both now knew that Dancer would make a difference, a very big difference.

Meanwhile, Dancer had slept for hours, judging from the darkness on the window, as he tried to focus his eyes. The ever present Nurse Ann and Dr. Hay were standing before him.

"Good to see you awake, James now let me get your temperature and pulse", Nurse Ann said as she inserted a thermometer into his mouth and felt he pulse while looking at the time on her watch.

Dr. Hay came forward and looking at the results of Nurse Ann's numbers on her recent temperature and heart check. "These look good, James. Your supper should arrive at any time." Just then a cart pushed by another nurse came through the door with the meals for the Joe, Ted and Dancer.

Dancer's bed was raised and special bedding allowed him sit up. He wasn't very hungry. He sat up to read the paper when he stopped. There was an announcement of Courtney and Marvin's engagement. If the lieutenant's bullet had struck his heart, he could not have felt worse. He wanted to cry, strike something, but it came to him that he wanted the best for Courtney. If she was happier with a rich man who could give her more than he ever could, so be it. He now understood what the will to live meant and for the first time felt the *Dear John Letter pain* that many others had felt before him that no medicine could cure.

Just before the back pain came, in his mind, he thought of the blond, green eyed girl that had shared Christmas with him and had given him a reason to forget all of the war memories that had kept him awake at night and remembering the loss of so many of his friends. Now they came back and he dreaded going to sleep where the memories lay and the nightmares were waiting. He knew the yelling and screaming would start again and that like before he could do nothing about it.

Dr. Hay and Nurse Ann watched Dancer though the door window as he moved the untouched dinner plate away and turned sideways in the bed. They both glimpsed the sudden anguish on his face and the pain from twisting of his back.

Dr. Hay looked at Nurse Ann and said, "I have seen this so many times before during Nam to boys who get a Dear John letter. That boy is suffering from something that our medicine cannot treat, he has a broken heart and I have no treatment for it, I am sorry to say. If he does not have the will to recover, then he will not recover no matter what we do. How he suddenly got it I don't know."

It was then that Courtney came through the doors down the hall. Both the doctor and the nurse turned to see her hurry her pace as she saw them outside Dancer's door. She saw the worried look in their eyes.

"Has something happened to James? Was his operation all right? Can I see him now, I...'she could not complete the sentence before the tears she had held back gushed out. Nurse Ann moved to her and held her close.

"Dancer's operation was a success, it just that there is something that is bothering him that we don't know about. If it goes unchecked it could slow down his healing progress or stop it all together. Can you help us?" she said as she stepped back from Courtney.

"Oh, I know what it is. The announcement of my engagement was in the paper. It was put in without me knowing about it by the parents of Marvin Smith. I came from UT as fast as I could when my Aunt Jill called and told me about it," wiping the tears from her eyes.

Nurse Ann and Dr. Hay looked at each other. Dr. Hay asked, "are you going to marry this Marvin person?'

"No," looking at them with a concerned look, "my parents want me to but I know that the man I love is here."

She paused, and looked at Nurse Ann, "I just hope he cares for me as much as I care for him," Courtney said finally getting control of her emotions.

"Visitations hours have passed but in this case, I will make an exception," Dr. Hay said as he stepped aside and opened the door into the room.

"He may be asleep and be careful when you speak to him. He could jerk the stitches loose," he whispered to Courtney, "try not to wake the other patients.

Courtney nodded her head and went quietly into the room. Dancer had turned over and was lying on his side facing the door. Courtney knelt down and gently stroked the side of his face. Dancer's eyes opened, for a moment he could not focus, and then he did. He started to rise but Courtney placed a hand on his shoulder and slowly pushed him down.

"Dr. Hay said you should not move or it could cause your stitches to come loose,' she whispered to the surprised and wide awake Dancer.

Dancer whispered "Courtney, I read your engagement announcement in the paper, it"...that is as far as he got.

Courtney placed a finger gently over his mouth and bent forward and kissed the surprised Dancer slowly on the lips. "The announcement was placed in the paper without me knowing about it by Marvin's parents," she said as she gently kissed him on the lips again.

"My heart belongs to you, James Dancer if you want it, I...this time she could not finish because Dancer place a hand behind her head an drew her close, kissing her and holding her close as he could.

Meanwhile at the door, Dr. Hay and Nurse Ann, who had watched the whole scene, looked at each other, with a knowing look.

It was the smiling Dr. Hay that looked, with a twinkle in his eye at the smiling Nurse Ann, as he said, "Nurse Ann I feel that our patient has been cured by the oldest remedy God ever put on this earth, a sharing love between a man and woman. Let them have thirty minutes before you ask her to leave, Dancer needs his rest."

"Dr. Hay, your prescription was perfect," Nurse Ann said as they walked happily down the hall.

Suddenly, a giant figure, Kana came through the hall doors, and held them open for Nada, Dancer's mother.

She smiled as she met Dr. Hay, "I don't know how to thank you for saving my son's life and his being able to walk again."

Before she could finish Dr. Hay replied, "It would have been impossible without your unique help. This is Nurse Ann she was the nurse in charge of the operation."

After exchanging greetings, "I am afraid it is too late to see Dancer. He has a visitor now and after she leaves in twenty minutes, he will have to rest until morning."

Nada then said in a low voice, "The visitor

is why I am here doctor. I must see Courtney before she leaves the hospital; it is of the utmost importance."

Dr. Hay, knowing and respecting the strange powers this woman possessed, turned to Nurse Ann, "When you tell Courtney it is time to go, do not mention his mother. The excitement added to what he has had already, will be too much for him. Take her to my office where we will be waiting. "

Nurse Ann nodded and Dr. Hay indicated for Nada and Kana to follow him to his office. She entered Dancer's room quietly and approached Courtney, who was holding Dancer's hand with both of hers as they were smiling, and whispering to each other.

She lightly touched Courtney on the back, pointed to her watch and the door. Courtney gave Dancer one last kiss, gently touching his face and followed Nurse Ann out the door. She explained the situation to Courtney as they went to Dr. Hay's office.

As Courtney stepped into the office, she was greeted by Nada with a hug and a nod from Kana. Courtney held Nada hands, "It is so good to see you both again." And looking at Kana, said, 'to thank you for saving my life and Ellis' life," the giant just looked at Courtney and nodded his head.

They stayed there in the office while Dr. Hay explained Dancer's condition and answering questions about how best to help him get well. Finally, Dr. Hay stood up, "It is time for me to make my final rounds, and you both can see Dancer tomorrow at ten."

He shook Kana's hand and asked, "Has anyone ever called you Tonto again?"

For the first time they all saw Kana smile, shaking his head, "No.".

As they were leaving, Nada and Kana took Courtney to the parking lot to her car. Nada said, "Before you leave Courtney, would you please let me see the necklace that James gave you for Christmas?"

Courtney took the necklace off and handed it to her. "James gave you this to protect you from any harm," holding the small dark stone in the middle up to the street light.

"Look at the stone in the middle and tell me what you see," she said as she handed the necklace to her. Holding it up to the light for the first time she saw the face of a white wolf with red eyes.

"Let me explain," Nada said as Courtney looked again at the necklace, "his name is Azar, the White Wolf of Death, and Stealer of Souls. He is a spirit wolf, hundreds of years old that protect anyone who wears this black charm and is loved by one of my people. We are an ancient race. If you look on my son's right hand palm you will see the sign of Azar that only appears when he calls it. You can command him. But be careful he is very dangerous.

Hold it in your hand and say, "Azar to me."

Courtney did as she was told. A short distance away, there was a blinding flash that momentarily blinded her. When she could see again a giant white wolf with red eyes was coming toward her. Suddenly a car, a black jeep,

without its lights on flashed by and if not for
Kana, who lifted them up and jumped between
two parked cars, would have hit Nada and
Courtney. However, it ran over the white wolf.
Courtney started to cry out until she saw the
wolf still coming toward them. He had run
through the jeep!

He leaped just before he reached them. He
went by Courtney into the extended hands of
Kana who held giant white wolf like a baby while
petting his head as it licked his face.

For the first time she heard the giant
speak, "Kana is glad to see you again too, Azar,
it has been a long time."

He put the giant wolf down and it trotted
over to Courtney. For some reason she felt no
fear. It stopped in front of her and looked in her
in the eyes for several seconds. Then he came
forward wagging his tail. She reached down and
rubbed his ears with both hands. The great wolf
responded by wagging his tail and licking her
hands.

Nada looked at both of them and smiled,
"Ah, Azar old friend, yes, it is my son, your
brother Dancer she loves and he gave her the
ancient black stone where you dwell as a bond
between them. You will now protect her from all
harm when called."

Turning to Courtney, Nada said. "He has
read your soul and he will be with you and
protect you as long as you need him."

"Remember, he will slay anyone or
anything that wants to do you any harm, when
you say, Azar Protect, he will appear as he did
tonight. He can read the souls of those around

you and will only slay the evil ones that wish to do you harm. You will need him in the future."

Then turning to Azar, she said, "Home, Azar," and there was another flash and he was gone. Courtney looked at the necklace; it felt warm, and in the middle of the black stone was a white wolf with red eyes. Azar had gone home.

Nada hugged Courtney as she and Kana left in a waiting car. Courtney started to go to see Jill but it was late and she had to go back to UT for an English test tomorrow. As she drove back, her thoughts went to Dancer and the feelings each shared. She was so happy she could shout it out. She felt better than she ever had in her life. But in the back of her mind was Nada saying that she would need Azar in the future. It puzzled her but she discarded it and thought of seeing Dancer again.

Miles away going through a dark mountain road, Nada looked at Kana, "We have done everything we can to protect her, tonight I will look at her future and see if there is anything else we can do. The car running over Azar and trying to hit us was no accident. We must find out more."

Kana nodded and settled back into the seat.

Chapter 17

Courtney had spent the night with her Aunt Jill. It took almost two hours before the two stopped discussing what had happened at the hospital between her and Dancer. Finally, Jill hugged her happy niece and closed the door quietly. As Jill quietly slipped under the covers, she could not see Carty's smile. He was glad things were working out between Courtney and Dancer too.

The next morning, Courtney and Jill were in the kitchen preparing breakfast and talking about Dancer and what they were going to bring when they visited him at the hospital on Sundays.

Neither one noticed Carty, who came down the stairs fully dressed, but they were startled when he kissed each one on the cheek, took a cup of coffee, the newspaper and went out the door. He did not want to know the plan they were working out for poor Dancer. Being bed bound as he was he could not run if he wanted to. He stopped before he got into his car, drank a sip of the hot morning coffee, on second thought, who would want to run from a girl like Courtney

Courtney left at ten the next morning to see Dancer. When she came into his room he was sitting up expecting her. He opened his arms and she rushed to them. Neither one said anything for a long minute they just held each other. She made sure she did not put any pressure on his back. Courtney spent an hour there with him hand in hand just looking at each other speaking in low voices about what each other liked and what they could do together.

"When you get better we can get physical," Courtney said looking a Dancer, who responded with a startled look.

Courtney laughed and moved her head back and forth, "No, not that kind of physical. I mean for example we can play tennis, swim, and run or go bowling together."

Dancer had never played tennis and knew nothing about bowling. He saw the twinkle in her eyes.

"I think you want to play games that you think you will beat me in," Dancer replied with accusing look.

Courtney had smiled, looked at him in the eyes and said "Maybe."

They both laughed and hugged each other.

In the hall Dr. Hay was about to enter the room when Nurse Ann, who was at the door looked up, "Give them another five minutes doctor. I believe Dancer is on his way to complete recovery because of the medication he is receiving at this moment."

Dr. Hay looked through the door window at Dancer and Courtney, "You are absolutely right Nurse Ann, but Coach Carty and the basketball team are about to arrive. Please go in and tell Courtney that she can come back later."

Nurse Ann informed Courtney about the coming of the basketball team and left. Courtney looked at Dancer and gave him a long kiss and hug. She quickly stood up just before the door opened and Carty and the team came in.

Carty look at Courtney, "I keep interrupting you don't I," he said with a knowing smile. Although Hound, Ellis, Forest and the rest of the team did not know what it referred to, they all laughed at the way Courtney's face turned red.

Courtney hugged her uncle and chatted to the rest of the team and explained she had to go back to UT for classes. Then the team circled Dancer's bed and began telling him what was going on at NTSC, Northern Tennessee State College.

As they left his mother, Nada and Kana came to see him and so it went except on weekends when Courtney spent most of Saturday there. And always on Sunday afternoon she and Jill would bring fried chicken, biscuits and gravy along with an apple pie that they had baked that morning before going to church.

They always made enough to share with Dr. Hay, Nurse Ann and the other patients in Dancer's Room. It was so good that several patients tried to get transferred to Dancer's Dinner as the hospital staff called it. Dancer was the most checked patient for vital signs in the hospital on Sunday.

As the team left on one visit, Hound looked at Coach Carty, 'Coach if I ever have to stay in the hospital, I want a nurse like Courtney, I mean what else would help him recover so fast."

Carty looked at Hound and smiled while the whole team laughed going out the door after Forest, looking back at Hound said, "Look in the mirror," to which Hound pushed him through the door.

Dr. Hay was right. Dancer began rehab within a week. On weekends began to walk slowly with Courtney down the hospital hall and Courtney would push him back in a wheel chair. The following week they made a similar trip around the hospital. As the days went by, Dancer was able to walk longer and was able to do special exercises under the watch of Nurse Ann and the PT nurse Rachel Branham. Courtney was amazed each weekend at the progress that he had made during the week before. It seemed that everyone knew that she was the reason for Dancer's quick recovery except her.

After Courtney had walked with Dancer back to his room on a rainy Saturday, she remembered that she needed to stop by the bank today before it closed. She told Dancer she had to leave now. He held her close and they kissed lightly in the hall before he went into his room.

In the room he was feeling good. Now he could get out of bed and walk without help or pain. Even though he felt good he tired quickly in his walks, but he was getting better. His recovery was slow but it was sure. Now he lay in his bed, he took a deep breath and thought it won't be long before he could run and a little time after that he would be able to practice basketball. Then he could play in his first college game ever. The thought of it excited him, but not as much as Courtney always did.

Courtney was late seeing Dancer and she

stayed longer that she should have. As she got out of her car it was almost dark and beginning to rain. As she stepped into the bank, she froze. All around her everyone in the bank was on the floor with their hands out stretched. She turned to go out and stood face to face with sawed off shotgun pointed at her by a man in a clown face.

"Well, look what we have here, good to see you again missy, I have been thinking about you since we escaped from jail," the clown said as he pushed her into the bank.

"Now sit down and don't move a muscle, or you will die," he said as another clown dressed man came from around the teller's desk, with a canvas sack in one hand and black revolver in the other.

He stopped, put the pistol in his belt, grabbed Courtney up from the floor with one arm and held the canvas sack with the other. Using his shoulder they went out the bank door to a waiting black Dodge with both of its rear doors open and its engine running.

He threw Courtney through the opened rear seat door and rushed around to the other side drawing his pistol as he went. Reaching the other side door he raised his pistol and resting it on the roof of the car motioned the other clown to jump into the back seat. With Courtney between them, they slammed both doors and one man yelled to the driver, "Get the hell out of here, now!" They sped away down a side street to a road leading up into the mountains.

Courtney was scared and barely able to breathe because she was mashed between the two. "It's time you got to know us again," the

261

clown who had grabbed her took off his clown mask, "Billy Jack's the name."

On the other side Willie, took his clown mask off and said, "How lucky can we get. You know because of you, that big Indian almost killed us and because of you now the cops will be afraid to shoot at us or even come after us. But I can't say the same for you," he said with a cruel grin. ."

Billy Jack looked at her with the same cruel smile and said, "It's get even time."

She was afraid, but knew that she had to keep her head for a chance to escape. She had no doubt of their intentions. For the first time Courtney noticed that there were two men in the front seat. The man driving was watching the road. From the back he had dark black hair cut in a flat-top. When she looked at the other man she was totally surprised, he was an Indian with braided hair and a dark brown skin.

The driver glanced back at Courtney, "What is a girl doing in here? You never said anything about a kidnapping. I think we should stop and let her out before this turns into more trouble than we can handle."

'Shut up and drive; it is none of your business; you still want your cut for your daughter's operation don't you. You just drive," Billy Jack said to the driver. The Indian said nothing and stared straight ahead. The driver turned off from the highway onto a narrow dirt road leading into dense black forest. They stopped when they came to a clearing surrounded by group of tall cedars and oak trees.

As Billy Jack got out of the car, Willie began building a small campfire.

Looking at the driver he said, "Frank, you, Dark Eagle and the girl sit on the blanket on the other side of the fire."

Courtney looked at Frank, a thin man with close cut hair, glasses and wearing green army pants, boots and an old army field jacket. Dark Eagle, dressed in similar fashion, was as tall but with wider shoulders. He had dark black eyes and hair that was now down to shoulders. His stoic brown face showed no emotion as he looked at her.

Then Frank turned to face Billy Jack and said, "Look, just leave us out and take the money. Just turn us and the girl loose; we won't say a thing."

Billy Jack had a cruel smile, "I know you won't." and shot Frank, who saw it coming but could not dodge the bullet. The Indian quickly stepped forward and caught him and lowered him gently to the blanket.

He aimed the pistol at the Indian for a moment, then turned and walked to the other side of the campfire and started talking to Willie.

The Indian looked at Courtney now with sadness in his eyes and voice, "My name is Dark Eagle and my friend's name is Frank Cross. I ask your forgiveness for being part of this crime."

As he began to look at his friends wound, Courtney replied, "I know that you had no part involving me. What I do not understand how you both got involved with someone like them?"

Dark Eagle moved his head back and forth

knowing that what they had just been involved in was wrong, "Frank has a twelve year old daughter that will go blind without an operation on her eyes. It is a very expensive operation that he could not pay for. They offered us enough money for the operation as our cut. This was the only way we could possibly come up with the money in time."

Then shaking his head again with doubt, he added, "But I fear we have doomed you along with us."

Back at the hospital there was excitement everywhere about the bank robbery. It was not until Dr. Hay came into his room and said, "Dancer, I'm sorry to tell you this, but bank robbers took Courtney hostage a short time ago. I know"...

Dancer stood up, "I need my street cloths now!' he said looking at Dr. Hay, who without hesitation, turned and raced into the hall. In minutes he handed Dancer his clothes and in less than that Dancer was going out door forgetting his injured back, but remembering Courtney as she looked at him and going out the door a short time ago. He was determined that no matter what he must do it would not be the last time he would look into those green eyes that held his soul.

The press had left and Sheriff Ray Clark and Deputy Tim Smith were busy going over maps of surrounding area. Sheriff Clark, wearing his large bifocal glasses looked up, took his glasses off and closed his eyes. "I am afraid we will not find them in time to save Courtney," he said with a worried look. "We have nothing to go on."

Deputy Smith, a younger athletic young man with a flat-top haircut and gray eyes said, "I am afraid you are right, sir."

Just then Dancer burst into the room; he was breathing hard and it took him a moment to catch his breath before he could speak to the startled men.

"I can find Courtney. I just need you to drive, now!"

Without a word, Sheriff Clark jumped up, while buckling on his pistol, looked at Deputy Smith and ordered, "Get the shotgun and rifle! I'll get the car. You meet us in front, Dancer."

Deputy Smith caught up with Sheriff Clark before they got to the car and asked. "Sir, who was that and how do you know what he is talking about?"

Reaching for the door, Sheriff Clark looked across the car at his deputy and answered, "That was James Dancer, and I saw him get off of the bus when he first got here to go to college. He has a Silver Star, Purple Heart and other medals from Nam with the 101st. I also have season tickets to Northern Tennessee Basketball games and Coach Carty goes to church with me and I know a lot about him. If he says he can find Courtney, he will find Courtney."

Deputy Smith, now informed about Dancer, said "Yes, Sir," and drove the car to the front of the police station where Dancer quickly got in the back seat and leaned forward between the seats.

Dancer looked at the men and cautioned, "What you see tonight cannot be told to anyone!

265

Do you understand and don't ask questions?'
They both nodded their heads.

Dancer leaned back, held his right arm out and his right hand palm up. He moved it in slowly in across in front of him. Suddenly the palm glowed, "Take a right here."

As they turned the sheriff and deputy just looked at each other and said nothing. They followed the directions that Dancer's glowing palm directed until it turned off down an old logging road deep into the dark forest. Smith turned the head light off and slowly drove the car depending on the moon light and Dancer's directions to guide them.

Dancer whispered, "Stop." It was then that they saw a glow of a campfire a good distance away. Smith parked the car behind a clump of cedar trees to prevent the car lights that came on when door was opened from being seen. Dancer took the rifle and Smith the shotgun. On Dancer's hand count they opened the three doors at the same time and closed them quickly while holding the door handles open, making almost no noise.

As they quietly closed the car doors, Sheriff Clark whispered to Dancer, "Is that their camp?"

Dancer nodded yes and directed his palm toward the fire. It glowed. It was then that Clark and Smith saw the outline of a glowing wolf on Dancer's palm. Again, each exchanged glances but said nothing

Dancer moved closer to Smith and Clark and whispered just loud enough for them to hear, "Follow behind me closely. There are stumps and branches that could make noise. The rain has wet the leaves enough to prevent any noise from stepping on them. I have been through this before in Nam. We need to stay close together to decide what to do when we get there. Any questions?"

Smith and Clark nodded no and turned to follow Dancer into the darkness. Both were glad that he was leading because neither one could see more than a foot in front of them.

Courtney had been talking with Dark Eagle while he tried to stop Frank's bleeding. "Frank and I served in Nam together, the reason he limps is because he knocked me out of the way and took a bullet that would have killed me."

As he finished wrapping the wound of the unconscious Frank Cross, he looked up at Courtney, "When they start toward us, I'll throw dirt in their face and try to get a gun from one of them. You run for the woods as fast as you can."

He looked at Courtney with a sad look, "I know it is a long shot, but it is better than nothing," and looking down at Frank his wounded friend, "if he was able he would do the same."

Courtney looked at the Indian who was on his knees trying to stop the bleeding of his friend even more. She was thinking the of the courage he had to give his life for someone he had never met until a few hours ago. Now it was her time to do something.

It was then that she remembered the necklace she was wearing with the black stone home of Azar. She took it from her hand and held it in the fire light. There he was the white wolf with red eyes, Azar the White Wolf of Death, The Stealer of Souls.

As she held it up, Dark Eagle asked, "What is that?"

Courtney gave the necklace to Dark Eagle, "Look into the stone, what you see?"

Dark Eagle did so and his hand trembled and his eyes were wide as he handed it back to Courtney. "Is that Azar, the White Wolf of Death, The Stealer of Souls I thought he was only a legend told by the Ancient Ones?" he asked as he tried to stop his shaking hands.

Courtney nodded he head, "Yes it is Azar, and I have seen him. I will call him to protect us."

Dark Eagle looked at Courtney, "He will probably take Frank and me too because we were involved in this, but do it, stop them, they are evil men."

Looking across the fire she saw Billy Jack and Willie burning some bank money. It was then that Billy Jack and Willie stood up from the fire and looked across it at Courtney and Black Eagle.

Billy Jack smiled, it was a cruel smile, "I guess you wonder why we are burning money, I bet they think we're crazy don't you, Willie."

Willie was laughing, "They don't know how smart we are. Tell her, Billy Jack."

"I'll do just that Willie," Billy Jack said with a confident grin. "We are burning some money and paper so that they will think all of the money was lost in the fire. Then think Black Eagle and Frank, got into a fight over the money and"... He pointed the pistol at Courtney.

Then he continued, "You two shot it out, killing each other and her. How is that for a story? But before that happens, I aim to take her into the woods for some fun."

Courtney thought it was time to act. She held the black stone up and said "Azar! Protect."

Arriving across the clearing, Dancer, Sheriff Clark and Deputy Smith held their fire because Courtney, Frank and Dark Eagle were in the way. Dancer had the rifle with the scope and started to fire at Billy Jack when he saw the bright flash and cloud rise up.

He knew what that meant and what was about to happen. Turning quickly to Clark and Smith and warned, "Be still, you are about to see something few men have seen and fewer have lived to tell about."

Billy Jack and Willie were blinded by the flash and when the smoke cleared there was Azar looking at each of them.

"Well, Willie, look what the girl has called to protect her. Time to get our heavy stuff Willie," Billy Jack said as he brought an AK-47 from around inside his coat, "this big dog wants to play; show him we can play."

As he said that, they both opened up with their fully automatic AK's. Dark Eagle threw himself in front of Courtney and the unconscious Frank Smith protecting them from any stray bullets.

The smoke from the rifles, and dirt thrown into the air, blinded everyone for an instant. When it cleared, Billy Jack and Willie both seemed frozen to the ground with unbelieving looks of terror on their faces. It would be the last thing they ever saw. Billy Jack started to run but the white wolf's great leap reached him before he could turn around.

What happened next amazed everyone; he went through Billy Jack before he could flee. He was instantly outlined in a blue glow and collapsed face down to the ground where never moved.

Meanwhile, Willie had dropped his AK-47 and grabbed Courtney. He held her in front of him between him and the crouching Azar.

"That's it big dog, one move and this knife I have at her throat will end her life in a minute. Now back off we are...."

Willie let out a scream, throwing both hands in the air. Courtney fell to the ground and felt Azar fly over her going through Willie. He fell face first beside her.

Courtney was stunned, trying to get up when she felt Dancer's arms around her as he lifted her off of the ground and held her close.

Sheriff Clark and Deputy Smith had moved out of the wood and were going toward Dancer, Courtney, Dark Eagle, and the unconscious Frank Smith.

Dancer said, "Stay where you are," and then he left the two, silently approaching Willie who was holding a knife against Courtney's throat. Dancer pulled his knife from his leg sheath and in one motion threw it at Willie. What happened next was beyond belief. The knife, streaking and leaving a red trail, hit Willie in his arm that held the knife. He screamed as Aztar leaped through him turning him blue as he fell next to Courtney who had fallen when he let her go.

Clark and Smith started toward the group when something else happened that stopped them with open mouths. Dancer held his hand up and the knife flew to his open hand, leaving a red streak behind it. They looked at each other, shook their heads, thinking if they had not seen it, they would not have believed it, and no one else would have either.

Aztar took two giant strides and leaped at Dancer. He put his giant paws on both sides of his neck.

"Azar, thank you for protecting Courtney and the others," he said as he rubbed Azar's ears.

Sheriff Clark and Deputy Smith, stupefied, did not move.

Azar, followed by the others, ran toward the little group by the fire. Courtney and Dancer hugged each other and turned toward the group. Azar looked at everyone in the group, and focused his gaze upon Dark Eagle. For a second they stared at each other, and then Azar wagged his tail and turned toward Courtney.

"Azar has searched your soul and found it true," Courtney said as she nodded her head toward the giant white, red eyed wolf a few feet away from her.

Courtney went down on one knee and hugged Azar.

"You have saved our lives Azar, but it is time for you go home."

Understanding her he wagged his tail and moved backward.

"You will be called again when we need you," she said and spread her hands whispered, "Home Azar."

There was a bright flash and he disappeared.

In meantime, Sheriff Clark had called for an ambulance for Frank Smith, and faced the action he dreaded most, the arrest of Dark Eagle and the wounded Frank Smith. The three of them had graduated from high school the same year, had played basketball, football together and been drafted at the same time. They did their basic training together. Later Dark Eagle and Frank served together in Viet Nam. He found out after he was discharged that Frank had pushed Dark Eagle out of the way in a firefight taking the bullet meant for him in the leg. The leg wound was the cause of his limp.

Dark Eagle stood up and faced Sheriff Clark, a man he respected and a friend for as long as he could remember. Now Clark had to do his duty. He figured that Clark dreaded this as much as he did. Dark Eagle tried to make it as easy as possible for him. He stepped forward and put his hands out to be cuffed. The sheriff took a deep breath and reached behind his back for the handcuffs.

Dancer saw the look that each had. Both dreaded what the sheriff must do. Then he looked at Courtney who was watching what was about to happen to Dark Eagle and Clark. She had tears in her eyes. This told him that Dark Eagle and Frank had no part in the kidnapping. He had to do something fast.

Dancer stepped between them and shook

Dark Eagles extended hand. "I don't know how to thank you and Frank for saving Courtney," he said.

Turning to Sheriff Clark, he asked, "Isn't there a reward out for the return of the money and the capture of both of the robbers, sheriff?

Before he could reply, Courtney stepped close to Dancer and shook Dark Eagle's extended hand then turned toward the sheriff and said, "That's right sheriff, without Dark Eagle and Frank, I shudder to think what would have happened to me."

For once in his life, Dark Eagle had a surprised look on his face as he looked at Dancer, Courtney and Sheriff Clark who broke out into a wide smile. "Hey, that's right; there is a large reward out for the capture and the return of the money."

And with a large smile of relief on his face, he added, "It should be enough to pay for the operation on Frank's daughter. "

He put his arm around the startled Dark Eagle who was still speechless and said, "You deserve it, without you and Frank stepping in, it could have been a different story."

Deputy Smith took this in and said nothing. After all who would believe the truth?

One ambulance arrived and the EMT said that Frank Smith would recover. The corner arrived and pronounced Billy Jack and Willie dead and left following another ambulance that would take them to the morgue. Sheriff Clark, Deputy Smith, Dark Eagle, Dancer and Courtney walked toward their parked car. Courtney and Dancer lingered in the back and walked slowly hand in hand. Before they got to the car, Dark Eagle turned and met them.

He looked at them, shaking his head and speaking with a slow voice, "I do not know what to say. I have seen things that few would believe. You have given my friend and me a new life. He has a way with words that I do not, he would know what to say. The Great Spirit did not give me a way with words. I do not know how to thank you for what you have done for Frank and me. You have saved his daughter from being blind."

Turning to Courtney, he said, "You are very brave and have the Spirit Wolf Azar to protect you. Until tonight I thought he did not exist, but he protected us and using powers that I have never seen destroyed those who would bring the wearer of the Azar necklace harm," he said bowing his head.

And then looking at Dancer, he said with pride, "You too must possess powers to have guided the sheriff to us through the rain and darkness," and then he gripped Dancer's hand with his own and bowed.

Dancer nodded to him and held his right hand in front of him. The image of Azar glowed red in the dark.

"My mother is Nada, Keeper of Secrets. It only appears on my hand when it is called."

Dark Eagle smiled, "Aaah now I understand. The tales told by my grandfather about the Ancient Ones were always true."

Weeks later, Sheriff Clark and Deputy Smith were enjoying a clear sunny day on a bench outside the sheriff's office when a little girl rode up on her tricycle and stopped in front of them.

She asked, "Are you Sheriff Clark and Deputy Smith?"

Sheriff Clark nodded his head, and said "Yes, we are now, what can we do for you, little girl?"

"My daddy is Frank Smith; you all saved his life and helped raise the money for the operation that allowed me to see again."

Then starting to move away, she added, "He said that I should always thank you when I see you thank you," she yelled over her shoulder, as she peddled away.

For a moment, Sheriff Clark and Deputy Smith just looked at each other. Finally Smith looking at Clark, "You know, sheriff, we have been called heroes by everyone. Heck, we even got an award from the county. Sometimes I wonder if we should tell the truth."

Sheriff Clark stood up and stretched, yawned and then looking at Deputy Smith, said, "Well, I thought about that too. Now let's see, would you believe a story about a giant white wolf with red eyes, that came out of a cloud, and was shot by two AK-47's and the bullets went right through him, or that he killed two robbers by jumping through them and turning them blue, and then disappeared into a cloud and that the two robbers, according to the corner, each died of a heart attack at the same time? Dancer threw his knife about thirty feet and hit the man holding a knife at Courtney's throat, and then it came back to him in a red streak?"

He turned away from Deputy Smith and

asked, "Finally, who would believe a story about a young man whose hand had a glowing red wolf on it that showed us the way to the robbers on a rainy dark night, down an old logging road in the mountains and could throw a knife that glowed thirty feet to hit a target we could not even see well and the knife came back to him in a red streak?"

Deputy Smith stood, smiled and put his arm around Sheriff Clark, "Since you put it that way, it makes me feel like a real hero. It is my turn to buy lunch at the Huddle." Then he turned to look at Clark, "I want to be just like you, sheriff."

As they continued walking down the street, Sheriff Clark took his deputy's arm from around his shoulder and looked at Deputy Smith, "Don't hold your breath expecting a raise."

To this Deputy Smith just looked ahead, smiled to himself and said nothing.

High in the mountains, far away Nada smiled as she looked out the window at the mountains far away, "You have done well Azar," and then turning away, she said, "Now I must use a promise and dreams to protect my son what is going to happen to him in the future unless I do something about it."

Lee Stewart and his Seven Disciples

An excerpt from one of Lee Stewart's journal entries in the possession of the author follows: "We (Biliter, Flanery, Burchett, Raney, Tuggle, Wes Perkins, Deputy U. S. Marshal, Henry Lewis, Sim Saylor, Greenbury Thomas, Wils and Irvine Browning, J. W. King, Mack Clem, Henry Stepp, Cam Cornett and Oscar) left the residence of Henry Lewis at 4:00 a. m. and raided the waters of Line Fork and Big Leatherwood. We assisted the Deputy Marshal to arrest several men. On Leatherwood Creek, we found the following outfit:

        400 gallons of still beer:
        11-55 gallon fermenters:

1-50 gallon copper still:
1 wood still cap:
1 flake stand:
1- process keg;
2-16 gallon kegs;
3-500 gallon fermenters;
1 axe; 1 hoe; 1 pair rubber shoes;
20 feet 1" iron pipe;
10 gallons of low wines;
1 bushel malt corn;
1 funnel; 1 mash rake;
2 rolls of rubber roofing;
1 still house 14 x 16;
1 stir stick; 1 shovel.

He notes: Which were destroyed. Did Smithy had been arrested for this outfit. We crossed several mountains and did a lot of walking, stuck a path on top of the mountain and followed it to Lick Branch of Stoney Fork of Big Leatherwood in Perry County, near Delta. There were:
1-60 gallon copper still;
8-55 gallon fermenters;
1-5 gallon wood still cap;
1-9 coil ¾ inch copper still worm;
1-16 gallon process keg;
2-16 gallon kegs;
1 stone still furnace;
2 copper still arms;
50 pounds brown sugar;
1 stove burner (iron);
1 funnel; 1 axe; 1 maul;
1 wood still cap; 1 frying pan;
2 stir sticks;

1 still house 12 x 16 covered with boards and all indications that it had been used for 5 or 6 years and had never been disturbed. It was understood that it belong to Dave Lewis, and he was arrested. We destroyed this and did a lot of hunting. About this time rain set in and did not stop any more till we arrive at the depot at 4:30 p. m. We could see smoke and found a number of places, but we could not find the stills, and some of the places were recent too. There were good paths everywhere. We came to the main road toward the Poor Fork, Roy, Guy, Raney and some of the others had found 8 gallons of moonshine hid behind some logs. Rain was still pouring and we were tired. Wiles Browning had killed a rattlesnake, the first one I had ever seen in the woods. We decided to quit as the weather was bad and we were worn out—having not slept any and had been in the rain for several hours and were wet to the skin. We left Dione for Harlan at 5:15 p. m. and arrived at 6:08 p. m. Fare .65. We stopped at the New Harlan Hotel. I wanted a room with a bath—got it all right, but there not a lot of heat and very little warm water. I did take a jay bird bath and nearly froze to death. My clothes were wet. I put my clothes in Roy's room, and it was dry, but my other clothes were still wet except nature had dried them to some extent. I slept pretty well.

R.R Fare .65: B. 1.00: D. 1.00: S. .75: L. 1.50 New Harlan Hotel.

The Cherokee Trail of Tears

Nunna Daul Isunyi
The Trail Where They Cryed

In the late eighteenth century, the Cherokee established a written constitution, a legislation, and Supreme Court. They also settled land in the southern states prospering on farms. White Americans sought their removal in order to use their land "more efficiently," the discovery of gold on Indian land now near Dahlonga, Georgia in 1829 increased the demand to remove the Cherokees.

The Indian Removal Act of 1830 passed congress with one vote. President Andrew Jackson signed the act into law. It was enacted by his successor President Martin Van Buren who allowed Georgia, Tennessee, North Carolina and Alabama an armed force of 7,000 made up of militia regular army and by volunteers under General Winfield Scott to round up about13,000 Cherokees into concentration camps at the U. S. Indian Agency near Cleveland, Tennessee before being sent to the West. Most of the deaths occurred from disease, starvation and cold in these camps. Their homes and farms were won by white settlers in a lottery.

In the winter of 1838 the Cherokees began the thousand mile march with scant clothing and most on foot without shoes or moccasins, the march began in Red Clay, Tennessee, and the location of the last Eastern Capital of the Cherokee Nation. The Cherokee were given used blankets from a hospital in Tennessee where an epidemic of small pox had broken out. Many died from the disease.

Because of the disease, the Indians were not allowed to go into any towns or villages along the way. This forced them to go around towns and travel a greater distance in the harsh winter.   After crossing Tennessee and Kentucky, they arrived in Southern Illinois at Golconda about the 3rd of December 1838.

Here the starving Indians were charged a dollar a head to cross the river on "Berry's Ferry" which charged twelve cents to cross the river to everyone else. They had to wait until everyone else that wanted to cross the river did so. They were forced to take shelter under "Mantle Rock," a shelter on the Kentucky side, until "Berry had nothing to do."

Many died huddled together at Mantle Rock waiting to cross. Several Cherokee were murdered by locals. The killers filed a lawsuit against the U.S. Government through the courthouse in Vienna, suing he government for $35.00 a head to bury each murdered Cherokee.

The removed Cherokees initially settled near Tahlequah, Oklahoma population the Cherokee Nation eventually increased and today the Cherokee are the largest American Indian group in the United States.

The Gray Wolf

Dancer's wolves were the Gray Wolf. The Gray wolf travels in packs of four to seven. There is a definite hierarchy in the pack centered on the Alpha pair, such as Cat and his mate, who mate for life and are the only members of the wolf pack to breed each year.

Howling is the type of vocal communication for which wolves are the most famous. The sound seems to captivate our imagination and remind us of the mysterious aspects of nature. Wolves howl to greet one another. Definite boundaries and call the pack together. Before a hunt howling may serve to excite and unite the pack members before setting out. Wolves howl more when it's lighter at night which leads to the concept of howling at the full moon as Hound did after too much moon shine (The Liquid Type)

When chasing a prey, wolves can run as fast as 30 miles per hour. When hunting, wolves pick out the sick or injured animals as their prey. They leave healthy, strong animals to reproduce and flourish.

The greatest threat to gray wolves is fear and misunderstanding. Recent TV shows and movies have acted to increase this fear. Only a small fraction of livestock farms in wolf range suffer losses due to wolf activity. However, recent court decisions have allowed the hunting of wolves which will reduce their population annually

The Dream Catcher

According to legend, the night is filled with dreams both good and bad. The dream catcher when hung over or near your bed singing freely in the air, catches the dreams as they flow by. The good dreams know how to pass through the dream catcher. Slipping through the outer holes and slide down the soft feathers so gently that many times the sleeper does not know that he/she is dreaming.

The bad dreams, not knowing the way, get tangled in the dream catcher and perish with the first light of the new day. The Keeper of Secrets and others had the gift to use the dreams to tell the future. Dancer's dreams after Viet Nam were so bad that at times his bad dreams came through catcher and he would then describe them while still asleep.

His mother, Nada, sends dreams to those who need to defend Dancer, Courtney and his friends.